On Distant Ground

On Distant Ground

A NOVEL BY

Robert Olen Butler

ALFRED A. KNOPF   NEW YORK   1985

THIS IS A BORZOI BOOK
PUBLISHED BY ALFRED A. KNOPF, INC.

Copyright © 1985 by Robert Olen Butler

Library of Congress Cataloging in Publication Data

Butler, Robert Olen.   On distant ground.

1. Vietnamese Conflict, 1961–1975—Fiction.
I. Title.
PS3552.U827805   1985   813'.54   84-48517
ISBN 0-394-54040-9

Manufactured in the United States of America

FIRST EDITION

For M.

On Distant Ground

David Fleming and the Army lawyer who would defend him bent, and together they laced their jogging shoes, a gesture that felt vaguely fraternal to David and made him uncomfortable. They didn't run yet but sat on the bench on the hill up from Fort Holabird. David looked out to the southeast, to Baltimore harbor, the morning fog slung down even to the tops of the cranes along the quays. He wanted to run to slow this beating of his heart. The vengeance that the Army sought frightened him in a physical way, in spite of the detachment of his mind.

"I heard on the radio that the Mekong Delta has been cut off," the lawyer said.

There was a tone of sincere sadness in the voice that drew David's attention. It struck him how little he knew of this man, Carl Lomas. Like David, an Army captain. Like David, thirty now and in the service a little longer than he'd expected to be. Superficial things. After the Army stirred itself into wrath, David had been repulsed by the civilian lawyers his father-in-law had sent to him and he'd settled for this man, appointed by the convening authority. Lomas kept his profile to David and the sadness lingered in this silence. A foghorn called from the harbor.

"I hadn't heard," David said.

"The Communists are going to win now," Lomas said. "The South's done for."

"It always has been."

"I've got some friends there who are gonna have a bad

time under the boys from the North." Lomas's mouth tightened. David tried to sympathize with these unknown Vietnamese but he didn't know how. He himself had no friends there. No one. Just a stranger—the man he'd freed—Tuyen —and it was Tuyen's side that was going to prevail. No friend at all, really.

"I was in Saigon much of the same time you were," Lomas said.

"Ah," David said, wondering when they could start to run. He was acutely conscious even of the physical differences between them. Lomas was thin, small-boned, dark, his cheeks beard-black even though they were shaved closely. David was thick, thick-necked, thick-armed, like an athlete just a few years past his prime and a little out of shape, and his hair was the color of the pale yellow legal pads that Lomas had written on all through the pretrial hearing.

"Are you afraid now?" Lomas said, turning on David the same tone of sadness he'd used for Nha Trang.

The question was both unexpected and apt; for a moment David saw himself as Lomas saw him, and he answered the question with a frankness that he did not want to have in these matters. "Yes," he said.

Lomas nodded and did not speak. David realized he'd been led to confess his fear by what was no doubt a cross-examiner's rhetorical trick. He knew he should resent that. But he also sensed Carl Lomas's compassion for him. And though at some point in his life—before Vietnam—David would have resented the compassion even more than the trick, now he did not. When he realized this, his fear sharpened: the change in him—whatever it was—was connected with his finding Tuyen and freeing him; the Army could not help prosecuting him for this softening of his heart. He looked away from Carl, out to the harbor again. The cranes had vanished in the fog.

"Why don't we run now," Carl said.

"Yes. All right."

They rose and stretched a final time and began running down the hill. The quick ecstasy of downhill was lost on David, for in his mind he stood motionless before the investigating officer waiting for the charges to be made. And David's knees started to hurt, bone grinding against bone, as he and Carl ran toward Holabird Avenue. The pain made him think of Jennifer in their apartment back up the hill. He hoped she was able to fall asleep again after he left. She was due to give birth very soon to their first child, but she insisted he go out and run. He reasoned that the time away from her was unavoidable anyway: there were contingency plans to shape with Carl. The charges—if there were to be any—would be made within the next few days.

They reached the bottom of the hill. On the long flat run along Holabird Avenue, past the post's main gate, past the storefronts and commuter-crowded bus-stop benches, David's knees stopped hurting. His body was tight but the pace was good and the balance of air-needed and air-taken-in hung perfectly in his chest like a plumb line, still, calm. "Is the pace too fast for you?" David asked.

"No," Carl said. "It's just fine."

"Stiff?"

"Yes."

Up ahead a small dog strained at a leash, yapping at them as they approached, and they moved off the sidewalk into the street, single file for a time. When they were back on the sidewalk, running beside each other, Carl said, "Shall we take as a premise the . . . possibility of charges?"

"You don't have to talk like that with me," David said; too sharply, he realized, though he felt a twist of pleasure in somehow taking back with his manner his earlier profession of fear. But this little pleasure also wiped away his appreciation of Carl's compassion and he was left with only a petty defiance and he wished he'd not spoken. "You can talk straight," he said but with a conscious gentleness.

"I'm sorry," Carl said.

"It's all right."

"We have to assume there'll be charges. *I'd* bring charges if I were the colonel."

"What will they be?"

"Major Hedberg wants to crucify you."

"That was clear," David said.

"He thinks he can get 'aiding the enemy.' "

David let these words slip through without considering them closely. It was the very speculation he'd been waiting for since the hearing closed yesterday; it was the worst possibility that the hearing had presented to him; it was the charge with the most severe penalties, allowing even death. But now that Carl had finally acknowledged this possibility between them, David instantly let it pass.

They ran in silence for a time and then David heard Carl say in a faintly breathless voice, "You've quickened the pace too soon."

David knew at once it was true. He was running faster now. Too fast for himself as well. His breath was shortening. "Okay," he said, and he slowed. I'm afraid again, he thought. Trying to run it off. He waited until he knew his voice would be strong and steady and he said, "So they want my ass."

"Maybe the colonel will go for 'dereliction of duty.' That we could live with."

"Do they have a case for aiding the enemy?"

Carl didn't answer at once. Their turn toward Sparrows Point was coming. They slowed and jogged in place at a light, then crossed Holabird Avenue and headed down a new street, a long stretch of Baltimore row houses, each house with the same cast-iron balcony, the same marble steps, each changing only in pastel color, the row as restrained and noncommittal as a jury.

When they were in stride once more, Carl said, "They've got witnesses at each step of the way. You inquire after this guy Tuyen. Several times, several places. You know he's a key member of the Vietcong infrastructure. You track him down, making your own way even to Con Son Island. You

find Tuyen, commandeer an ARVN jeep and an ARVN lieutenant with it, and you force your helicopter pilot to land in
the bush and you let Tuyen go free."

Carl stopped speaking and David knew the man wasn't
toying with him; he knew Carl was trying to reason all of
this out for himself as well. So David waited without anger,
in spite of his anxiety. He could see, far off, the steel mill at
Sparrows Point, the place where they would turn. The stand
of stacks was heaving smoke against the fog. David could
not wait for Carl's mind to piece things together at its own
pace. "So does that add up to aiding the enemy?" he asked.

"It adds up to a charge perhaps. The charge . . . I don't
know. There's the question of motive."

"Yes?"

"A question even I have."

David didn't know how to respond to this. It had come
up often between them and David had been vague or silent
before the question.

"It's going to be hard to keep you off the stand if it goes
to a court-martial as aiding the enemy."

"They've got to prove it."

"Well, the 'aid' itself—in an objective sense—is already
there. You're not trying to deny the basic events."

David didn't answer. No. He wasn't trying to deny them.
He knew Carl wanted an artful lie from him. He knew Carl
was gently suggesting some better story. Most of the witnesses—the key ones especially—were Vietnamese. Faceless depositions. If David could come up with something
good, something plausible, he might have a chance. But he
couldn't do that. In spite of Jennifer, in spite of his nascent
child, in spite of his own deep conviction that he had been
justified. It was just that he wasn't sure himself what had
happened in him, and he didn't know how to lie about it.

Carl said, "I'd never suggest that a client . . . not be hon-
est about . . . facts."

There was a pause, as if David was supposed to partici-
pate in this line of reasoning. But he said nothing.

"If I could just speculate a moment about you. And your reticence . . ." Carl paused again, but only briefly. "You were an intelligence officer . . . You knew this man Tuyen was well placed in the VC infrastructure you wanted to destroy . . . Perhaps you had a plan—a delicate plan, one that you didn't want to talk about for . . . ah . . . security reasons. Even when there was an inquiry like this. Perhaps your plan in Vietnam was to turn this man Tuyen into a . . . what do you call it? A mole? An agent for the US. Maybe you got to doing this a little too much on your own . . . A plan of your own that didn't work out too well . . . So you were a damn fool, operating without authorization, without even telling anyone at that point. A damn fool is all . . ."

All this had come from Carl a phrase at a time, a stride at a time, and listening to him began to make David weary. He refused to respond. He couldn't bring himself to embrace this lie, as artful as it seemed to be. But what good would it do anyway? "I guess I am a damn fool . . ." he said.

"Yes?" Carl said, his voice lifting in hope.

"Because I can't make any sense out of . . ."

"You've got to think all this out before you say anything," Carl said, cutting him off. They took two strides, three, before Carl added, "You want a chance to spend some time with your first child before you're a grandfather, don't you?"

Now David felt a spike of anger, just as his foot hit with his stride. He lifted up and the anger vanished, his other foot hit and the image of his child jarred back into him, he lifted and with his next stride he almost snapped at Carl to shut up, but instead he clutched these thoughts, flung them away, and he ran, he ran and said no more, he ran waiting for the release of the third mile to come, waiting for the body chemistry of jogging to give him a few moments free from fear.

. . .

David stood in the bedroom door with his limbs still thrumming from his run and he watched Jennifer sleeping. She was lying on her back, the sheet rising up where the baby slept inside her, but her shoulders and head were twisted around, as if she really wanted to be on her side. Her long yellow hair—as fine as any infant's—was splayed on the pillow and her high cheeks were flushed. She stirred. Her nostrils flared briefly and she angled her head as if trying to get a crick out of her neck. The stirring resonated in David. He moved his shoulders, touched the doorjamb. At that moment he felt connected to his sleeping wife and he wondered if this was anything like Jennifer's feeling for the child. He thought of the child sleeping inside her body, its dreams—simple dreams? or infinitely complex?—moving its limbs, reminding Jennifer of a connection, just as David was reminded. His mind imagined how this might feel, but his body could not.

Then Jennifer was awake. Her eyes were open and she smiled at him slowly, as if he had paid her a subtle compliment. She held out her hand to him.

"I'm just back," he said. "I'm sweaty."

"I don't care," she said. When he moved to her and sat on the bed, taking her hand, she added, "I'm sweaty too."

"How are you feeling?"

"Stretched."

"Did you sleep?"

"Yes."

"Did you dream?"

"I don't remember."

"That's good," David said. For several weeks she'd been dreaming of him: he was trapped inside a wall, caught in the plaster, his face and hands pressed there, as if against a window; she tried to touch his twisted face but she felt only the cold slick surface of the wall. "How's the little one?" he said.

"He was running when you were."

"Yes?"

"I'm feeling more certain it's a boy."

"You know I don't care at all," David said, though he realized this was a lie; and with the realization, he felt compelled to reinforce it. "If it's not a boy it would make no difference at all." This time the words were actually painful for him and he said, "Do you really feel certain?"

"I think so."

David clung to this thought but after a moment Jennifer began to laugh quietly. "What is it?" he said.

"You asked me if I was certain and I said 'I think so.'"

David was still caught up in his yearning for a son and he didn't understand.

With a slow, explanatory cadence, Jennifer said, "I was saying I thought I was certain, but I said it uncertainly."

David couldn't rouse enough interest in this little paradox to respond to her. He felt suddenly cut off and his fear bled back into him, starting in his chest, flowing into his limbs.

"It's not important," Jennifer said.

"What isn't?" His voice sounded small.

"My little self-contradiction . . ." She squeezed his hand as if she'd felt a kick inside, but she said, "Did it go badly with Carl?" and David knew that her squeeze had been, instead, an insight she'd had into his pain.

David paused to wonder at her sensitivity to him. He thought how much he loved her but how rarely he had any sense of what she was thinking. Not as she did with him. Did that mean she loved him more than he loved her? He squeezed her hand in return. "It was all right," he said. "About like I'd expected."

"Does he think you'll be charged?"

"Yes."

"With what?"

"Aiding the enemy."

Jennifer squeezed at his hand again and she closed her eyes slowly. But she made no sound. David knew her bravery was for him. No tears. No expressions of her own deepest fears. And David realized that he was sensitive to her now, sensitive to the way she was protecting him. At this moment he did indeed know what she was thinking.

"I love you," David said.

Jennifer opened her eyes.

"I'm amazed sometimes at how far I've come," he said.

"How far?" Her voice was husky.

"Before I went to Vietnam, I couldn't even imagine feeling like this. I . . . my father was in me . . . I couldn't find even a trace of this kind of feeling for anyone. Not really . . ." He stopped speaking as his thoughts approached Tuyen. Again Tuyen. David had been caught by a few words on the wall of an interrogation cell and they had grown in him until he did the thing that brought him to his present jeopardy and then he'd come back from Vietnam and fallen in love at last. Jennifer touched his cheek, cupped the back of his head, pulled him to her.

He lay against her and the sweat of his running and of her sleep was warm and slick between their faces. He laid his hand on her belly. The child inside did not move. "I hope it is a son," he said.

Later that morning David sat waiting for Jennifer in the obstetrician's outer office, the only man among half a dozen pregnant women and two sleeping children in strollers. Just this—sitting here with these women and children early on a weekday afternoon—made him keenly aware of the threat against him, how he'd been plucked from the natural course of his life. One of the women was reading a newspaper, the front section held up high before her face, but David did not look at it. He hadn't read a paper in several weeks. He found he'd lost his taste for news. He watched the sleeping children for a time, but they meant nothing to him and he stared at his hands. He should have stayed in the apartment. He should have tried to read or sleep or eat. He clenched his hands and watched his knuckles grow white. He looked at the table beside him full of copies of *Parents* and *American Baby*. The newspaper rustled and it drew his glance. The lead front-page headline was about the road to the Mekong Delta, but David didn't even read those few words. He looked at his hands again and squeezed now at his mind, his feelings, tried to squeeze them dry. What was all this for? The South was falling and he was being prosecuted and for what?

He closed his eyes and he knew what he would see. The prosecution had witnesses at each step except for one. The beginning. He saw the interrogation center. In Bien Hoa, down a dusty road with palm fronds drooping in the heat and chickens clucking, dust and tropical stillness, the center was just a sleepy courtyard and a few low buildings. One of the buildings on the courtyard had a row of iron doors, the holding cells. David thought of his first visit there. He and a CIA team had made a capture of some suspected VC cadre, members of the infrastructure, the shadow government the Communists were setting up in the countryside. David spoke excellent Vietnamese from a year in Army language school and he wanted to carry the investigation forward himself. But the suspects were turned over to the South Vietnamese for interrogation at this place. On the first visit to the center, he saw one of these prisoners after questioning. It was in an inner room, windowless, a waiting room with the faint hum of a generator beyond a closed door. The Vietnamese commandant had escorted David and a CIA man into the presence of the suspected VC. The VC had just finished a session. He stood in the center of the windowless room and he was naked. All the hair on his body had been shaved off and there were white spots on his dusky skin. David looked at two of them on his throat and he knew there were others, lower on his body. But David did not even glance at those, as if they were an indiscretion of the man himself, like being naked. The man blinked mindlessly there while the commandant talked to Trask, and David listened to the electric hum beyond the door and he watched the man's eyes.

But David felt as empty as those eyes. He had no compassion for the torture the prisoner had obviously undergone, no sense of his pain or his fear or of the damage done to him. Neither did David regard him professionally, as Trask and the commandant seemed to do. David had no sense of this man as the enemy, the foe of freedom for the South Vietnamese, defiantly silent, with the blood of Americans on his hands. David looked at these dark, empty eyes, this tiny, naked brown man, and he had no feeling at all. That was the irony David could see now, as he sat among pregnant women, waiting to be made a prisoner himself. It wasn't until weeks later, a second visit to the center, low-keyed, administrative, that he was finally moved.

On that visit, after a meeting with the commandant that consisted only of small talk and paperwork, David had stepped out into the courtyard. He was thinking of getting back to base, getting out of this heat and into the air-conditioning of the officers' club, when he saw the door of one of the holding cells standing open. From the most casual curiosity he paused and went to the cell to see what it was like.

The cell door was iron with only a single observation slit covered by a metal flap. David looked down the row of doors. Every flap was closed and latched. He pushed the door open and stepped in.

The air was hot and close and stank of urine. The cell was a six-foot square. In the back wall was a stone shelf to sit on. In the corner of the concrete floor was a hole about nine inches across. Against one wall was a wooden stand, presumably for the guard to leave a rice bowl at mealtime. David stepped into the middle of the floor and pushed the door partway closed. The cell went dark and the rancid air thickened. There were no windows. He looked up, but the ceiling was lost in shadows. There was no wisp of air from that direction. His body reacted with an abrupt directness to the cell. Sweat flowed from him with the suddenness of blood, absorbing at once as its own the stench of the cell, sickening him.

But David stayed. He did not move. He wiped hard at the sweat around his face. The door was not completely closed. There was still a faint light, a light the prisoners did not have. The sweat returned to his face, amplifying the smell again. He wiped hard with his sleeve and he looked toward the uncovered hole in the floor. His mind cried: why am I staying here? But instead of turning, leaving, he moved to the stone shelf, he bent to it, extended his hand, touched it. His fingers recoiled. It was warm with a thin layer of slime. The prisoners slept here, waited here, for questioning, for the pain beyond the door of the windowless room.

David was growing dizzy in the closeness of the cell. He backed away. There was a brief smell of concrete that touched a kindred smell of his own past, of the New York subway. A further connection, a sudden thought: graffiti. Perhaps the walls had graffiti. A VC prisoner left in the compacted, stinking dark of this place to wait for interrogation— what would he write or scratch on the walls? What, in his solitude before torture, would he say? David began to search the sweating walls carefully. In several places were smudged areas, as if words had been there but had been removed. Of course the authorities would remove them, he thought. The obscenities, the Communist slogans, the outcries of hate, would not be left as solace to the next prisoner. Even if there was no light to read them, not even the mere existence of the words was granted the tenants of this cell.

David was soaked now, not just in sweat, but soaked in the smell of urine and feces and a dense, unmoving staleness. David could not—dared not—draw a full breath. He started toward the door when he noticed the wooden stand. Perhaps a few words had been overlooked. He went to the stand and pulled it back from the wall. Suddenly there was a flurry of hundreds of brittle feet. David jumped back as dozens of cockroaches darted from behind the stand. They crossed his feet and he kicked out at them, stamped at them, drew back from them. The prisoners were not alone in the darkness of the cell, and in the darkness the roaches would have no hesitation in exploring a man's body. Most of them had disappeared down the hole in the floor now. Some crouched in the corners. David went back to the wooden stand and looked behind it. There were three Vietnamese words scratched faintly into the sweaty wall. They were *"ve-sinh la khoe."* They meant "hygiene is healthful."

David stared a long time at the words. A VC prisoner, spending time in this cell, waiting for an interrogation that he must have known would either break or destroy him, with all the words of the world to proclaim here, to bellow here, to rage here, had crouched in the dark with the cockroaches and scratched out that hygiene is healthful. An image of the prisoner was instantly born in David: the detachment of the man's mind, his unassailable irony, his courage. There was no face yet, no form, but a sense of the man himself, very clear, clearer to David than any friend.

An aide to the commandant appeared at the door. "You looking at our cells?" he said, smiling a stock-friendly Vietnamese smile.

"Yes," David said, the word very small.

The man glanced at the wall. "You find something?"

"No."

"This cell was vacated only this morning. We haven't gone over it yet."

"You go over the cells after each prisoner?" David asked.

"Very closely," the man said.

"Is this morning's prisoner still around?"

"No. They took him to Saigon to question. We think he is a very big man."

"What was his name?"

"Pham Van Tuyen."

David had a complex feeling at the name: he was glad to have it; he wanted, even then, even at the first, to meet Tuyen; he resented the name's being spoken by this aide whom David knew would be Tuyen's mortal enemy; he found himself afraid for Tuyen, as strongly as he might fear for himself, fearful especially now that Tuyen had been taken to Saigon.

David placed the stand against the wall, glimpsing Tuyen's words one last time. And as soon as the words were covered, the reverie faded, David heard the newspaper ruffle again, heard a cough, a door open, feet scuffling. Jennifer stood before him in the waiting room and David looked at her. He returned her smile but she was very distant now, he looked at her as if she were the memory, a woman he'd known long, long ago.

The courtroom was small and almost empty. The colonel had not yet appeared. David sat very still and Carl was leaning near, speaking in a low tone to him about something, but David didn't hear a word. He found an old reflex coming back and it made him feel comfortable. He simply shut Carl out. He knew the man had nothing important to say at this moment, was speaking only from his own nervousness, and so David detached from him. David felt alone in this place and that let him control his breathing, control the quaking in his chest, let him even feel for a moment that he'd never set a VC prisoner free, had never gone to Vietnam. He was alone here in the way he'd been alone for most of his life before Vietnam, deliciously alone, even when he'd been in a room full of people, even when he'd been in the presence of his father, whose own eyes fully acknowledged no one. David stared at the picture of Gerald Ford hanging behind the judge's bench. He imagined that was how the people of the world looked to his father—a world of Gerald Fords—of portraits of Gerald Ford—vaguely benign, a little goofy, ignorable. David's own aloofness held no judgment, but it was as instinctive as his father's. And now he found that he hadn't lost the knack. He could even look over to the prosecutor's table and see Major Hedberg, his hair parted down near his ear to cover his baldness, a vain man, his eyes large behind his Army-issue horn-rims, a vain man who wanted to destroy David. David thought: if I were bald, would he be as hard on me? David smiled faintly at this. Hedberg did not seem to be a threat at all. Let him hang me for my follicles, David thought, and he was calm inside, utterly calm. He would write on the wall of his cell before the hanging: bald is beautiful.

The military bailiff called the court to attention and David rose, Carl beside him, Hedberg and his aides rose, the colonel came in. The colonel was gray and crew-cut and during the hearing always calm but not quite grim, a rampike, a hardwood tree standing alone in a field, someone for whom David suddenly had a surprising sympathy, one solitary figure for another.

But as the courtroom sat and the colonel began to read his report, David shut even this man out. He had no patience for the procedural matters—the list of rights he'd been advised of, the validation of depositions—the colonel had no sense of priorities—and David found himself calm still, not impatient, just waiting, waiting through a summary of the evidence and he was alone here again.

Then David was on his feet, standing beside Carl before the colonel and the gray face darkened, became now actually grim, and the man said, "In that Captain David Bates Fleming did in the province of Phuoc Thuy in the Republic of Vietnam . . ."

David sensed Carl tighten next to him and his attention pulled away from the colonel; he fixed on Carl, as if they were running together, as if the pace was suddenly too fast and Carl was struggling. David knew what was happening —that Carl was already anticipating the worst—and David wanted to whisper to him, Slow down, Carl, you're going too fast, we've got a long way to run. And at this David lost his detachment. He was no longer alone in the room. Vietnam, Tuyen, the long process since, Jennifer: all these rushed back into him, seized him, dragged him to the colonel, opened him once more to the words, to the danger, and the colonel was saying ". . . by helicopter and set him free. I am therefore recommending that you be tried by a general court-martial under Article 104 of the Uniform Code of Military Justice, aiding the enemy."

David heard a faint gasp from the back of the courtroom. He knew that he himself appeared calm, that his surface was placid. The charge burrowed into him and it would have its effect but right now all he was conscious of was the gasp behind him and of the past few minutes as he'd found again the detachment of his mind that he'd once held as a critical part of his truest self. But he realized that he'd isolated himself so effectively in this place that threatened him that he'd not even thought of his wife. It was Jennifer's gasp. And he was saluting the colonel now at his dismissal and he was turning and he saw Jennifer rising in the back of the room, rising with one hand over their unborn child and her eyes wide with a fear that he felt once more as his own.

"Why did you do it?" Jennifer said.

David had thought she was asleep, for she had grown very still beside him in the bed, in spite of her almost constant discomfort. Instead, she had been working up to this question. She spoke it gently, a little sadly. With the same tone he said, "When was the last time you asked me that?"

He heard her turn toward him but he did not look at her. He kept his eyes on the darkness that thickened against the ceiling like heat.

"A couple of months," she said.

He let that reply stand as his answer.

"But the whole pretrial hearing has happened since," she said.

"I don't know how to answer the question."

"Didn't anything come to you, listening to the case?" Her voice was still quiet but the gentleness was gone.

David tried again. He opened himself to possible answers, but all the words that came were very familiar. "I didn't go to him intending to set him free. I wanted to meet him."

"You're not an impulsive man."

"I know I'm not."

"Then when you met him—why did you let him go?" Her voice was louder now, growing frantic.

"I found him by a stream. He'd already escaped into the jungle on Con Son Island. I found him myself and he was there and I spoke to him at last and then I just took him where he . . . belonged . . . I don't know."

"You can't say these things on the witness stand."

"I know I can't."

"You took him where he belonged?"

"It's not that . . ."

"Who was he to you, anyway? A stranger . . ."

"I don't know who he was."

"Was he a father figure or something?"

"No," David said and from the lack of vehemence in his answer he knew this was true. He knew from Tuyen, as well. He was nothing like a father. At the very beginning, starting with the words on the cell wall, there was in David no feeling of meek comfort that a son would have before a surrogate father. David's interest had been caught by this man as an equal. But the strength of David's feeling, the obscurity of its source: he had no answers.

"Then what was it?" Jennifer drew her face closer to David. Her voice trembled.

"I don't know."

"You've got to lie."

"I don't know what to say."

"You can think of something. Lie. You have to lie."

David thought of the story Carl wanted to feed him but he said nothing.

"They could kill you for this," Jennifer said.

"They wouldn't."

"They could."

"They can't figure out my motive either. They could convict me of a lesser charge."

"What?"

"Dereliction of duty maybe."

"It's still prison."

"Maybe not."

"Dammit, David." Jennifer rose up on one elbow and, as she did, she barked wordlessly in either anger or pain. Then she said, "Dammit. You can't go to prison now. We're just starting."

"Do you think I *want* to go to prison?"

"You seem to think you're above all this."

"I'm not."

"You're passive. You're just passive now." She tried to sit up.

"Please don't," David said. "Please rest." He sat up quickly, stroked at her hair, tried to ease her back down onto the bed.

"Don't," she said and she swiped his hand away. She began to weep.

"Please . . . I'm not passive . . . I'm as scared as you are."

Jennifer clutched at his hand. "They're going to convict you," she said.

"We don't know that."

"How will you defend yourself?"

David had no answer for this question. "If I lie," he said, "it would mean going onto the stand. If my heart isn't in a lie, if I don't have every detail at my command, Hedberg would destroy me in cross-examination. And then the attempt to lie would be an issue. Hedberg would have what he wants. It's better for me to be silent. Better to make them prove their case. I don't know how to lie about this."

"You were in intelligence and you don't know how to lie?" Jennifer was sitting now, holding her belly.

Even more serious to David than being convicted was her sitting up, her agitation. "Please be calm," he said. "Please don't get up."

"Was this 'make them prove their case' stuff Carl's suggestion?"

"No."

"I didn't think so. He knows you don't have a chance unless you tell them something they can relate to. Spy work. Whatever. Lie, dammit."

"I'm only an effective liar professionally. This is much too close to me. On a witness stand and fighting for my life I can't imagine how I'd lie about what I did. Don't you understand that?"

"Then what are we going to do?" Jennifer's anger had broken like a wave and now her voice grew quiet again, full of despair; she lay back down.

David was more thankful that she was resting than he was distressed at her despair. "We could run away," he said, an unpremeditated thought. As soon as he spoke it, the idea depressed him.

"Run away?"

"Get in a car and drive to Canada."

"Couldn't they extradite you?"

"I don't know."

"We make our child a fugitive along with us?"

"No." David lay down and looked again into the darkness above the bed. He thought of Clifford Wilkes. Wilkes was an enlisted man working for David's intelligence operation in Vietnam. Wilkes had deserted. He'd deserted while still in Vietnam. He was last seen driving an Army jeep down Highway 1A toward Saigon. A deserter who stayed in Vietnam. David wondered where he was now. Maybe Wilkes would understand why David set a VC prisoner free.

"David?" Jennifer's voice was very small.

"Yes?"

"The baby is coming now."

David had been able to find no concentration for natural childbirth training, and so he sat in a windowless waiting room that smelled of cigarette smoke and floor polish. He was thankful he was alone here. He assumed that all the other fathers-to-be were with their wives, coaching their breathing, mopping their brows. Jennifer was strong. She was calm. David loved those qualities in her and they gave him this time alone. He knew that if she had not been able to give him this kind of time, they would never have married. Before Jennifer, before Vietnam, solitude was his keenest joy, his first instinct, his habitat. He placed his hands on his knees and sat very still, waiting for his child to be born, and he consciously thought of the places where he'd often been alone. Truly alone. The Cascades. Camping in the mountains. But suddenly David saw those mountains from one remove: he thought of himself in Vietnam, lying in a tent in Nui Dat, and as he lay there he thought of the mountains. He was in Nui Dat working with the Australians. He lay shrouded in mosquito netting listening to the trees move above him in the dark. A night bird twittered near the tent and on that night he let the images come, the Cascades, the creak of fir as he came near to sleep, the falling away of all human contact, the rush of rain against a fast, cold stream, a mountainside quiet with evergreen and implying nothing of men. For a short time he let that present wood—the tropical wood—suggest the earlier. Then Tuyen came to him. He'd been seeking Tuyen in the Australians' area of operations, but he'd been delayed and the delay worried David. Tuyen might finally be questioned to the end, to death, and that could happen anytime. David lay in his tent and the Cascades did not quite fade, but Tuyen was there too, the face of Tuyen turning to a cell wall, his mind seeking refuge somewhere. David thought: is he remembering a wood like mine? Is he holding on just as I am? Is he pressing his face close to the concrete wall and clinging to a jungle guerrilla camp where trees lean against the night sky and his comrades fall away and the wide forests hold his quick mind softly, smoothing his irony into peace?

David had gone far down this tunnel in his mind and he

began to retreat: from Tuyen's dreams of solitude and safety; to Tuyen's mind in his cell; to David's own mind in his tent in Vietnam, imagining Tuyen's mind; to the Cascades; and David leaped back from Vietnam, across the mountain stream that ran in him then as now; and David rose up from the Naugahyde chair and paced the waiting room like an expectant father from a cartoon. He stopped as the door swung open.

"Mr. Fleming?" the nurse said.

"Yes."

"Congratulations. You have a son."

"Yes?" The leaping in David's chest would let him say no more, ask no questions.

"Your wife and child are both doing fine."

David nodded and the nurse smiled and turned, the door clicked shut behind her. David was motionless for a moment and then he lunged to the door, jerked it open.

"When can I see him?" David called after the nurse.

She said, "I'll let you know," without pausing or turning even her face to him.

David went back to the chair and he waited, for a time, in suspension: he had his son, but the child was just a word still, an abstraction. Jennifer was doing fine. He had a son. But what did that mean? For the present it meant that no other thoughts intruded. Nothing of the trial, of Vietnam, of trees or mountains or of Vietcong prisoners. David simply dangled in this room, in the still air, and he did not turn one way or another until the nurse returned.

"You can come see him now," she said and she led David down a corridor full of doorways until the doorways turned into a long hallway of glass windows. Beyond the windows were rows of high cradles each containing a tiny body, each with a name in large letters, all written by the same hand. "Go on down to the far end," the nurse said and she went through a door and between the furrows of infants.

David continued to the far window, which looked into an open space at the edge of the nursery. The nurse who had brought David here—he recognized only her tortoise-shell glasses, for her face was masked—came into this area and something was in her arms. David squared around, pressed against the glass, only moments to wait now, only moments, he watched the nurse approach and her arms came out and she lifted what was in her arms and there were limbs jutting out, arms, legs, feet, toes splayed, and David's own face. His own face rose before him. Tiny, a replica, the rough places smoothed away, the eyes puffy, but it was David's face. All the subtle contours and relationships—the width of the nose, the set of the eyes, the thin-lipped stretch of the mouth—all these were unmistakably from him, were part of him, broken off now, reshaped, externalized. And the thickness of the child's neck, the thickness of the arms, the calves of his legs, his feet. These were all David's. The baby's limbs stretched out and the child cried, a single tone, like a jungle bird, a high clear tone, unmodulated, rising to a peak with no break in its sound. The face contracted with the sound and David felt his own face grow tight, his own eyes narrow as if it were he himself crying out; his own throat vibrated faintly with the sound. David felt exposed. This tiny, other self made the surface of David's body grow sensitive, as if he were naked; more, as if the outer layer of his skin had been painlessly stripped away. He felt himself lifted up by the nurse a brief moment and then drawn back and carried away. Even after the space beyond the window was empty and the baby was gone, David remained pressed there, focused on the place where his son had appeared moments ago as briefly and comprehensively as a lifetime flashing before a drowning man.

David and Carl were jogging. Their route was already familiar to David—down the hill, out Holabird Avenue, down to the steel mill at Sparrows Point, and back. David wanted to fill this hollow of familiarity with his son. To run and think of his new son: that might wipe away every trace of his

present jeopardy, for a time at least. But Carl was striding
with him, the trial was striding with him, step for step.

"How's it feel?" Carl asked.

"What?"

"Fatherhood."

"Okay," David said, thinking something much stronger.
He felt stunned by his child.

"When are they coming home?"

"From the hospital?"

"Yes."

"On Monday," David said.

"Big day."

"Yes."

They ran for a few blocks in silence. The air smelled of
bus fumes, though none was in sight.

Carl said, "I see that the South lost a regiment of para-
troopers at Xuan Loc."

"I'm not reading the papers lately," David said.

"No?"

"I've lost my interest."

"I was in Xuan Loc for a while."

"I think I *prefer* to have no interest," David said.

"Sorry."

"That's not why I said that."

"It's okay," Carl said. "You're right anyway. The Vietnam war is half a world away, eons old."

"If that were so, we wouldn't be jogging here as lawyer
and client."

Carl grunted in reply and after their turn toward Sparrows Point he said, "Have you been thinking about the . . .
ah . . . analysis I made last time we ran?"

"About trying to recruit a double agent?"

"Yes."

"I've thought about it."

"Yes?"

"If I lie, Hedberg will have me for breakfast."

Carl grunted again, as if he'd stridden into a hole.

"You know there's an irony at work here," David said. "A big one."

"What's that?"

"That the Army should be prosecuting me for this. I helped kill a prisoner over there, you know."

"When?"

"Somewhere along the line. After I'd grown interested in Tuyen, I think. But before I'd started really trying to track him down. This had nothing at all to do with that. In any way. That's ironic too."

"What happened?"

"I had an enlisted man working for me named Wilson Hand. He got snatched by a little party of VC out at an orphanage we used to visit. The VC had him for about a week and we got a lead that he was still being held in the area, that a VC suspect might have some information on where he was. I took my other EM with me—a guy named Clifford Wilkes—and an MP who helped us out, and we went to the local National Police compound. When the prisoner wouldn't say anything but made a little semantic slip that suggested he did know something, we all went out in the woods to scare him. We put a cloth over his face and poured water on it—not a fatal technique at all, not at all. But he had a bad heart. The Vietnamese lieutenant with us told us that fact only after it was over. We were clumsy. Stupid. The man died." David hadn't thought about all this for a long time. Even as he told it now, there were very few clear images of the incident. The fractured sunlight coming through the canopy of trees. The stream running nearby, where the water came from. The man's face contoured beneath the handkerchief like a plaster mask. Wilkes, his eyes wide, holding the man down. Little else. David tried to remember the man himself, but he had no definite image of him. Even at the time he'd had none. He did remember that the prisoner was of the indistinct age common to many Vietnamese—anywhere between thirty and sixty. The man was small, but no more so than any Vietnamese.

The man had been bland and inaccessible. And David had felt nothing for him, neither during the interrogation nor after the death. He'd felt no real remorse, no loss; the man had hardly existed for him. The remorse David did feel—and it was keen for a time—was over the fact that he felt no remorse. "Why isn't *that* what's coming back to avenge itself on me?" David said.

"The answer's simple."

"Yes?"

"For the Army, you're the antidote to all that." Carl said no more, as if David would instantly understand. David did not, but before he could press the point, Carl said, "The Army had a gutful of self-condemnation in the Calley trial. Your mystifying bit of compassion is far more provocative to them. That's what they really want to prosecute. That's what they really can't tolerate. What the hell's this whole institution for? What's the *real* crime in their eyes? Being too tough or too soft?"

They fell silent as they jogged in place at a traffic light. The morning sky was clear except for the steel mill's column of smoke, unified from a dozen smokestacks and swept to the west, as if the mill were in motion. David said, "The more mystified they get over what I did, the angrier they're going to get."

"You're a smart man, David. You'd make a good lawyer."

"But the letter of the law insulates me from their anger, doesn't it?"

"Forget what I just said."

"I didn't want to be a lawyer anyway."

The light changed and they were running again. Carl said, "You've got to make some decisions without any more hesitation, David. The real thing is starting now and it won't last long."

"But they took so long getting to this point. After it all came out—flagging me, putting their case together, how long already? It's been a couple of years and . . ."

"What's your point, David?"

David didn't know. "Maybe I convinced myself that this thing never would actually get around to happening."

"There's an inertia involved here. What made it so slow before will make it fast now."

"I still can't go on the stand. I still don't think I could pull off a lie elaborate enough to explain all this away."

"Okay," Carl said. "What have they got? The most crucial witnesses are Vietnamese. Really, the linchpin is the helicopter pilot. The lieutenant you forced to help you on Con Son had not a clue as to what you intended to do with Tuyen. You could have come to take Tuyen off and kill him for all he knew. The helicopter pilot is the key. And he's just words on paper."

"Where is he?"

"He lost a leg in a crash," Carl said. "He's in some military hospital in the Delta . . . Too bad that crash wasn't a little more thorough."

"Could we plead to a lesser charge?"

"Every charge is based on a motive. And what's yours? You got intrigued by this man? From a piece of graffiti? This is the Army, David. In ten minutes of cross-examination Hedberg would have you admitting to a sneaky admiration for the Communists. In twenty minutes you'd be a radical revolutionary yourself. Prosecutors are trained to fill holes with anything they want. And your story is full of holes. And not even you know what to put in them."

David felt a flutter of panic in his chest. He wanted to run faster, to sprint, but he held back.

Carl said, "I've raised this before, David, but it's all we've got at the moment and I want to press it. We should bring in a couple of character witnesses. Let me work with them. Paint you as a superpatriot."

"Whatever you want."

"Who is there?"

"I was a loner in Vietnam."

"Not entirely."

"The last time you wanted people I was close to, there was no one."

"How about your enlisted men? How about Wilkes?"

"He deserted in Vietnam."

"Ouch."

"They'll try to blame me for that, as well. Right?"

"Of course. They'll say you filled his mind with the very anti-American sentiments that prompted you to free the prisoner."

"There's Wilson Hand. I got him back from the VC. In okay shape, too."

"Right. I've got a line on him. He's running a little security business in Manhattan. We'll get him down here . . . Anyone else? Your commanding officer at Homestead, before you transferred to Saigon?"

"Major Dole. I guess so. But he was a weak man. Or maybe it was just his weak stomach. He spent his tour of duty fighting the GI shits and he had no energy to pay attention to much of anything else. I don't know what good he'd do."

"You have any CIA friends?"

"Still on that?"

"No," Carl said. "But they'd lend some sort of credibility to an unusual event. Maybe. I don't know. Authorized loners. Given to indirect plans. If you don't go on the stand, at least we can hint at things . . ."

"There was one guy. Kenneth Trask. I worked with him in Saigon for a while. Not a friend, really. I don't know what he thought of me at all. He might have been my friend, he might have hated my guts."

Carl fell silent once more and David realized that at these moments he never knew which way the man's mind would turn next. We're mysteries to each other, David thought.

Then Carl said, "I have one more idea."

"What's that?"

"I want to alert the press."

"The press?"

"I want to get the national press interested in what's going on here."

David stopped running. He halted even before his reaction to this suggestion was clear to himself. "No," he said, the response beginning to elaborate itself in David: that would be a crowd he could never be alone in; he'd face the vast, unspoken scrutiny of subway riders and breakfast loungers all over the country. The press would destroy any chance David might have to go through this thing in the way he'd always felt the most comfortable in his life.

Carl was approaching, having jogged on a few yards before he'd realized David had stopped. "No," David repeated.

"Listen," Carl said. For the first time he spoke with a tone of impatience unmitigated by any sympathy. "Do you have a death wish or something? I don't want to preside over a suicide here."

"Do you want to drop me as a client, counselor?" David said.

Carl recoiled slightly. He seemed to be groping for words but David spoke first. "You don't like the way I feel compelled to sort out my life, then you don't have to represent me."

"It's not that, David. I just have a great deal of respect for you . . ."

"Then respect what I say I have to do."

"Respect's the wrong word . . ."

The wry bluntness of this response held David silent long enough for him to soften his defiance. Carl must have done the same with his impatience, for he suddenly smiled. "Affection's the right word. I like you and so it makes me upset to see us giving you away to the prosecution. The Army wants to do this thing privately, for its own satisfaction. If the trial stays private, they won't have any pressure on them at all except what they put on themselves. And that would go against you."

"I've got to be private too," David said. "It's even more important to me."

Carl puffed and looked around him in the street as if he were trying to find an objective bystander to appeal to David. Then he said in a low voice, "We better run. We're cooling off."

David nodded and they ran, falling instantly into step, and they didn't speak again until they'd turned at the main gate of the steel mill, the air full of the smell of naphtha, and they'd started back toward Holabird. Then Carl said, "The law is full of passionless language. Sometimes you'd never guess from the way laws are expressed that they have anything to do with human beings."

David waited out one of Carl's tantalizing pauses. They ran and he might have grown irritated at this, another of the little rhetorical tricks that Carl seemed to enjoy. But instead, David had an impression of sincerity about this man, that Carl did indeed care about the people he defended. Then, just as the alternative began to take shape—that this impression was a sham, was the very purpose of the rhetorical trick —Carl spoke again.

"But there's a law in California," he said. "A test of whether murder has been proved. I think it's pretty close to human life. For a murder conviction to be appropriate, the prosecutor has to prove what's called 'implied malice.' And the test for implied malice is when, as the law says, 'the circumstances attending a killing show an abandoned and malignant heart.'"

They were beginning to run up a slight rise and their breath was growing short. Carl puffed and said, "It doesn't have to be murder for that to have meaning. My God, have I been close to a couple of people in my life who've had just that, abandoned and malignant hearts. Haven't you?"

"What's your point?" David said, conscious of throwing

Carl's earlier challenge back at him, conscious also that what
the man said was true.

"No point really."

"Is that so?"

"Maybe I was thinking about these people who want to
see you crushed."

"I don't want to go on the stand to lie and I don't want to
be the plaything of the national press," David said as firmly
as he could.

"I wasn't getting back to that."

"I can't worry about anyone else's heart, Carl."

"I'm going to do the best I can for you."

"I'm sorry if I'm making it tough."

"And for your family."

It was a cheap trick and David knew it. But his anger at
Carl for using it was instantly obscured by the image the
man had summoned of a family. No longer just a wife. The
boy existed separately now. And the separateness that
David felt so sharply was not the separateness from Jennifer's womb, but from David himself. That feeling of being
externalized. And Carl finally had his way. There was this
boy to protect and the pulse of fear quickened in David. He
tried to open his mind to what Carl said must be done. But
even with a son he could not change what he was. "No lies,
no press," he said.

Early that evening David lay alone in the bedroom. He'd
seen his son again that afternoon, through the glass. The
child was in his high crib and he kept his eyes open wide,
not sleeping, more alert than the others, as if he had some
special knowledge. As David lay in this room, which was
dim with the twilight, he wondered if even now his son was
staring just like this into the space around him. David felt
blank, as blank as an infant's mind, as his son's mind. For
the past few hours David had touched his child's face in his
thoughts so often that it was hard now to see it anymore.

He'd turned to the vision too often. He might expect this to distress him, but it did not. He knew he would be able to refresh his impressions of the face tomorrow. Tomorrow he would even hold the child himself. And for the present David was weary. He was content to mimic his son's emptiness. His son was alone now that he was born and no one could get inside him, his eyes saw only vague shapes, the voices about him had no meaning, he had the blessing of infancy—this benign aloofness.

And then David's own father came. The man came to David's room with the slanting walls under the eaves of the house with the pin oak and David was twelve years old and he'd been listening to shouting downstairs. His father came up the stairs and the door opened and the man was a massive silhouette in the doorway, the bare bulb in the hall spreading a penumbra of light behind his featureless face. And then the figure was gone, the lightbulb swung, waving shadows across David's bed. The man was gone forever. And after that there were more years of voices from downstairs. Other men's voices. All smoother voices than his father's, all stronger voices than his father's; he remembered his father's voice as harsh and inexpressive, like a badly dubbed foreign film. But maybe that was the problem. David was supplying the voice himself. Where had he heard his father answer someone's question? Are you married? someone asked. A woman's voice. His father would never lie. David remembered that, but not with any admiration. He never even created the lie of love for his son. Are you married? the woman's voice asked and David heard his father say: I have a son; he has a mother; she is his natural mother; I am the boy's natural father; the mother of my son and I both live with him; but she herself would put all of this quite differently. "Go away," David whispered on his bed in Baltimore. Months would pass—sometimes many months—without a specific image of his father. David felt he was in control even now, even on this night of his own fatherhood.

Sounds began outside. Through the open window came

the voice of Dan Rather. Fragments of sentences: refugees, Saigon, fears, advancing Communist forces. Someone was watching the fall of South Vietnam on the patio of the garden apartment next door. David rose up and closed the window, and by the time he returned to the bed, his father was gone, replaced briefly by an image of highways clogged with Vietnamese—a cliché. David closed his eyes, confident he could detach again. But just as a mind will pick a casual remark, an overlooked image, from the day just passed to cause a dream at night, David now could not shake an issue raised by Carl from their run; a minor issue, really, but it would not yield. David had been a loner in Vietnam, close to no one. Certainly no one who could testify for him. That was the issue, but David went further. There had been a woman. For just a few months. Suong. The words from the television linked to this thought of her: the panic in Saigon, the South Vietnamese in flight. She was in danger now. She was frightened. He hadn't thought of her for a long time, not since his return from Vietnam. Even before that. He'd known her early in his tour of duty, for perhaps three months. Having thought this much about her, David felt he was in control again, he could turn away now, he could forget her, could regain his emptiness. But instead he remembered; he chose to remember.

They'd been lovers briefly. The only Vietnamese woman he'd slept with. She was wealthy, part of a very wealthy family with strong political connections. David's thoughts were without context still. He could see her face: her eyelids rounded from the French blood in her family, her jaw strong for a Vietnamese, a surprisingly Western face but for her tawny skin and the long, straight black hair and the tilt to her eyes and her wide, sullen mouth. He saw the sullenness of her mouth in this image—but it was only sometimes sullen. Then the image grew specific. He sat with her in the grounds of the park off Nguyen Binh Khiem Street, near the National Museum. Her mouth was sullen then, she seemed sad. But she would not talk to him about it and he didn't

press it. She felt dizzy, she said. From the morning heat. A
monkey cried out in a cage in the Saigon Zoo on the other
side of the park. David and Suong had walked in the park
and hadn't spoken much. When her dizziness passed, they
went into the museum, but they sat again in an exhibit room
surrounded by scowling mythological heads of the Khmer
and Cham. The Vietnamese who passed through the room
glanced sharply from the statues to David and Suong and
back again.

"Do you know why they do that?" Suong asked, reading
his thought.

"Why?"

"Any Vietnamese girl with an American is thought to be
a whore."

Lying in the bed in Baltimore, David tried to remember
if he'd been making love with Suong by this time. Yes, he
decided. For about two months. This was late in their brief
affair. He'd said to her, "The people in the street didn't look
at us."

"In the streets, they don't care," she said. "But the people who come here do care. They feel this park is still their
own."

"Do you want to leave?" David asked.

"Certainly not. I knew this would happen."

Was she strong now? David wondered. As she was then?
Now that her country was falling? He rose up from the bed
and tried to pace Suong out of his mind. He'd considered
her long enough. His closeness with her had ended
abruptly. Not long after that day in the park. Perhaps she
hadn't been as untouched by the scorn of her countrymen as
she'd seemed. Perhaps they'd finally made her feel like a
whore. It was she who broke off the affair after all. He had
known enough about himself to soon feel relieved that it
had ended, but it had been her choice. He remembered a
quote he'd found from Christopher Marlowe later on. He'd
read a great deal in Vietnam, though he'd hardly opened a
book since. But he'd found a quote from Marlowe used by

T. S. Eliot as an epigraph to a poem: "Thou art guilty of fornication. But that was in another country. And besides, the wench is dead." David stopped pacing. He'd savored the ironic appropriateness at the time—the sense of all the GIs and their Vietnamese women prefigured by an Elizabethan playwright. But now he wondered if she was indeed dead. It was certainly another country, a far country. David lay back down on the bed. He'd put another quote in one of his notebooks before he'd left for Vietnam. He'd been self-consciously literary at times during that period and he smiled in faint ridicule of himself at that. The quote in his notebook was by Thomas Fuller: "He is miserable who dieth not before he desires to die." Was she dead now, Suong, in the fall of South Vietnam?

He remembered their first meeting. David was in Saigon following some leads on a VC supply line. He had to see a high-ranking USAID man, a Mr. Craig, for some help. The CIA man David had worked with—Trask—had recommended the USAID man, had even set up a meeting at a dinner party at Craig's house. It was there that David met Suong and he remembered the night as it had happened. He approached the house in the thick, steamy dark. The stretch of street was residential and lights were isolated and dim. At Craig's villa there was a cluster of American government cars, half a dozen pastel Ford Falcons. Three local policemen stood guard outside the iron gate.

David entered the grounds. He drew near a tree and stopped. Across the narrow front lawn was the villa, its lower level brilliant with light that pushed through the open windows and the screened porch. The second floor stretched up into the dark blur of trees and night sky. Party gabble and isolated surges of laughter and bossa nova music drained with the light into the yard. In an upstairs window David saw a glow, as if from a night-light. From the upstairs, too, he sensed silence.

People moved in the lower windows. This was as close as David wanted to be. Once inside, this would be the precise distance he would desire for his mind—outside, alone, under a tree, watching figures move behind windows. Then the door to the porch swung open abruptly and a man stepped out, a drink in his hand, an American. David drew back into the shadows as if this were an enemy agent. The man did not notice David but walked to the front gate and stood looking through it, not moving. David quietly slipped by and entered the house.

The bar was set up on the porch and an old Vietnamese man behind it asked him at once, "What drink you have?" The porch had only two Vietnamese women sitting in chairs beneath a lacquer screen. One was young and pretty, the other perhaps thirty-five and very plain. They smiled and nodded at him and he moved past them to the door leading from the porch into the dining room. There he paused, feeling the resistant press against him of congregated people in the far room. The dining room itself was quiet. The ceiling pulled his eyes up at once with its height. A paddle fan moved slowly overhead. The table below was being spread with cold cuts and fruit and raw vegetables by Vietnamese in white coats. A paunchy American was bending near and whispering to a Vietnamese woman in an ao dai before a wall of glass cases filled with Buddhas, Oriental vases, and plastic models of US Navy vessels.

"You looking someone?"

David turned and was dismayed to find himself within easy talking distance of the two Vietnamese women in the chairs. The older of the two had spoken to him and she allowed no time for an answer before adding, "I'm Miss Kim. This is my sister, Miss Quanh. I am a secretary at USAID headquarters. My sister work at City Hall."

David tried to deflect the woman by pressing her for useful information. "Do you know Mr. Trask? Do you know where he is?"

She repeated the name slowly, mispronouncing it almost beyond recognition, and then she was talking again about herself and her sister with no attempt at all at a graceful transition from answering his question to continuing her own monologue. "My sister is very beautiful," she said and the younger sister giggled. "Many Americans ask her to go with them to restaurants." David expected the girl to giggle again, but she didn't; she looked at him closely. "She is very young. I am the older sister. She asks me what to do." She paused, as if to let David consider all the things she might tell her sister to do. David began to think that Craig's advice couldn't possibly be worth remaining at this party. Then the older sister said, "You are a very handsome man," and she repeated it in Vietnamese. The younger sister giggled.

"Don't let them start flattering you," a voice said. David turned to find Trask. The man was David's age and had a snide, immobile face.

"I was almost out the door," David said.

"I saw you when you came in, but I was tied up in a conversation. Thought you'd stick it out more than five minutes."

"You misjudged me."

"Aren't you dazzled by the Saigon social whirl?" Trask said, smiling.

"No."

"I understand your feeling, naturally. But we sometimes have to bite the bullet in our line of work." Trask inclined his head slightly toward the living room and moved away. David followed. As they passed through the dining room, Trask took a drink off a tray held by a Vietnamese servant, stopped, and handed it to David. "Your disguise," he said in a mock whisper.

The living room was filled with what was, for David, the multitude of low-grade torments that are patched together to make parties. He followed Trask into the press of bodies, along a path that was constantly shifting and pinching shut and then opening again. The American bodies were gross and hearty, the Vietnamese bodies slithery and giggly. David tried to sidle quickly past them all. He was trapped, he knew, and so he placed his mind back outside, out under a tree; he watched from there, watched himself move in this room that was heavy with smoke and perfume and sweat, all catalyzed by the early evening heat.

He squeezed past a full-bird colonel telling his tiny Vietnamese companion how he could help her get into an American university. Then David shut out the sounds and he finally broke through the clutch of people and into a small, loose space almost at the center of the room, like the eye of a storm. Trask was there, waiting. He had a man with him who was obviously Mr. Craig. Trask beckoned with a stiff flip of the hand but before David moved to the two men, he paused and wiped the sweat from his forehead and glanced away, through a sudden break in the crowd and into the far corner.

A woman stood there. She was tall, much taller than the other Vietnamese women, and she was detached from the several men around her, aloof. She stood straight and still, the silk panels of her ao dai dangling loosely but not stirring. She laughed once, while David watched, but it was a full laugh. Then the bodies of the crowd shifted again and David's sight of her was broken.

At this, David rose up from his bed. This memory of Suong was like seeing her for the first time. David paced the floor. He was sweating, as if he were in a crowded room. He wiped at his forehead and he wondered where Suong was at this moment. But the curiosity was purely of the mind; his heart and body were still in the party at Craig's house and he lay back down on the bed.

That night in Saigon, David talked to Craig for a time. The man had taken him into the relative privacy of the dining room. They stood near a wide stairway leading to the second floor. They were far away from the stereo speakers and from most of the people and David could speak to him in a low voice. He explained to Craig why he was in Saigon. The man was vague but friendly, unable to help in specifics but useful for a general lead or two. David was feeling that this had all been a waste of time. Now that he'd escaped it, the crowded room repelled him even more intensely. Mr. Craig had a forced how-do-we-gracefully-disengage-this-conversation smile and David was ready to bolt. Then he felt someone brush past. The tall Vietnamese woman started up the stairs. Craig stopped her.

"Miss Suong," he said. "I have someone for you to meet." She turned slowly to face David, looking down from the fourth step. She smiled.

"Of course, William." She came back down, but remained elevated on the bottom step. Craig introduced David to Nguyen Thi Tuyet Suong, and he left.

"I haven't seen you here before," she said with a trace of a French accent.

"No." David wondered if he was detaining her and glanced up the stairs. She picked it up.

"It's all right. That can wait." She smiled.

"Your name is the loveliest of all the Vietnamese women's names. It means 'snow before the dawn,' doesn't it?"

She laughed, again a full, deep laugh. "Yes. How did you know that?"

"I speak Vietnamese," he said in Vietnamese.

"Very good," she said, still in English. "But do you really find it a beautiful name? I mean, to your ear. It's one thing to find enchanting the image of a name's meaning and it's quite another thing actually to hear beauty in the sound of a name."

"I don't speak the language *that* well. No," David said, in English again, pleased at her refusal to engage him in Vietnamese conversation or to praise his learning the language.

"I should think," she continued, "the sound of Tuyet Suong would inspire no feelings of beauty in an American's heart."

"Not in mine, at least. I admit it."

"For all the reputation Americans have for bluntness, not a man at this party would have admitted that straight out to me." She smiled only slightly, and she stepped down at last from the bottom stair. She was tall by Vietnamese standards, certainly, but if David were to hold her, her head would fall lightly on his chest.

"Did you want me to gracefully avoid the admission?" David said.

"No."

"Who told you most Americans are blunt?"

"I can't remember," she said at once. "Perhaps the same one who says to you that all Vietnamese are either beggars or crooks."

"Oh, him."

"Yes. He's the one. Is he a friend of yours?" She kept a very solemn face.

David nodded toward the living room and said in a low voice, "He's somewhere in that room."

Suong laughed. "It's good, then, that we are in here."

"Very good." They looked at each other a moment in silence.

"Are you new in Saigon?" she asked.

David felt, at the question, oddly sad. He appreciated her, but the feeling still caught him by surprise. "Not exactly. I've been here before, but I'm working about twenty miles out of town, out in the direction of Bien Hoa. I'm leaving Saigon tomorrow." He tried to read disappointment in her face but there was no trace of change. He suddenly felt her foreignness. It was just as well that he did, he thought, for there was an Air Force captain standing beside them now.

"Are you ready?" he asked Suong.

"Not yet," she said. David heard no warmth in her words to the man and she introduced the captain to him and climbed the stairs. Her black hair hung straight and long against the pale blue of her ao dai.

The captain drifted away with a curt nod and David lingered near the foot of the stairs. He felt foolish. But when

Suong descended a few minutes later, he saw her look around. The captain had his back to them and she came to David near the glass cases.

"You may get back to Saigon someday," she said. "My family would be happy to have you come by for dinner." She thrust a piece of paper into his hand and turned away. He looked at her neatly lettered address and glanced up to see her leave with the captain. David looked for Trask before he himself left, to ask who she was. Already David's comfort felt vaguely threatened. He didn't want to become involved with a Vietnamese woman. Still, he found Trask and asked the question, half hoping that she was a whore, someone he could easily put out of his mind.

"She's a very wealthy woman," Trask said. "Her father is dead now, but he and his brother once were very close to Diem, very influential. She's a friend of Craig's mistress."

"Is she the Air Force captain's mistress?" David asked. "Who?"

David had forgotten the captain's name. But Trask didn't need it. She had a reputation for being aloof, he said. She belonged to no one, at least to his knowledge.

David went out into the night and paused under the tree and he turned on his side in the bed in Baltimore and silence buzzed faintly in the room and he thought of Suong, saw her in that first moment standing with an aloofness like his own. The kinship he'd felt then for her had proved to be a lie. She would make love with him and turn moody and then vanish from his life, all in the space of just a few months. But that was in another country: his mouth shaped this phrase but he did not make a sound.

The whisk of brush on shoe filled David up. He concentrated fiercely on his shine, a military habit; he buffed and buffed and watched the reflection of his face sharpen in the toe of his shoe. He stopped at last and carefully placed it by its mate. His right arm was tight, the triceps ached, from the brushing. He turned to the table beside him where his brass lay. The Brasso he'd applied had clouded and dried and he took a fresh handkerchief and he began to polish. His captain's bars first—easy to shine, the two metal parallel bars glittering at once in the beam of morning light from the bedroom window. He stopped and held the bars aloft, angling them this way and that, letting them flash so sharply that he expected them to make a sound, a crackling sound. But the apartment was very still. He paused, his hand fell, he was conscious of Jennifer's absence, of the distance now, the unreality, of his son. It was Monday, the first morning of his trial.

He returned to his task and all thoughts vanished. He polished the other set of captain's bars and the US insignia and the Intelligence Corps insignia—difficult, the central circle full of convolutions. He used a cotton swab to polish the Brasso out of the crevices. And then the buttons on his coat, using the swab again to make the wings of each American eagle shine.

Then he dressed: his black cotton socks; his tan dress shirt full of starch, the collar stiff against his neck; his black tie, the knot made perfectly; the green pants with the black officer's stripes down the legs. He reattached the brass to his coat, handling the pieces only by the edge, then carefully buffing away with his handkerchief even the faint margins of fingerprints, once the pieces were in place. He touched his Vietnamese service ribbon over the breast pocket. The ribbon was yellow with vertical red stripes, the colors of the South Vietnamese flag. But he did not let himself think about that country or its fate. This ribbon was out of line and he adjusted it to make it exactly parallel with the flap of the pocket. He put on his shoes, lacing them carefully, and then his coat.

He stood in the center of the room and he was wrapped with minute precision; this order, this containment, was a gift from the Army; he felt no fear and an hour later he stood just like this before the colonel and heard the specification of charges once more, aiding the enemy, and he sat beside Carl to listen to prospective jurors being interviewed.

For a time he heard little, had little in his mind. But eventually his sweat softened his collar; he shifted in his chair and felt the wrinkles in his pants created by the way he'd been sitting; he accidentally brushed his shoe against the table leg and he knew a scuff mark was there. The time went on and the words droned around him and he thought about Jennifer and about his son coming home this afternoon. David Junior. That was the name they had decided on, at last. Jennifer and David Junior would be home today.

"Do you have a family of your own?" Hedberg asked.

David looked up. The major was talking to a prospective juror. A young sergeant with wire-rim glasses and a pale mustache was sitting in the witness box. "Yessir," he said.

"Wife?" the major said, not looking at the sergeant, his back to him, his face angled toward the ceiling.

"Yessir," the sergeant said.

"Children?"

"No sir."

"And what nationality is your wife, Sergeant Booker?"

"She's Vietnamese, sir."

David found himself intently studying the sergeant, his own interest surprising him a little bit. The man was nervous; he kept stretching his neck as if his collar were chafing him; his thin hands kept darting to his face, scratching, smoothing the mustache, plucking an earlobe.

"She's Vietnamese?" Hedberg said.

"Yessir," the sergeant said.

"Would you say you have a special affinity for the Vietnamese people?" Hedberg said.

The sergeant's face contracted in confusion over this.

"A special feeling or affection," Hedberg said, patronizing the man, clarifying the hard word in the question.

"I don't know, sir."

David knew from the sergeant's tone—and he realized Hedberg knew it, too—that the sergeant did indeed have a special feeling for the Vietnamese. That's why I was drawn to him, David thought. Because of last night, my memories of Suong.

Hedberg turned to the judge. He said, "The prosecution desires to challenge this juror peremptorily."

The colonel nodded. "Sergeant Booker, you can step down. Thank you very much."

The sergeant dipped his head and rose. Hedberg crossed back to his table and David wondered what had just happened. He knew the prosecution had a limited number of peremptory challenges and one of them was invoked very quickly here. What did Hedberg think he knew about David? The sergeant had a Vietnamese wife, presumably a special feeling for the Vietnamese people, and the major expected this to prejudice him in favor of David. If the sergeant had opposed the war, that would make sense. But a South Vietnamese wife would likely fear, even hate, the Communists. Surely that would make the husband more receptive to the prosecution's case, if anything. But the major challenged the juror. David felt fidgety. This man Hedberg thought he knew something about him, about his deepest motives, and David didn't know what it was. Hedberg sat at his table and pushed some papers around, complacent, smug, full of this secret, and David almost jumped up, almost leaped across the courtroom to seize him by the throat and squeeze his thoughts out of him.

Carl's hand was on David's arm. "Are you all right?" he whispered.

David turned to Carl and he felt now the trembling in himself, heard himself breathing heavily.

David carried his son into the apartment, Jennifer shaky at his elbow, and he laid his boy in the crib. Away from the glass and metal of the hospital nursery, home among the cartoon wallpaper and stuffed animals, Jennifer leaning against him, her body restored to its former slender state,

David felt even more keenly that the baby was a detached part of himself, as if it had been his own body from which this boy had been plucked. The tiny face was alert and placid, seemingly conscious of David but unmoved by him. More details of the face: the faint cleft in the chin, the rise of the cheek; it was minutely David's own face. And the hands. One of the boy's hands came up fitfully and fell, drawing David's attention, and the proportion of the fingers, the shape of the nails, were a man's. This shocked David. He expected the hands to be a child's, the fingers stubby and homogeneous. But David extended his forefinger and let these tiny fingers lie on his knuckle, and the round thumbnail, the elongated nails of the other fingers, the tiny moons there, were copied meticulously from David's own hands. He bent low into the crib and kissed the child's hand. He felt a touch on his back and it startled him. He'd forgotten that Jennifer was in the room. He straightened up.

"He's beautiful," Jennifer said softly.

David didn't want to cheapen this moment with words. He nodded and tried to cut her out of his awareness.

But she surprised him by saying, "I feel weary. Let's go outside and sit together."

David was not ready to leave the child but he said nothing; he followed his wife out of the tiny second bedroom and through their living room and kitchen and out onto their garden-apartment patio. He paused near the door, but Jennifer went on, into the patch of grass. She stopped and moved her shoulders slowly as if her muscles were stiff and she lifted her face a bit and breathed deeply. "I've felt so cooped up," she said.

David's thoughts lingered in his son's room. But Jennifer was on the patio again, coming to him, and he knew there would soon be time for him alone with the boy. "Let's sit," she said. "Let's just sit a little while and clear our heads."

They sat beside each other on a wrought-iron settee and David took Jennifer's hand. She puffed, as if in exasperation.

"What is it?" he said.

"Why are human beings so damn irrational?"

There was a pause and David said, "You really want me to try to answer that?"

"I knew from every damn book I read that there'd be a letdown. You'd think that if I understood that so well, I'd be able to control it."

"You can't."

"No, I can't."

"Why not?"

"I don't know why not. Maybe because I *should* be let down. After all the things I went through, the final resolution is something that's overwhelmingly *separate* from me. The climax left me just like I was. *I* should be different after all that. *My* body should be new after that, *my* mind should be new. Something. The baby's beautiful and I love him very much, but he's his own person already and I'm nothing but what I was."

David wanted to say something to help, he wanted to be gentle, supportive, and yet he couldn't find any words. Indeed, all he could think of was that he felt some of the things Jennifer wanted to feel for herself. He didn't feel different in that his essential qualities were made new, but he did feel intensified, as if his own life and self had been projected into a form that he could touch and hold and speak to. Yes, he knew Jennifer's sense of separateness; this child was separate, vulnerable. But David felt the unceasing impulse to reach out and touch the child and he knew that the touching would close a circle, would come back to him. He said, "I don't know what to say."

"My father called me at the hospital," she said.

"He did?"

"Yes."

"Well, I guess he couldn't overlook this."

"No." Jennifer's voice was very small now. The rush of her earlier words seemed to have dissipated. Her quiet thickened around them and he found he much preferred the more voluble phase of her postpartum depression.

She said, "He made a point of telling me he'd left a board meeting when he got my wire."

"I'm sure he did leave one," David said. The intent of his remark was lamely sarcastic, but Jennifer seemed to take him seriously.

"You think so?" she said.

David turned to his wife with an ache for her apparent need to believe this. "Sure. He left a board meeting."

"I wanted to tell him that we could use a few bucks. I really did. But I couldn't." Her words were speeding again. "He's always made me ask for things."

"I know. It's all right."

"I've always had to ask, to crawl to him, and then there's always that little pause before he replies . . . I can't stand asking, David."

"We'll be all right, Jen. Really. We don't need to beg your father."

"I wish I could have asked."

"Don't. Please."

"Okay," she said. "It's all right. It's just his nature. He'll surprise us with a check."

"That's how he likes to do it." David hesitated at this. It sounded as if he were excusing the man. He wasn't. Jennifer's mother had died almost ten years ago, and it wasn't until she was gone that Jennifer had any real understanding of how cold her father was. The mother's fire had reflected on the man all through Jennifer's childhood. He'd been there in the background when the mother was loving her daughter and so Jennifer had always assumed he'd been part of it. He wasn't. He played handball now once a week with his son, the Wall Street lawyer, Jennifer's brother. And that was his family. Jennifer would no doubt inherit a great deal of money when he died, but right now the man mostly ignored her. "We can do without his money," David said.

"The things I want for our son . . ."

"Someday."

"The way my father drives himself, he'll be dead in a

year or two anyway." After saying this, Jennifer raised her face and closed her eyes. "Oh my. Listen to me. I'm sorry. I'm sorry to talk like that."

"He's not worth your guilt," David said.

Jennifer did not respond to this. She kept her face lifted to the sky, her eyes closed; a casual observer would think she was sunning herself. David strained to sense her mind and he had no idea where his wife's thoughts were heading.

Then she said, "Maybe he's made our marriage what it is."

"What do you mean?"

"Do you think we'd be as close to each other as we are if we didn't both have such hateful fathers?"

David felt Jennifer's words tugging him in the direction of his own father, but David would not yield. The man was a stranger, unrecognizable. This time not even the flicker of a face appeared to David. Instead, he thought of the child that lay in the apartment, a child David knew clearly was his own.

Jennifer said, "I'm too tender and too grumpy to make love tonight." David said he understood and they kissed and went to bed. He lay in the dark, thinking, for a time, about his son, about each tiny teacupful of air being drawn into the boy's body, expired, drawn in again. Then Suong came unbidden. The link was obscure and David did not even seek it. He had no real feeling for Suong, but he found he was eager to think of her.

David had been transferred into Saigon and one of the first things he did was to use the phone number from the slip of paper Suong had given him at Craig's party. Fragmentary images of the early meetings spun now through David. The house—large, five stories, near Cholon; the family was turning the ground floor into a nightclub. Her face smiled down from the second-floor balcony as he fumbled at the front-gate latch. She led him up winding stone steps and she wore a flowered blouse and loose black silk pantaloons that rippled around her bare feet. Her feet caught him now. He saw her bare feet stretched beside her as she sat on a divan. The Vietnamese women preened their feet as intensely as their hands and Suong's toes were slender and the nails were long, perfectly oval, meticulously painted. He regretted that they were forced to bear her weight. He stole glances at her feet as he sat before her on an overstuffed couch, and a polished brass mobile tinkled at the balcony door while he ate strips of mango from a lacquer tray. She talked about all the people in her extended family living in the house, all except her father, whose picture sat nearby on a tiny Buddhist shrine. "He died too soon," she said. "He was a very important man." A young Vietnamese man, perhaps twenty years old, bowed his way into the room, smiling and mumbling hello. He picked up the serving tray, and after he was gone, Suong said, "That was my sister's boy. We have to pay ten thousand piasters a month to keep him out of the army."

It was the boy who finally focused David's thoughts. The boy chauffeured David and Suong on the trip to Nha Be, out into the countryside southeast of Saigon. It was still very early in their few months together and David and Suong had kissed for a time one night on the roof of the house but they still had not made love. David desired Suong, he liked her very much, but he had no idea what her culture expected of him in expressing these feelings. Then at some point she suggested they go to Nha Be for a day. Her uncle had a vacation house out there and they could have some time away from the family, she said.

And so they sat close to each other in the back seat of one of the family's cars and Suong smelled like the rain. They left Saigon through the triangular wedge of District Four, the shanties and low, open-mouthed shops cluttering the route. But when they crossed the Kinh Te, a tributary of the Saigon River, the city stopped abruptly. They were out of Saigon and passing among rice paddies and clusters of banana trees. The paddies here were filled with water brought from the branches of the Saigon River that snaked and scrolled through the countryside.

Suong chatted lightly with David, pointing out a tree she thought he might not know or naming a stream that they crossed.

"You know this countryside very well," David said.

"My uncle has had the house for a long time. My family has always used it as a retreat."

They entered the district of Nha Be and Suong's nephew turned off the main road and onto a dusty lane. The paddies were giving way to the tentative beginnings of settlements, but the little houses gathered only in infrequent, sparse clumps. At an isolated, larger house behind a high gray wall, the car slowed and stopped at an iron gate. The nephew got out to open the gate and David looked off to the left and saw a large ship, a tanker, sitting in the middle of a field. The land was flat to the tree-bristled horizon and one of the twists of the river had placed the vessel out among the farmers and the water buffalo.

The car pulled into the courtyard and a woman servant —a young woman with a white scar running from her right ear across her cheek and down to her jaw—greeted David and Suong at the door. Behind them, the nephew closed and bolted the iron gate.

The woman led them into the house. The front room was large, dim, confusing in its mixture of the Orient in vases and lacquerware, the West in an ornate chandelier, and ancient Rome in its mosaic floor and bare, cool, stone feeling. The servant left them, continuing on into the dining room while David and Suong lingered under the chandelier.

"Do you like it?" Suong asked, smiling at him.

"Yes."

They walked through the house, its ground floor rooms laid out consecutively. They passed through a dining room with a stairway at one end leading upstairs, a sitting room, and a large kitchen. The servant nodded at them as they passed her at the stove. They stepped out the back door and into the shelter of a trellis that was thick with jasmine and shaded the waters of a tiled pond. In a tiny pagoda, with a sanctuary barely large enough for a single supplicant, a meditating Buddha sat in a slice of morning sunlight, the trays of food before it full, the incense faintly smoking.

Suong led David around the pagoda and behind it was a gazebo, its far side nearly at the foot of a slender inlet from the Nha Be River. The two sat on wicker chairs with the inlet splashing gently before them, mimicking the river where a sampan scudded past. The distant bank held a vague jumble of shacks.

They sat and Suong said nothing for a long while and David was intensely aware of the quiet. Though he'd been living in Saigon for only a few weeks, he had already absorbed its background roar so completely that this release now was striking. The quiet lay on the countryside like Suong's hand lying on his arm. He felt her hand keenly, as well. To his left he could look past her delicate profile and across a field, a clean, distant view, the view reckoned and amplified by a lone house with its Buddhist swastika finely etched against the sky. A dog barked somewhere in the distance. There was a chirping in the roof of the gazebo. David looked at Suong.

"Where is your uncle?" he asked.

"He's away on business."

"I'd like to thank him for letting me come here."

"You're entirely welcome," Suong said, squeezing his arm. She paused, then said, "It is a very nice house. Very safe. When President Diem was overthrown and the city was dangerous, especially for those who had close connections to the president, my father brought us out here to stay. He and my uncle played checkers in these chairs every day while we listened first to the distant gunfire and then the distant silence, which we knew was even worse."

David and Suong stopped speaking again. They were

holding hands now. As the morning waxed on, the heat was growing more oppressive. Far off, clouds were gathering, white still, but cumulous, mounting high above the horizon. The air grew dense. David's limbs were heavy and he became sleepy.

"Do you hear the bird in the roof?" Suong asked.

"Yes."

"It's a wild parrot. It's had a nest there for two years now."

They rested quietly, holding hands, for a long while. Then Suong turned to David and said, "Are you ready to catch our dinner?"

"Catch it?"

She rose, went into the gazebo, and emerged with a bamboo fishing pole and a can of small shrimp. "In the inlet," she said.

David took the pole from her and walked down the inlet. The finger of water had straight, parallel banks about eight feet apart. The water was yellowish brown and he doubted that he could catch anything edible in here. But he hooked a shrimp on the line and cast it into the middle. The cork bobbed in the chop of the water for only a few moments and then it disappeared with a jerk. David pulled the pole evenly and firmly and a large, sleek gray fish he didn't recognize rose flopping from the water. Suong laughed. "You see what a good fisherman you are?"

He cast half a dozen times in the space of ten minutes and caught half a dozen fish, each about two pounds. As he fished he felt very calm, with the hot sun on his face, the gentle rise and fall of Suong's laughter, the quiet, empty fields. He had never fished much in the States, but the repose he felt by the muddy inlet was akin to the repose he felt up in the Cascades. He looked at Suong as he cast a seventh time. She stood on the opposite bank not far from the gazebo. The wind blew the flaps of her ao dai and ruffled the black silk of her pantaloons. She was standing very still, one arm akimbo, the other raised, bent at the elbow, hand curved gracefully up into her long, flowing hair. Her face was in shadow but her dark eyes shone clearly.

"How much do you expect to eat?" she asked.

"Why?"

"I'm only one Vietnamese girl. You have six fish and are seeking more. Are you starving?"

"I'm fishing now for the sport of it," David said.

"We have no freezer here."

"I'm fishing now to prolong this moment."

She smiled slowly. "There will be more moments. Come inside."

They ate the fish at the long dining table, a paddle fan moving slowly, silently above them. The fish was cooked simply and had a delicate, sweet flavor. They ate Vietnamese egg roll, wrapped in rice paper; goose stuffed with rice noodles and seaweed; fertilized chicken eggs, with a rich taste like duck eggs; and mangosteens with ice and sugar. They drank raisin wine, dark brown and very smooth, from an unlabeled bottle.

When they finished eating they sat in silence for a long while, looking at each other. David felt no pressure whatsoever to speak or to act and he appreciated this woman deeply. Suddenly he heard a crack of sound. David started, hearing in it a VC rocket.

"It's just thunder," Suong said.

The sound was metallic like a rocket but it had reverberations, the echoing crackle, farther off, of thunder.

"Will it rain now?" he asked.

"Not for long. The rain in the months between the dry and wet seasons never lasts long." She rose.

The rain began, building rapidly in force. Suong stood over David, smiling down at him for a moment, and then he, too, rose. They held each other and kissed long and deeply and then held each other again as the rain washed over the house. They pulled apart just far enough to see each other's face and David wanted Suong very much but he knew to wait, knew that a decision was shaping behind these dark eyes; he felt her thrumming with the process of it. Thunder cracked nearby. David started, but there was no flicker at all in Suong. Her hand came up and she touched David's cheek and she smiled. With the touch, he knew she had decided. She took his hand and led him up the stairs and into a bedroom looking out over the river. She closed the door and in the pale gray light they undressed quickly, rushing like the rain outside.

David remembered the pressure of her on his body and the soles of her feet moving over his ankles and the calves of his legs. She did not make a sound nor did he but she held him with great strength and the rain stopped abruptly before they were done and still there were no sounds except the ruffle of the sheets around them and the smack of her kisses which grew noisier, more childlike, as they went on and finally David and Suong squeezed together and then they parted. She curled against him and was very still and after a time it was as if she had vanished, and then he fancied that he could hear the Nha Be River running outside, just as he always thought he could hear a stream in the Cascades whenever he wanted, no matter how far he was from one. He listened to the river until she whispered, "I didn't expect this to happen."

"I didn't either," he said and that was true.

"I didn't expect this at all," she said.

Suddenly David was conscious of thin tracks burning on his ankles. It puzzled him only briefly. They were cuts from Suong's toenails. This made him smile. It had been a surprise, yes.

"I feel filled up," she said.

In his bed in Baltimore, his wife sleeping nearby, David shuddered. He turned on his side and wiped the memory away. That was easy, now that he and Suong had touched again. David felt a vague guilt, as if he'd slipped quietly away from Jennifer tonight and had found a woman. But Suong was in another country, a far country, and she might even be dead. She'd certainly disappeared from David's life with the abruptness of death. He felt a tremor of ease and pleasure over the day in Nha Be that he'd just remembered. How could something that began so well have ended so soon, he wondered. He shifted again in the bed; he lay on his back.

How good had that first time with Suong actually been? Its unexpectedness had been good. But his experience of Suong, of Suong herself, had been very brief, really. There had been a river, sleek gray fish, rain, stillness. None of these were Suong. He remembered lying beside her in that upstairs bedroom in Nha Be. She was asleep now. He lay awake, sweating profusely in the close room. She was right. The rain did not last long. Nor did it provide any relief. It only accentuated the heavy wetness of the air. Then with great ease on that afternoon in Vietnam, an ease that could have alarmed David but did not, his mind turned to Tuyen. He wondered if Tuyen, too, had trouble turning off his detachment. When the man made love with a woman, was part of him aloof? Did the same quality of mind that let him write the words in the cell make him feel his isolation from a woman, from the physical entering of a woman? Yes, David thought. Tuyen would feel that way. David knew his mind. Knew it well. Tuyen was lying in a cell at that very moment, he thought. Tuyen was sweating in a close cell, cursing with a placid face the rain that comes but brings no relief.

Outside the courtroom the next day was Kenneth Trask. He waited near the trunk of a tree, inconspicuous as an assassin, but David noticed him at once and he turned to Carl. "Did you bring him here?"

Carl followed the flick of David's head and, when he saw Trask, said, "Who is he?"

"You don't know?"

"I don't," Carl said and David decided that he believed him.

"It's Trask," David said.

"Your CIA friend?"

"Yes."

"I'll never be able to convince you I didn't . . ."

"I'm already convinced."

"Well, I'll be damned," Carl said softly.

David turned and Trask was watching him but had not moved from where he stood. This was part of the dominant impression Trask had always given—the absolute control the man had of every movement of his body, and presumably of his mind and feelings. He gave the impression of not even blinking without premeditation. This memory of Trask made David wonder what the hell he was doing here. He crossed to the man.

"Hello, Fleming," Trask said, his voice flat, his hand coming out only after the words had faded.

David shook his hand and said, "Hello, Trask. What are you doing here?"

The man did not respond for a moment. His hand had retreated, his face was bland, faintly smiling. Then he said, "I was up here at Holabird on a little business. I knew you were under fire and I thought I'd drop by and see how you were."

"Forgive me if this surprises me about you."

Trask laughed. "That's just the reason I was interested in you. Not many people refuse to take my crap."

"How'd you hear about my little problem?"

"You being ironic?"

"About what?"

"The size of the problem."

"Of course I am," David said. "I'm no fool."

"That's how I heard. Your situation is very well known. Even around the Company."

"They don't have any sympathy for me at the CIA, surely . . ."

Trask smiled. "More so than the guys in the haircuts . . . but no. My visit is personal, I guess."

"You're not telling me I've won *your* sympathy."

"I wouldn't say that. No. My curiosity, certainly."

"Curiosity about what?"

"Oh, lots of things . . . Why you did it, for one."

David turned around to look at Carl. He was nowhere in sight. David turned back to Trask. "My lawyer got you to come here, didn't he."

"No." The word came instantly, firmly.

"I don't believe you."

Trask's face grew immobile again. "This was my own idea, Fleming. You want to have coffee?"

"No."

"How about sitting on that bench over there."

David hesitated. He should walk away from this man. He still had no intention of constructing a lie for his own defense. And if Carl and Trask were themselves telling the truth, David had no real interest in catering to Trask's personal curiosity about him. But he felt vaguely drawn to Trask for a reason he could not identify and he said, "Okay."

They sat on a bench before the military court building and the air was thick with the smell from a plant at the south edge of Holabird, an industrial smell like overripe peaches.

David said, "I don't see why you should risk my telling you to go to hell."

"Do you think that would bother me?"

"No. I guess not."

"Now that you bring it up, *I* don't see why you'd be willing to just sit and chat with me."

"I don't have an answer for that right now."

"We did work pretty well together, particularly once you got into Saigon for good." Trask said this reflectively, as if in search of David's motive for tolerating him.

"Not that either of us is given to nostalgia over that."

"Look, David, I regret that we fell into this little game of ours, sniping at each other. We had some pleasure from that in Vietnam and it even served a purpose, kept us on our toes. But I didn't mean to get into that here. I'm not given to nostalgia. You're right. But I hope you never completely believed the light you kept putting me in, in our little games with each other. I respect your abilities. No emotion in that. I think you did a good job, especially for an Army agent. I really was up here doing some business. I'm on the Vietnam desk, Stateside, and I get up here now and then. I heard about what was happening to you and I came by."

This sustained burst of what seemed to be sincerity disarmed David. He wanted to speak, wanted to be conciliatory with Trask. But he could find no words to say. He half expected Trask to give him a fixed stare now, to turn the little speech into just another tactic to keep David off balance.

But Trask persisted in his sincerity. He apparently perceived David's speechlessness, for he took the burden back onto himself. He said, "I don't really care what made you snatch that prisoner and set him free. I didn't come here to talk about that, if you're not inclined to do so on your own." He hesitated briefly, as if to see if David did want to speak. David remained silent and Trask said, "My curiosity be damned, then. *Whatever* it was, my own sympathies lie with the talent, with the man, and not the fumbly institution that thinks it runs him . . . Does that surprise you?"

What David was thinking was that this must be how Trask would go about turning a respected counterpart in the KGB into a double agent. The same tone, the same expression of sympathy, the construction of the same mutual foe. But David did not use this against Trask. He said, "No. It doesn't surprise me."

"Then I'm losing my touch." Trask smiled. "I didn't think I was so transparent."

"Don't worry, Ken. It doesn't surprise me once you say it, but it never would have occurred to me."

Trask laughed. "Well, that's comforting."

The two fell silent and David didn't know what to say. Trask didn't exert any pressure, made no silent demands; he crossed his leg and watched a car pass in the street. David tried to understand what it was that had drawn him to this man a few minutes ago. Perhaps it was the association with Saigon. As soon as this thought came to David, he knew it was so. Saigon meant Suong. Trask was even at the party the night of the first meeting. David had sat down with Trask because he was an indirect link back to Suong.

"When did you leave Saigon?" David asked.

Trask turned to him and his manner changed utterly. He had instantly reverted to his wordless, unblinking stare. He was willing to give only the information, only the emotions that he had decided to give.

David said, "I ask because I thought the other day of someone we both knew and I wondered whatever became of her."

"Who's that?"

"Nguyen Thi Tuyet Suong."

There was no movement in Trask's face, as if he didn't recognize the name.

"The woman we talked about at Craig's party that night in Saigon. Remember? I'd just met her. She was a friend of Craig's mistress."

Trask smiled. He seemed to relax again. His voice softened. "Oh her. You remembered her, did you?" He cocked his head, showing that the affair was something he hadn't been aware of.

"So you didn't know quite everything that went on in Saigon?" David instantly regretted saying this. Not because it broke the truce between him and Trask, but because it seemed to turn Suong into a sly elbow-prod between a couple of men home from the sexy Orient.

"I must have missed *that*, at least," Trask said.

David turned his face sharply away from the man's grin.

"No big deal," David said.

"As a matter of fact," Trask said, "that tour only lasted six or eight months more for me. I don't recall seeing Miss Suong again . . . I think she dropped out of sight, for a while. Now I understand why."

David felt flushed. He wondered how long he would

have to wait before he could break off this meeting without letting Trask think this talk of Suong was the reason.

"You were a lucky man," Trask said.

David said nothing.

"Listen." Trask pitched his voice low, seemingly intense now in his concern. "I know you've got a lot on your mind, Dave. I won't keep you. But I want you to know that I'd like to be of assistance to you, if you ever think how. On a personal basis. One on one. For a man whose professionalism I respect. I don't give a damn about all the institutions. For me, this work is personal. A select group of professionals who work together, make things happen. I like it for that. For the sport. Here's a phone number." Trask gave David a plain white card with a phone number typed on it. He said, "Give me a call if there's anything I can do to help you."

David nodded and Trask was gone. Left behind was not even a clue as to what the man had really been up to. David decided this had been Trask's final, devastating victory in their long-standing game of oneupmanship.

David and Jennifer sat together in the living room. She curled against him and they sat quietly while the baby slept in his bedroom. They'd sat down here while the early evening sun through the window still filled the far wall. Now the room was dim and they'd hardly spoken a word. David felt comfortable with Jennifer. He felt no need to speak. She demanded nothing. Her body against him disappeared from his awareness and when she shifted briefly he realized that he'd forgotten about her. With the memory of Nha Be so fresh, this reminded him of Suong curled against him in the upper bedroom of her uncle's house. He found, this time, that the memory of her was faintly distasteful. Just as he'd been drawn to Trask because of his link to Suong, David now was faintly repelled by Suong because of her link to Trask; to Trask and to all of the grasping, hustling people who had filled Craig's villa that night in Saigon. But his present withdrawal from Suong was more than just bad associations. It was Suong herself. She'd dropped him abruptly and as his mind drew near to their last time together, he backed off. He knew how little had been foreshadowed on that night. It wasn't necessary to go over any of this. Suong never spoke of them, but obviously there were demands being made on him that he never perceived. He squeezed at Jennifer, held her closer. He was content here. His only regret was that they hadn't made a pallet for the boy so that he could be sleeping here beside them instead of in a separate room, so that David could see the boy, could touch him, could strain to hear his dreams.

"Do you still find me attractive?" Jennifer said, low.

"Of course."

"I don't feel attractive."

"That's nonsense." He said this gently.

"It's just that . . ."

"It's just the postpartums."

"When I asked you if I was still attractive, you didn't even look at me."

"I have a very clear memory of you," David said, still not looking.

"From before the baby."

"From this morning."

"Look again."

David turned his face to Jennifer. She had twisted her lower jaw out of place and had crossed her eyes. "Just as I remembered you," he whispered.

Jennifer laid her head on David's chest. "All I get are lies," she said.

David began to feel restless before Jennifer's need, restless and ineffective. "I'll be back," he said.

"I'm in pain and you have to take a leak," Jennifer said, her voice clinging to the joke in this statement. But David had a strong sense of the other element, the undercurrent of genuine distress in her. He admired her attempt to cope with it, but he did not stop to go back to her. He went into the bathroom and closed the door. He stood in the middle of the floor until he heard a sound from the living room. Jennifer had switched on the television. She was distracted, at last. He wouldn't have to bear this depression of hers that seemed so alien to him: only then did he realize that it was this he was hiding from in here. He stepped to the toilet and flushed it.

Out in the hallway he knew where he belonged. He went into his son's room and closed the door against the mutter of Walter Cronkite. He crossed to the crib and waited for his eyes to adjust to the glow of the night-light. The boy was sleeping on his stomach, his face turned away. The shape of his son's head made David's hands rise, made his hands anxious at the vulnerability of the child. David reached into the crib, lightly touched the back of the tiny head; the head fit his palm; he felt the boy move and he withdrew his hand at once. It hurt David to think he might trouble the child's sleep. But he wished his son were awake so he could hold him. He felt tight; he realized that he was hardly breathing. It was painful for him here, yearning like this for a child whose very presence should resolve the yearning, not heighten it. David drew back, crossed the room, went out into the hall, and the first word he heard from the television in the other room was "babies."

The word drew him quickly to it and he found Jennifer sitting on the edge of the couch. She was lit by the TV screen in the dark room. She leaned forward and David looked to see children on the screen. The images before him, the words being spoken, were disjointed, but he understood that these were orphans of the Vietnamese war. A shot of the children; a shot of Tan Son Nhut Airport in Saigon; a jumbo-jet airliner; the head of an American man, a civilian, talking; "Most of these children had American fathers"; children's faces, the voice continuing but the faces clearly half American now, a little boy with the tilted almond eyes of a Vietnamese but a long, thin nose; a little girl with the round Oriental face but her dark hair tightly, minutely curled. The traces of long-gone fathers. And mothers who were where? Dead maybe. Whoring to the end on Tu Do Street maybe. Children. Faces. The plane raced along the runway, the camera following until it stopped on the CBS News correspondent, with the microphone before him and the plane arcing into the air behind him, and the man spoke of a life for these children in a free land with new parents. David's feeling at this was complicated. But he did not try to understand it fully. What became clear on its own was enough: there was a feeling of gratitude for his own son; there was a sense that for the boy to be sleeping in the bedroom was not so painful a separation after all.

David's declaration of "not guilty" to charges of aiding the enemy went very easily. He rose before the judge, his legs were steady, his voice was clear, he was hardly aware of moving and speaking at all. Sitting again at the defense table, he thought he should try to study the jurors. Hedberg began his opening statement and the words were what David expected, recounting the event, portraying Tuyen's importance to the VC cause, hinting at a radical streak in David. The jurors—five officers, from full-bird colonel to first lieutenant, and one staff sergeant—sat with parade-rest attention on Hedberg, and David tried to focus on these six faces that would finally turn on him in judgment. But he could not. His mind wandered, almost idly; he considered trivial things: Hedberg's bald head, the soft lip-smack of the court stenographer's machine, David's own gathering urge to urinate. He thought of standing in the bathroom last night to escape Jennifer; he thought of the hallway and then the TV set and the baby lift, Vietnamese orphans being flown out of Saigon, snatched away from the advancing Communists. Orphans with American fathers. He thought of his own son. He saw the traces of the fathers in the faces of the children on the TV. He wondered if perhaps a father saw his own child on the TV last night. He wondered if many of those fathers had no idea that such a child existed, the pregnancy following a single night with a short-time girl.

Then a scrambling began in David's chest, a furious scrambling even before his mind shaped the thought that prompted the feeling. He held the thought back, he focused instead on Hedberg; the man was finishing his statement, returning to the prosecution's table. Carl was rising to give what he had warned David would be a very short statement because he had little to work with. David felt exhausted. He could not hold his mind steady. The scrambling went on inside him, made his hands clench on the tabletop, and then his mind spoke clearly to him: he himself had a child in Vietnam. More: a son. More: a son with his face. Suong broke off their affair because she was pregnant and David never knew: that was his thought. A patriot, Carl was saying. Unquestionably loyal, Carl's voice said. David's limbs were very heavy now. He could not lift his arms. The burden of proof, Carl said, and David's mind cried. There's no proof, no proof that she was pregnant. None. This is a fantasy, unfounded. But it would not go away. He tried again to concentrate on the people around him. Carl was saying that David could not have willfully aided the enemy, that it would run counter to David's clearly demonstrable background, record, philosophy, and character. A son like David Junior. Somewhere in Vietnam, taking breath into his lungs, sleeping in a dark room. The image was of an infant. But then David realized that the child would be older. The child would be perhaps four years old now. David wouldn't let himself reckon the passage of time, the month when Suong might have become pregnant, or the day; he saw sleek gray fish leaping from the water, the panels of her ao dai blowing, he heard distant thunder. A child, he thought. My child. He thought of the Communists advancing on Saigon. Whole regions were being cut off. The end was near. His child was there. And David felt the panic beginning to bleed inside his head, spreading in him, and he knew he had to stop this now. He stiffened and he thought very clearly: there is no way for me to know, no way to ever know; I have one son, one son is all that exists, all that could exist, anything else is utterly unknowable. He squeezed hard at his mind, drew himself away, raced deep into the woods in the Cascades, there was no one else, no one. And he felt his mind grow suddenly calm. There were people in the world, but they had nothing to do with him. That was always the way it had been for David. It was still so. His chest felt tight, but he was all right now. His chest was tight from his breath held in and he let it out sharply and he was conscious of the sound he made. The six faces on the jury turned and looked at him, but they were far, far away.

After a dinner in mindless silence, David stayed at the kitchen table and Jennifer disappeared. He was blank. This detachment held no pleasure in it, though at least he was untroubled. The TV began in the other room and he felt a twist of irritation at Jennifer. But immediately he blamed himself. He had cut short any talk of the day in court. He had kept to himself. He knew he was unable to give Jennifer what she needed. It was his own fault. But the television continued to bother him. He heard the familiar phrases again. Saigon. Vietcong. The North. Fighting. Advancing. This threatened him, he knew. He did not want to consider the fall of Vietnam. Soon the country would be shut off forever. Shut off from what? his mind demanded. What meaning did that have? Shut off from America. That wasn't the point, he knew. Shut off from *him*. And what meaning did that have? David stood up. Even as he did, voices began to pop in the other room; Jennifer was changing channels.

David waited. He was sweating. Now a voice was talking about babies. "Two weeks into Operation Babylift," the voice began, and David strode from the kitchen, through the hallway, into the living room.

"Dammit, Jennifer," he said, knowing how loud he was,

how harsh. Her face turned to him, her eyes wide in surprise. David said, "Turn that damn thing off."

She opened her mouth to reply but no words came. "This was the scene on April fourth," the TV announcer said, "when an Air Force C5A jumbo jet crashed soon after takeoff from Saigon's Tan Son Nhut Airport, killing one hundred and seventy-two passengers, mostly orphans."

Jennifer's face swung toward the TV screen. David looked too. He saw the smoking wreckage of a plane. Then a row of tiny body bags on the ground. David stepped to the TV and turned it off. "I don't want this machine on again when I'm in this house," he shouted.

Jennifer began to cry. David's anger drained away and in his mind he saw children's bodies strewn across a rice paddy and then his son began to cry in the bedroom. Jennifer raised her face but her own tears did not stop and the child cried and David hung for a moment between his wife and his son and then he moved away from Jennifer, toward the hallway.

Jennifer rose. "I'll go," she said sharply.

David turned to her. "Please," he said. "I'm sorry I yelled at you. Let me go."

His apology came as a surprise to himself and obviously to Jennifer. Her body stiffened but her face softened at once and she and David moved to each other and held each other briefly. Then he said, "I was the one who frightened him. I'll go."

He went into his son's bedroom. The cries filled David up and suddenly he feared the boy was hurt; he saw his son in the wreckage of a plane, crying just like this. He bent into the crib and picked him up. The tiny body seemed to have no weight at all. The body was so delicate that David felt angry: how could he be expected to protect anything as vulnerable as this? But he must. He held the child close, patted the child, walked around and around the room, squeezing his own mind shut, trying to keep any thoughts out except for an awareness of this warmth that lay against his chest, this child that would not grow calm. Then David could resist no longer. The idea of another child, a child in Vietnam, rushed into him and he stopped in the middle of the floor. This son in David's arms cried against his shoulder and the phantom son cried in his head and he detached himself enough to calmly consider the unexpectedness of all this. David was surprised. Surprised that pure biological fatherhood should have so strong an effect on him. David Junior was here in his arms, insistent. The strength of David's feeling for the child was surprising to some degree, but this other child—the mere idea of another child—should not be this insistent, should not ravage him. His mind tried to hold its distance but the C5A smoking in a rice paddy made David want to howl in despair. Was a child of his on that plane? Was it indeed a son, like this one in his arms, a fragment of David himself? And was that part of him dead now, stuffed into a body bag? No, he cried to himself. The child would be with Suong. The child existed even now. And that ravaged David, too. A son: instead, he tried to see a little girl, the image of Suong, but he could not; he felt with great certainty that it would be a son and that very certainty made him believe that it was true; instantly he believed in the transcendent knowledge of his own fatherhood. These were feelings unlike any he could ever have imagined for himself.

The son in his arms cried on and David grew conscious of this sound now and he felt he had to attend to the child he was sure of. That made sense. He thought that perhaps David Junior needed to have his diaper changed and this seemed to offer a refuge to David in its very banality. The problem was only a dirty diaper.

He laid the child on the changing table and shushed softly at the contorted face. He felt the diaper and it was dry and suddenly these cries began to slash at him. They became the cries of his Vietnam child; the boy was on the plane that crashed and for one brief moment David actually wished for that, wished that any child he'd had were on that plane. A clean break, the independent physical reality squaring itself with the only possible emotional reality. But this thought instantly horrified David. He drew back from it, drew back from himself. He embraced that strange biological link. The alternative, he saw, was indifference, indifference even to a child's death. How could I want a child of mine to die? David demanded of himself. How could I not want to see, to touch, to hold a child of mine? Another face, just like the one that lay before him, rushed into his mind: the skin was duskier, but the thin mouth, the wide nose, even the pale yellow hair were the same. His son.

David looked down at his American son on the changing table. He stroked the child's head, bent to him and kissed him, whispered to him not to cry, to trust his father, to please grow calm now. And the boy's tears began to slow, the boy's crying snubbed to a stop, and David straightened up. The child's T-shirt had ridden up and David saw the dark fluid, the color of blood, clotted at the navel. It was a natural thing, the remnant of the umbilical cord, but it brought tears to his eyes, made him softly curse the strength of his own love. It would have been better, he thought, to live a celibate life than to ache for another like this.

The next day a deposition was read into the record from a Mr. Tho, a man David could hardly remember, the man who gave him some information on Tuyen at the Saigon interrogation center. Hedberg sat on the stand and read Tho's English-language answers in response to the questions read by the assistant prosecutor. Hedberg seemed to be enjoying his part. He put on the Vietnamese accent inherent in the deposition, contorting his face as if in thought before giving some of the tentative answers, focusing hard and clear on the questioner in the damning parts, thoroughly mugging his way through the deposition, and David stopped watching, only half listened. The case began to build up: David sought Tuyen in Saigon; he was told that Tuyen had been moved down to Ba Ria, in Phuoc Thuy province; David pressed for information, persuaded Tho to let him see Tuyen's file.

Then the prosecution called Major Morello. David turned in his seat to see the man come from the back of the courtroom. He was natty in his dress uniform and except for his round, swarthy face and thick arms, he did not bear any resemblance to the Major Morello who'd been David's commanding officer in Saigon. He walked with the almost prim step of a Stateside officer. His uniform was wildly out of place; David saw Morello in his patterned sport shirt and chinos, his feet up on his desk at City Hall in Saigon, his casual secretiveness speaking of all the complexities of Saigon operations. Morello was being sworn in and he didn't look at David, not even a glance, and David vaguely recalled that the major had somehow put Trask down in their first meeting. David, transfer orders in hand, had gone to Trask first when he got to Saigon because they'd already begun an operation together, using some leads David had generated out at Homestead. Trask drove David over to City Hall, where Morello had his office. They approached from the side, the old French building's narrow cupola rising against the empty morning sky, pulling away from the scrolls and pinnacles of the roof and facade. Passing into the building's shadow they turned abruptly under an arch and emerged into a tiny street behind it. There was a low latticed row of offices and at the far end of the street was an iron gate joining the offices with the main City Hall building and blocking entry.

Morello was speaking in the courtroom, but David's focus shifted away from the man. The major had humbled Trask in some way, but this little street behind City Hall held a much clearer image. There was a crowd of people there. They were all Vietnamese, all clucking and gabbling in hushed tones, their attention directed downward before them in the center of the street. David did not push through the crowd but skirted it. Morello's Vietnamese assistant, Mr.

Uc, was standing apart from the others. David approached him.

"What is it?" David asked.

"A man has jumped from the roof of the City Hall. He has tried to kill himself."

"Who is he?"

"It's all right," Uc said. "It's just a Vietnamese worker, a clerk."

"It's all right?" David repeated, not knowing if he was being sarcastic.

"He's no one important," Uc said.

David still didn't understand and his face must have shown it, for Uc tried again. "There's no trouble," he said. "It's nothing political."

Morello was talking to the courtroom about City Hall. The surface of David's attention rippled with the man's words, with the now familiar voice, but the surface grew calm again and then David saw the crowd behind City Hall parting and the man who had jumped emerged on a stretcher. He passed in front of David, a smear of red on his forehead, his face cream-colored and the texture of rubber. He looked up at David, still conscious, with an odd look on his face. He was perhaps fifty, his hair cropped close; and the streak of blood, the look—a subtle, abandoned look— startled David, stirred him. It's Tuyen, he thought for a moment. All the interrogation is done, they've finished with him. The face passed and David turned to see the stretcher jiggling and rolling between the two attendants. David felt his muscles grow tense, as if before movement, as if before pursuit, as if before running after the man, asking him his name. But the fantasy passed quickly. The face was that of a stranger. David had never seen Tuyen's face. This man was not important. Uc was speaking.

"He was broke and his wife left him," Uc said. "I think it was too many children. No one says so, but that's what I think. He had nine children. Too many. I'm modern that way."

And it was foolish, the fantasy. Impossible. Foolish, too, to see a man who despaired and tried to take his own life, and then confuse him with Tuyen. Tuyen would never take his own life. He had too great a sense of irony. Too much detachment from terror. After all, that's what his message was, in the cell. The man who passed on the stretcher—his face—was clear now. The look was a look of profound bewilderment, for he still lived. He had hurled himself to an ending, but remained. The look was bewildered: not even this would be easy for me, he was thinking. And Tuyen could never be the man on the stretcher. Tho's file said that Tuyen had revealed nothing to his Saigon interrogators, not the slightest detail, even under what the file called "strongest questioning," a euphemism that had sucked all the strength from David, made it difficult even to hold the folder before him. Tuyen would never reach the level of despair that this clerk with nine children had reached, no matter how relentlessly he was tortured. Tuyen would be all right, at least in the sacred privacy of his own mind. David realized that he wanted to believe in that. Yet even as he thought this, David felt that it would be better for Tuyen to be the man on the stretcher. That man would be at rest soon; he was drifting away even then, his awareness ebbing, his life beyond recall. He would be dead before nightfall, while Tuyen was in a cell, under strongest questioning. David himself felt suddenly vulnerable. That, too, was foolish, he thought. He blamed it on the strain of being in this country. But his intensely personal fear for Tuyen persisted, his mind vibrated uncontrollably, like a muscle held tight for too long and then suddenly released. David looked around him. The sweating facade of City Hall, the dingy alley, small slim people moving around him, an iron fence, a stone arch, heavy hot stinking air, nothing of what he loved, no stillness, no stand of trees, no escape from all people.

"He asked me if I had ever become friendly with any of the enemy operatives I'd interrogated." Morello's voice.

David shook his head. The trial had rushed back upon

him and he didn't know why. But his memories had turned bad anyway.

"Friendly?" Hedberg said.

"That's the word he used."

"Friendly with whom?"

"Friendly with the enemy."

Carl stirred beside David, as if he were about to object. Hedberg seemed to be leading the witness; and David couldn't remember saying this to Morello. It didn't sound familiar at all. But Hedberg went on into a line of questioning about David's access to sensitive material and Carl never did rise and David put his elbows on the table and laid the heels of his two hands against his eyes. He had no defense in this trial. He could not invent one and Carl could not invent one and all David could do was turn his face away and write ironic phrases across his own mind. And he wondered if Tuyen had a child.

In the dark, in her bed, Jennifer wanted to make love, and they began. But while David's body obeyed, his head filled with the past. Nor were his thoughts sexual, even though he found himself in Nha Be, in bed with Suong. He knew why his mind had returned to this room. It was time to make a final judgment on the matter of a Vietnamese child. He had to examine the evidence. He and Suong had not made love before Nha Be. The possibilities began on that afternoon. For a moment he assumed that this examination was an act of futility. How could he know if she was fertile on that day? He stood at the prosecutor's table and confronted himself sitting as a witness on the stand and he did not know what to ask. Then he thought to develop the circumstantial evidence.

Did you use any protection on that afternoon? he asked himself. Did you do anything to prevent a pregnancy?

He answered himself: No, I did not.

So you could have gotten her pregnant?

You ask me to speculate. Stick to the facts.

Answer the question, dammit.

Yes. Yes, I could have.

Could *she* have had some protection?

It's possible.

All right. I let you put that in the record, at least.

But wait. She said that our making love was unexpected. She stressed that. How unexpected it was.

In what way was this said?

In what way?

Wistful? Worried?

Wistful, yes. Worried? Yes. Maybe that too.

She could have been pregnant.

She said she felt filled up.

After you were lying apart from her?

Yes. She felt filled up even then.

Could this have been a premonition?

It's possible.

Jennifer pounded on David's back. "I love you," she cried.

He lowered his face on the witness stand. He felt guilty over Jennifer's love, over his own distance from her.

"I love my child too," Jennifer cried. "I really do."

David said to himself on the stand, Did she ever say anything that would suggest she was pregnant?

No.

Are you certain she never said anything?

Not clearly so. I believe I would have responded at once, though, if she had.

How would you have responded?

I don't know.

At some point, she would have known the truth. Let's go back to the final days with her.

We spent an afternoon in the park near the National Museum.

What was her mood?

Odd. She told me that the people in the park assumed she was a whore.

Could her pregnancy have prompted that observation?

I don't see how.

Anything else about her mood?

Yes. Not her mood, exactly. She felt dizzy. Sick to her stomach.

"Are you okay?" Jennifer said.

"What?"

"Was it good for you?"

He knew in a vague way that she was talking about their lovemaking. "Yes," he said.

Jennifer kissed him and pressed him gently off her and turned away.

David lay on his back on the bed. He picked up the thread of the prosecution's case: You say she felt sick?

Yes.

This was when?

Near the end of our affair.

How long after Nha Be?

I don't know exactly. A couple of months. Maybe three.

Long enough for her pregnancy . . .

To begin to affect her. I guess so. Yes.

At this point, do you still hold that she was not pregnant?

I don't know.

You don't know? And what about your final meeting with her?

David sat up in bed.

"What is it?" Jennifer said.

"Nothing." David lay back down. He wanted to find some other reason for the end of the affair. Some other, clear reason. But the last time he had seen Suong he'd felt closer to her than ever before.

It was the evening that the nightclub opened in the lower floor of Suong's house. The place was floodlit and two Saigon policemen directed arriving cars into parking places along the street. The facade surprised David in its old-fashioned air, though the signs were neon and garish. A fake front with a canopy extended from the door as if it were copied from old American gangster movies, and a young Vietnamese man wearing white gloves opened the stained-glass doors for the guests.

David entered the club and looked for Suong. On the far side of the room, beyond the horseshoe of tables, she stood with two Vietnamese men. David admired her for her solitariness, just as he'd admired her the first time he ever saw her, standing aloof in the crowd at Craig's party. Then he made his way through the crowded tables and across a central dance floor. Suong saw him approach and stopped her conversation abruptly. As he reached her she dipped her head briefly, a gesture that at the time struck David as quaintly Oriental, a mock-humility, for social situations, but recalling it now the gesture seemed to hold more. She'd found out she was pregnant. She felt slightly ashamed.

But her face rose at once and she took his arm. "David, I'm so happy you could come for this," she said, then turned to the two men. She introduced them to him. Both were ARVN officers and both were wearing wide-lapelled suits and brightly colored shirts. In turn they each smiled and pumped David's hand. "I was just speaking to them about some business. But this is really my uncle's responsibility." She tightened the grip on David's arm and the two men bowed slightly and said good-bye and drifted away.

When they were gone, David felt the tension flow out of Suong; but more than that: she seemed to grow weak. "I'm not up to this tonight," she said. "I'm tired."

She was tired? David demanded of himself on the witness stand.

There are many reasons to be tired, he answered.

Suong said no more. They turned together and looked around the club. David was the only American. In the reds and blues of the color wheel he seemed to be in a room full of adolescents at a prom. The Vietnamese were tiny, smooth-faced, elaborately restrained. The men all wore the same sixties-cut suits and pointed shoes. The thick-knotted ties made their wide shirt collars ride up nearly to their chins. The women wore ao dais and stood erect and quiet near their posturing men. The Vietnamese band on the platform nearby began to play "Rock Around the Clock" and a few couples went to the floor to dance the jitterbug. The dancers met and parted to arm's length in fancy, jerky little steps.

"Who are they all?" David asked.

"Most are the friends of my sister's husband," she said. "Army officers. Others are my uncle's associates. Some are friends of my father, from business, from the government. A few others."

"I understood that dancing was illegal in Saigon."

"It is for those who cannot pay," she said in a flat tone. "Our government is very corrupt." She turned her face to the band, four long-haired Vietnamese boys who played with what struck David as a vague lethargy.

"Let's go upstairs," Suong said, her voice weary.

David followed her into the back corridor on the ground floor and up the stairs. They climbed five floors to the roof. The area was partially enclosed and David felt blindly about among the dark masses of stacked furniture for something to sit on. "Is there a light?"

"Do you need it?"

"No," he said, as he found a wicker settee standing alone. He pulled it to the edge of the dark, where the enclosure ended and the moonlight took up. They sat down, their legs in the light, and David put his arm around Suong. She seemed to be thinking for a time and then she laid her head against his shoulder. He kissed her hair.

The evening, which began cloudy, had blown itself clear and the moon was nearly full. The breeze was warm that moved the treetops beyond the balustrade and brushed Suong's hair against his face. He kissed her again, her passive forehead. Bombs thumped on the horizon. David looked out over the dark rooftops of the city. Far away a swath of sky went orange from a flare, then faded into dark again. From still farther came another rumbling from the B-52 strikes. But the lights and the sounds seemed as remote to David as auroras, as heat lightning. The crack and flare out beyond the city, beyond the river, in the countryside, only localized David the more strongly in the comfort of the shadow of the roof.

Then Suong spoke his own thought. "I feel distant from things," she said.

"I know what you mean," he said.

As prosecutor, David laughed at himself over this. Did you really know what she meant? he demanded.

No, he answered himself. Obviously not.

"Do you feel far from your home?" she asked.

"Yes. But I feel that way even when I'm there."

"I can't imagine America," she said. "I've tried, but I can't imagine it."

And do you know why she'd tried? David asked himself.
No.

Because she was pregnant. She was trying to see herself living in America with you.

She said, "I don't think now that I'm as worldly as people tell me I am."

David felt he understood her very well. He said, "Those people have no claims on you. Your ability to separate yourself from all of that is what drew me to you from the first."

She looked at him. "You understand how I am?"

"Yes."

Jennifer spoke.

David turned to her but the words he heard were slurred, from a dream. She shifted in the bed and fell silent.

David went back to his memory but there was very little more. The rest of that night at Suong's house held no clear words. He left her on the roof. She said she was tired, she would stay there for a while. He said he knew the way out. They kissed and there was a sudden surge in her kiss—a good-bye, he later realized—and he went down the stairs, across the dance floor, and he noticed on the way out that the Vietnamese boy in the white gloves holding the door was Suong's nephew, the boy who'd driven them to Nha Be. David thought: they've bribed his way out of the army for this? Then he went into the street and listened for the bombs. The band was playing loudly and the sound of laughter came from the nightclub and there was no other sound to be heard. He looked up toward the roof, but no face appeared. Suong was sitting there, he knew, but she was out of sight, out of reach.

And he never saw her again. He'd called two days later and a woman—an old woman, by the sound of her, probably Suong's mother—had answered the phone. Suong was out of town. No, her return was unknown. No, she had left no message for him. He tried to reach her by phone several more times in the following weeks and it was always the same: so sorry, we do not know when she'll be back; so sorry, she said nothing about you; no, we don't know where she is.

And he found himself puzzled and a little angry at the way he'd been sealed off from contact with her. But soon— very soon—he found himself feeling relieved. He'd never intended to become involved with anyone in Vietnam; now external conditions had forced him to pay attention to his own good sense. At the time, it had never occurred to him that Suong had gone into seclusion because she was pregnant. She was pregnant and she had thought it over and she had decided that she didn't want to go to America, she had decided that she didn't want to be with the father of her child. Or not David, at least.

David sat up in the bed. Jennifer stirred but did not wake. This was a simple completion of his own injury; his prosecution rested and no more words were necessary. The instinct that David had had in this whole matter was proven in his mind to be correct. He felt certain now that he had a child in Vietnam. Further, although he had no special proof, he was equally certain that the child was a son. And inexorably he was led to the final conclusion: he must find the boy; he must go to Vietnam and find his son.

The next day David was focused on his resolution but he had no clear thoughts. His mind could not get past the disparity between what he needed to do and what his present circumstances allowed. Carl's very presence beside him as they walked down the hill toward the day in court just made David's dilemma more vexing.

The two approached the front gate of Holabird. They walked past the guardhouse and turned down the street that led to the court building. Carl said, "David, I want to warn you about something."

"Yes?"

"This won't make you happy. But very soon you're going to be seeing . . . well, the press at this trial."

David stopped. The first reflex he had was what it had always been. He wanted as little of the outside world involved with this as possible. He wanted to stay apart. He said, "I told you to keep them away."

"Listen," Carl said sharply. "This trial is going badly already and it will get worse."

It surprised David how this, too, stopped him. Carl had spoken like this before. David knew in a formal sort of way that he was in great jeopardy. But this time the words chilled him, made him listen. He knew at once why this change in him had occurred. Finding his son in Vietnam: the trial was a threat to that now.

Carl said, "Hedberg has flown your helicopter pilot to the US."

"The man who took me to Con Son?"

"Yes."

"Is that going to make a difference?"

"It's going to make a good show. He'll point you out in person."

"I don't know how to lie to the press any more than I know how to lie to the court."

"You don't have to lie to the press. They'll do it for you."

"I'm in trouble, Carl." David said this matter-of-factly, in a steady voice, but behind the words David began to tremble. He'd been a fool. He'd thought he could hold himself apart. He could not do anything to change what he'd done or what the government knew about what he'd done; so he could only detach. He'd realized that this detachment wouldn't clear him, but it promised to let him get through the ordeal, and he'd just have to cope with the outcome when it finally occurred. And in the meantime he'd served the accustomed pattern of his mind, the way he'd always looked at things, and as a result he'd been able to remain calm; he'd been able to listen to the familiar flow of his life, just as if it had been a stream in the Cascades. Now things had changed. "I'm . . . I wish I could do what you think needs to be done, Carl . . ." Now David wanted something very badly and he could not act.

"David." Carl put his hand on David's shoulder. "You're not capable of the things that could radically alter your situation. I wouldn't even advise them. But maybe we can get some leverage at least. Play the good-hearted martyr for these press guys."

"I've got to get out of this, Carl."

"Please. Just be courteous with them. The press is incredibly emotional."

"I mean out of these charges. I've got to be able to . . . leave."

"Are you all right, David?"

"No, dammit."

"Are you having trouble putting your thoughts together?" Carl's speech became overprecise.

"I'm fine that way. You can really be stupid sometimes, counselor." David wanted to run. He thought of running, of turning on his heel and running away. Maybe it was that simple. Run. Get on a plane. Go to Saigon before it fell. It would fall soon. Run. Find the boy.

"Then come on," Carl said.

They approached the front of the court building. There were half a dozen people gathered there. Carl took David's arm. "Not now," Carl said to the reporters. "Sorry."

Voices besieged David, notebooks waved, David forced a smile, kept moving.

"We'll have a further statement later," Carl said.

Inside the front doors, feet scuffling behind, following, David said, "You've already talked to them?"

"I pointed them in the right direction to bring themselves up to date. There's only so much I can do." He winked at David and they entered the courtroom. The clatter of feet followed, chairs scraped at the back of the room, and soon the trial was in session again.

More depositions. An interrogator in Ba Ria. David remembered the man. A stocky man but faceless now; in a room in a building that was a former French primary school. A blackboard was still on the wall. David had missed Tuyen by a single day. Tuyen had been questioned and taken on to Con Son Island, the final stop for political prisoners, the home of Thieu's tiger cages, the cells where his foes were tortured, often to death.

The stocky man was introduced by his commanding officer, a major, as Pham Van Tuyen's interrogator. The three of them sat in this schoolroom and David said to the interrogator, "What was Tuyen like?"

In the courtroom the man talked, through another performance by Hedberg, about David's intensity, his desperation to know about this VC prisoner. In David's mind, the man's voice was suddenly very clear, speaking Vietnamese. "This Tuyen was tough when he came in. But I am tough too."

David looked away from his face as a smile began to shape. But David listened intently to the words, even though he knew they would be bad.

"He claimed to be a woodcutter," the stocky man continued. "He claimed to be from Honai."

At this point David still didn't have even a physical description of Tuyen. He only had the government's suspicion that he was important, and he had these lies that Tuyen used in order to deflect, even taunt, his foes.

"I was very thorough with him," the interrogator said. "I used what methods I had and he stopped lying to me."

David tried to keep a calm facade before this man, but the sense of Tuyen gradually being broken was very difficult for David to bear without showing the welter of feelings inside him. He imagined Tuyen standing naked in a doorway, his body framed in fluorescence, the hum of a machine behind him, his eyes blinking sightless, his flesh covered with the white spots from electrodes. But the features of Tuyen's face were blurred. David could not even discern his stature.

"He is no woodcutter," the interrogator said. "That was very clear. He is the man we thought him to be. It's all in my report."

"Was he tall?" David asked in a low voice.

"What?"

"Was he tall?" David's voice was harsh. "My Vietnamese is good. You understand my words. Was he tall? Was he short? Was he fat? Was he skinny?"

"Taller than me. Not as tall as the major," he said, nodding toward his commanding officer, who was still in the room.

David looked at the major and judged Tuyen's height. Then he said, "Skinny. Was he skinny?"

"Yes . . . No."

"Which is it? Did you look at him?"

The interrogator's veneer of toughness was crumbling. He was clearly confused. David knew the confusion was from trying to understand the intensity of this crazy American. That made David even angrier.

"Was he skinny or not skinny?" David's voice strained as he fought back the urge to shout.

"Not skinny. But not fat either. Medium build."

"Did you damage him?" David asked, gripping tightly the arms of the chair he sat in.

"How . . . damage?" The interrogator seemed shaken.

"Your thorough methods."

"I used the shocks several times . . ."

"I don't want to hear what you did," David said, rising abruptly from the chair. "I only want to know if his mind is damaged."

The major answered, "We're careful not to inflict permanent damage if further interrogation is expected. We sent the man to Con Son in reasonably good shape."

"Good enough to be questioned further," the interrogator added with a tone of relief, obviously deciding that that had been the source of David's intense concern.

This surmise of the interrogator was nowhere present now, though; not in this courtroom. Now the interrogator had failed to work out David's intensity at all. There was only the odd hostility of this American; his almost frantic interest in this high-ranking enemy official.

David felt his anger dissipate in the old French schoolroom. He looked from the interrogator to the major and back again and their confused, solicitous stares were alien to him beyond the slightest hope of comprehension. The room, its heavy air, echoes out in the hallway, all these struck him like these stares: alien, unknowable. He left the room, left the building; outside he stood somewhere and he thought of Con Son Island. It was beyond reach, out in the South China Sea. David knew Tuyen was cracking. He was on Con Son. The destruction was near of that pure, ironic, detached mind. David knew he must go to the island. This much was clear. At that moment, what he didn't know was how.

And so the prosecution followed the same logical sequence. The next deposition was from Mr. Uc, Major Morello's Vietnamese assistant. Deceased, since the obtaining of this deposition, Hedberg announced. Uc was the man David had turned to.

And Uc was dead. This distressed David. He didn't know why. He hadn't known Uc very well and what he did know he didn't much like. Morello had warned David that Uc was a wheeler-dealer and that was certainly how the man came across. Why should David feel fretful at his death?

"Captain Fleming ask me how he can get to Con Son Island," Hedberg said, reading Uc's reply to a question in the deposition.

Uc got him a helicopter. He made it possible to track down the man whose words on the wall had come to obsess David. But that was no reason to feel anything at the news of his death.

"I told him I maybe could get him there. Captain Fleming say he would pay very much. It was very important to him."

"Were those his words?" Hedberg's assistant read the prosecution's question from the deposition.

Hedberg wrinkled his brow as if in thought and then read Uc's answer. "No. Captain Fleming say, 'It's of the utmost urgency.'"

David stopped listening. This dead man was helping to build a case against him, threatening to keep him from his son. David grew angry at the man and then he knew why he'd been disturbed by the death. The man had died half a world away; he was utterly beyond reach now; life had gone on since David left Vietnam; striking events were occurring beyond David's awareness. All of this was declared by Uc's death; all of this told David that his son in Vietnam was real, was in danger, was unreachable, could be dying, even as David sat at this hardwood table in this tiny courtroom in this country that wanted him imprisoned or worse. David had to find a way out. He needed help and he thought of Trask.

.   .   .

Trask told David to jog and so he did. He went out alone the following evening. It was Saturday and he jogged through the dark streets along his accustomed route. Trask said he'd find him at the right moment.

David turned on the street leading to the steel mill and he ran faster down a slight incline, flashing from dark to streetlight to dark and he passed a parked car and his name, "David," Trask's voice.

David stopped and turned and came back to the car. The street was empty, the row houses were quiet, many were dark, and David got into the front passenger side of the car and closed the door.

Trask was behind the wheel. He said, "Hello, David."

David puffed in something resembling relief. Trask had come; Trask who carried the smell and feel of Saigon with him; Trask who, with David, had always been able to get unusual things done. But David realized how vague his own plans still were. He was not clear what he needed from Trask. "You said you'd like to help me," David said.

"Yes."

"How can you do that?"

Trask stared at David for a time without moving. David waited him out. Finally Trask said, "I didn't have anything specific in mind. Don't you?"

"I guess I was hoping for another burst of sincerity from you. You didn't drive up here to meet me in the dark so we could play our little game some more."

David's eyes were accustomed now to the dimness of the car and he saw Trask smile. "Okay," the man said. "I understand. But I really did think you'd have some definite plan."

"Not quite yet."

"There are certain things I *can't* do."

"What are those?"

"There's nothing I can do to affect the actual course of the trial."

"You couldn't testify, for instance? Make what I did part of . . ."

"That's right. I couldn't do that. I couldn't disrupt the process from *within*, let us say."

David sensed something in the phrasing of this, in the tone of the man's voice—a manipulativeness, a cynicism— that made more sense of Trask's character than the covert compassion that had been portrayed the last time. "You're here officially now, aren't you," David said.

Trask grew still once more.

"What is it you boys would want with me?"

"Now, David, you're a professional . . ."

"No I'm not."

Trask smiled faintly. "Well, you were once. I did mean what I said in what you call my last burst of sincerity. My own personal allegiance *is* with the individual."

"What have I got that you want?"

"It's not quite as official as you're making it sound."

"There are levels of these things. I know. Don't be coy with me."

"What I have to offer is limited. Your commitment to us is limited . . . What are you planning, David? Why did you call me here?"

Now David played Trask's role. He stared at the man without responding, letting him keep the burden of speech.

"All right," Trask said. "I understand how all of this is difficult for you . . . First what I *can't* offer. You have to cope with the trial itself. I can't touch that. But if you . . . Let's say you decide to do something rash. After that I can give you a little help. Once you take yourself out of the system, so to speak."

David almost laughed. The subtle boundaries Trask was trying to describe seemed ludicrous to David and he knew he could make Trask very uncomfortable by just playing stupid. But in fact he knew very well what the man was saying, and though it made the trial itself more frightening, it gave him some hope beyond that. He said, "If I were to run . . ."

"Yes. If that's a decision you make, there are certain things I can do."

"Like what?"

"A pathway, perhaps. Documentation. Help in . . . placing you in some work."

"You're talking about . . . where? Canada?"

"It's certainly the most appropriate place."

"What's your interest in Canada?"

Trask shrugged. "Not Canada, really."

"What would you want from me?"

"I saw an item on your trial in the Baltimore *Sun* today."

"Yes?"

"They're printing just facts for now. A medium-sized item. It moved on the Associated Press, though."

David felt itchy. He didn't like sitting here with Trask, he didn't like having to deal with him; thinking about his own name, the trial, being publicized around the country made David stir in his seat, made him consider leaping from the car and running away. But he forced those feelings back. He had a more insistent purpose that quickly drew him back to the business at hand.

Trask was still talking. He said, ". . . Certain groups will seek you out in a place like Toronto. Groups connected to the larger opponents you and I have dealt with before, Dave."

"Listen, Trask. How about your own Vietnam desk?"

"What do you mean?"

"You yourself aren't tracking the radical groups in Canada. You're here trying to recruit me for one of your colleagues. But my interests aren't in Canada. They're back in Vietnam."

The silence that ensued was pleasant for David in a way that reminded him of Saigon; so much so that he expected to turn his eyes and see a xich-lo flash by. He'd caught Trask off balance. He felt the man's mind racing in the dark.

"Vietnam?" Trask said.

"I want to go back."

"There aren't three weeks left for the South. Maybe not even two."

This declaration gouged a hollow out of David's chest. He felt frantic. His son would soon be lost. Then he said, low, "The trial won't last even that long."

"Vietnam . . ."

"But if I go and I get trapped there . . . You'd still be able to get any information I generated out of the country, I bet . . . You'd find that useful."

"Damn right. Of course." Trask leaned toward him, his hand came up between them. "I'm not saying you shouldn't do what you need to do . . . Is it that woman?"

"No."

"Well, whatever. I'm sure you know what you're doing."

"You don't have to give me that crap, Ken. I don't need convincing to go."

"Your intention is to get in and out before the fall?"

"Of course. I know if I get that done, I'm not nearly as useful to you."

"We all take our little risks," Trask said.

"My risk is that I don't get out in time. Yours is that I do."

"And if you don't, that you'll do anything for us."

Trask suddenly sounded cool to the idea. David felt a ripple of panic. And the source was more than Trask's seeming to pull back: David realized that he had to get through the trial before anything else; he might not even have a chance to get to Vietnam.

Then Trask's voice grew warm again. "Listen, David, I'd be willing to get involved in this just on the chance that you'll be able to do something for us. A little speculative venture."

"Good," David said, trying to keep his eagerness out of his voice. But the trial nagged at him. "Are you sure," he said, "there's nothing you can do about this . . ."

"Worse than that, I'm afraid. I presume you were going to say 'this trial'?"

"Yes."

"No matter how you handle this—play the good soldier and hope to get off or run away—you're not going to be able to go back to Vietnam. Not as David Fleming. Even if they acquitted you, the Army wouldn't let you go. Everybody knows what's happening over there."

David knew what Trask said was true. He had to squeeze at his will to speak. "So what are you saying?"

"You'd need a passport. Canadian would do."

"Yes?"

"Now we're dealing with time, David. Time in producing a document of that sort. You've got a time problem."

"How long?"

"Maybe two weeks."

"The trial could be over in two weeks. I could be convicted and on the way to Leavenworth."

"Another of our little risks."

"It can't be faster?"

"I won't be able to convince anyone this is a high-priority project. Even if it were, we're a big old fussy bureaucracy. You should know that."

"And a plane ticket?"

"I'll get you that, too."

"So is this it? Is this the okay?"

"You're going to get very nervous over this, David. Very impatient. I don't want you to phone me again. I'll get this thing done as fast as I possibly can. You're going to have to be patient. If you call me, we'll just terminate the situation."

"All right."

"Don't pull a muscle running now," Trask said, lifting his head slightly in dismissal.

David said no more but got out of the car. He resumed his run, heading for the steel mill which showed itself in the darkness as a grid of churning red. He would turn and run back home somewhere this side of that uproar and he won-

dered if he'd have the same chance in the trial, if the passport would come in time to let him turn and run away.

When David opened the front door of the apartment after
his run, Jennifer leaped from the couch and switched off the
TV. He stood in the doorway, the measured tones of a late-
night news anchor fading in his head, and he didn't want to
be angry but he churned at the idea of the South falling and
it was hard to keep still. He stepped in and closed the door
to the apartment and he went into the bathroom without a
word to Jennifer and he stripped and showered and dressed
and when he came out she was sitting on the couch in the
silent room and her head was thrown back as if she was
weary. He was in control now. There was too much to think
about and it was maybe even easier this way, easier than if
there'd been one thing, one worry; he felt very tired and he
wanted to sleep, knew he could sleep if he tried.
    "I'm getting fed up," Jennifer said.
    "What?"
    "Did you see what I did when you came in?"
    David expected his anger to return. He was conscious of
his own sensitivity over the news being forced on him. But
the anger didn't come. There was a weltering instead: his
son, the fall, Suong, Tuyen, Hedberg and the Army, the
waiting ahead of him, waiting for Trask to rescue him. And
David would have to ask Jennifer again to go into exile. And
for what? His child by another woman. David knew how
hard he'd already been on Jennifer with his silences, with
his demands; but what he wanted next would be far worse.
How could he be angry with her?
    Jennifer said, "I jumped up and turned the TV off as if
I'd been caught in some petty crime."
    "It's just that I . . ."
    Jennifer rose again, purposefully this time, and David
didn't finish his sentence. She turned to confront him. He
understood her anger, wanted to wipe it away, but he had

no desire for her to understand his own desperate state. He had no urge to hold her, no urge for her to hold him. He just didn't want her to be angry. That was all.

"I know you're going through a lot," Jennifer said, her voice clenched. "But I'm going through everything you are and more."

"I don't want to fight with you."

"I know you're a quiet man a lot of the time," she said and she was beginning to grow short of breath. "And that's okay with me. But your quiet is different now and it's not just my postpartum depression saying so, it's me saying so and I know I'm right. If I want to watch television so I can bring the warmth of a human voice into my life, then I'm damn well going to watch television and you're going to have to just buy some earplugs or put your jogging suit on and go out and . . ." She was shouting now and she paused and seemed to be struggling with how far to let her rhetoric go. ". . . And just run around the neighborhood till you're tired enough to sleep." She began to cry.

David knew she'd considered saying that he should just run and keep on running. He wondered if her tears were in frustration at not having the courage to say what she really felt or in pain at having come so close to saying what she could never possibly feel. He moved to her, knowing he should move to her; he put his arms around her, still an act of the will, still not seeking any solace from her, still fearing what was to come but not allowing himself to consider it fully for now. She let him hold her and finally she even put her arms around him. She'd not felt the thing she almost said, David decided. A brief regret flickered in him: it would be easier that way, if she would ask him to run away from her. But it was no longer just her. There was a child. Nor was it just his son: he didn't want to leave Jennifer. He held her more tightly against him. He wanted to be with her, though even now he was thinking of Monday in court.

.   .   .

David thought that perhaps he was, in a certain sense, quite mad. Lieutenant somebody—David had missed even the name—the Vietnamese helicopter pilot—was sitting on the witness stand; he was pointing across the courtroom and he was saying that yes, that is the man who said he would kill me when we landed if I did not put the helicopter down near the Long Khanh Mountains. This lieutenant had crossed the space before David just a few minutes ago, jerking by on his crutches, the empty pant-leg pinned up, the jury leaning forward, watching carefully. And yet David could not make himself hear the words. Perhaps this was madness. But he didn't believe that. Instead this was entirely reasonable: he had nothing to say to this man; there was nothing that could be done; the only reality was in David's mind; he knew what had happened on Con Son when he'd finally found Tuyen. He didn't need to listen. Even now he felt satisfied with what he'd done that day. David's attachment to Tuyen had been vindicated in the court of his own mind, though even there certain questions remained only vaguely answered.

David flew to Con Son in this lieutenant's helicopter and he knew what to expect: a prison on an island covered with jungle; a quiet exterior with little apparent security, for there was nowhere to run. But somewhere in the grounds of the main compound was a vegetable garden and in the garden was a door and behind the door were two low wooden buildings and in the buildings were catwalks running between rows of cells dug deep into the ground. The bars in the floor, covering the cells, smoked with lime—the lime was thrown down on the prisoners to punish them for speaking to each other and the dusting of lime on the bars smoked because the guards routinely urinated into the cells. These things were unquestionably true: David had heard them from several sources, one of them American, all firsthand, all consistent. And this was where Tuyen was being held. As he flew he knew he would find Tuyen on this day, and he tried to keep his mind away from the tough questions: find him for what? What could he do for Tuyen? What could he say?

David flew over the Mekong Delta and then he was over the South China Sea, scaled in dull jade like the flank of a dragon, and then the island appeared. The chopper passed low over its westward cliff and then climbed up over its rain forest which rolled and peaked and fell through a shroud of high mist, the jungles black without the sun, and then the sea returned, the south coast of the island, the green sea, a stretch of beach and the chopper turned sharply, descended, pulled up over a runway, approached a low terminal and touched down on the tarmac.

Now David had to improvise very effectively. The pilot would leave at a specified hour whether or not anyone returned. David looked about him. The airstrip was deserted but well kept. On one side was the sea; on the other, the high hills. David went into the terminal building and found a Vietnamese man in an army uniform. He was a sergeant. He approached David with great deference.

"Sergeant, are you in charge here?" David asked in Vietnamese.

"Yessir . . . That is, I'm on duty at the terminal building."

"Why is there no one else here?"

"We know when planes are due to come. Your helicopter wasn't expected."

"I must go to the prison at once. I have urgent business there."

"Sir?"

David showed him his credentials and identification papers and the sergeant went to a telephone in an inner office. After a brief exchange he hung up and returned to David. "Someone will come after you," he said.

"How far is it to the prison?" David asked.

"Not far by road. The other side of the hills."

David turned away from him and walked to the windows. He did not want to talk to anyone. A little village sat at the foot of the hills and between the huts and the airstrip were women moving in a small field, bending close to the ground, weeding their crops. David watched a nearby stand of coconut trees bending at the tops in the sea wind.

Time passed and the women moved evenly through their rows but no one came. David looked about the room. The sergeant had disappeared. David turned again to the window and found himself impatient with the women and their mindless, stooped march through the fields. But he knew that his impatience was from the strain of waiting. I am here now, he thought. Nothing will keep me from seeing him. David did not think further and the door opened behind him and he whirled to confront the sound.

An ARVN lieutenant approached and saluted him. "I'm Lieutenant Quoc. You want to go to the prison?"

"That's right, lieutenant."

"Come with me, please."

The lieutenant drove David in an open jeep through the village and onto a road that rose slightly as it curled around the hills and crossed a stream flowing from the tangle of the forest. They passed a chain gang clearing trees along the edge of the road, then took a turn that left all people behind. Far to the rear David could view the sea. Above him, its bulk palpable against his face, was the highest of the hills, thick with the rain forest. The road turned again and they passed another jeep parked on the shoulder. A soldier waved at the lieutenant, who acknowledged the greeting with a nod. David could see two soldiers with automatic rifles at a tree line that was created, no doubt, by earlier chain gangs. Again the hill and the road resumed their solitary articulation.

The lieutenant did not speak and David was glad for that, glad too that the man drove fast. The road began to descend into a valley. The trees fell away and in the cleared bottom of the valley lay the prison.

The prison was like a dozen outposts he'd seen all over

Vietnam. An indifferently maintained perimeter of concertina wire contained rows of low hooches and barracks, a cluster of administrative buildings, a tiny Buddhist chapel for the guards. The jeep descended to the valley floor, crossed a cleared no-man's land, and passed through the perimeter. The lieutenant stopped before the only two-storied structure on the prison grounds and he led David inside and upstairs.

The prison commandant, a colonel in a crisply starched uniform, received David with a handshake. At once David played his only claim to authority, his Saigon credentials and identification papers. The commandant looked at them closely. He nodded faintly and then said, "Ah yes. You are CIA." There was great admiration in his voice and David was glad for the man's confusion, for the commandant was suddenly receptive, was full of comradely warmth as he gave back David's papers and offered him a chair. It was difficult for David, in his relief, not to rush; but he held back, kept the same smiling, brittle slyness in his manner that the commandant now assumed.

"One week ago," David said, "a prisoner was brought here from Ba Ria. We believe he has information that would be useful in an operation that . . . my organization is interested in. I'd like to talk with the man, if that's possible."

The commandant spread his hands in a gesture of magnanimity. "Of course," he said. "I'm a great admirer of you people. I almost never get to see you here. Only sometimes the fruits of your labor." He laughed at this in a way that suggested he expected David to laugh with him. But David could not manage this. He nodded but waited quietly, without even a smile. The commandant let his own laughter fade away and he nodded at David sympathetically. "Of course," he said. "We are happy to cooperate. What is the man's name?"

David faltered. He'd come this far and Tuyen or news of Tuyen's final fate was only a few words away and yet he hesitated. But the last bit of fear at what he would find, of helplessness at what he would do, burned away and he said, "Pham Van Tuyen."

The colonel instantly frowned. He repeated the name while searching his desk. He found a piece of paper and said, "I thought that name was familiar."

"He's the one from this morning," Quoc said.

"Yes, lieutenant." The colonel nodded at Quoc, then turned to David. "This man Tuyen is somewhere on the island."

"What do you mean?"

Lieutenant Quoc spoke as the colonel looked at the paper. "He's escaped our direct custody. He was being moved from one security area to another this morning before dawn. He overpowered the guard and took a vehicle."

David struggled to keep his face impassive, his hands from jumping up before him. Tuyen had fought back.

"You must understand," the colonel interjected. "Security here is a unique thing. The man was clearly incapable —physically or psychologically—of committing such an act to begin with. But there is nowhere to run to on this island anyway, except back into our custody. Or to a death in the forest that would merely complete our work."

"Do you have any idea where he went?" David asked, looking at the lieutenant.

"The vehicle he stole was abandoned only a few hundred yards out the front gate. He'd run it into a ditch."

This chilled David, suggested that Tuyen's faculties were not sound.

The lieutenant said, "He has to be somewhere on the hill we passed driving in."

David remembered the army jeep by the side of the road and the men with their rifles in the tree line. He said, "His usefulness to you may be minimal once he gets to this island, but I need to try to talk to him for our own . . ."

"Please," the colonel said. "Don't misunderstand. We're searching for him. He can't go far on foot. Do you have time to wait for a while?"

"No, I don't," David said. "May I join the search?"

The colonel was startled at the request but immediately agreed. However, he insisted that Lieutenant Quoc go with him. David could not firmly resist the colonel and so the lieutenant and David went back outside and got into the jeep. The lieutenant whipped the vehicle backward and then they leaped forward. As the prison structures passed, David saw, in a remote corner of the grounds, a garden. The sight vanished as they roared on but the image lingered. There had been a vegetable garden and a wall nearby with a door and beyond the wall David had seen the tops of two low barrack buildings.

The jeep climbed and curled around the hill again. The lieutenant was speaking to David. "Do you want to join our searching parties?"

David looked at Quoc. "No," he said. "Drive me beyond them." David wanted to find Tuyen himself, find him alone. He had to decide where to look. I know his mind, he thought. Tuyen did not escape merely to die in the rain forest. David did not believe that of him, though Tuyen surely would prefer dying alone in the trees than at the hands of an interrogator. Maybe that was his reason. He knew the hopelessness of this island and he had withdrawn to meet his death in solitude. If that were so, the search was hopeless. He'd climb toward the top of the hill until his strength gave out and he'd die beyond all possibility of David's reaching him. But David could not let himself accept that possibility. He thought: if Tuyen still clung to the slightest hope of survival, what would he, what would I myself, do? First, he would have to find his way back out of the forest. David thought at once of the stream they'd crossed. If Tuyen could find that stream, he would prepare himself to follow it out to the road after dark.

"That stream," David said. "Not far from the village. Take me there."

The lieutenant nodded and they drove to the place and stopped and David stepped down from the jeep. He turned to Quoc and said firmly, "Lieutenant, I'd rather search on my own. If my guess is correct, the man may come out here. I want you to stay and watch in case he gets past me."

The lieutenant began to object but David left him quickly, moving by the side of the narrow stream until he entered the shadow of the trees. The stream turned and the jeep, the lieutenant, the road vanished. David stopped for a moment and listened to the water rushing in its channel; he listened and he felt calm; this place was familiar to him, a wood, moving water, and he knew Tuyen, knew him well, knew he would be drawn to this stream.

Up ahead the channel turned and the trees joined over the water, shrouding it in shadow. David continued his ascent, moving quickly, knowing that Tuyen would not come down this far in the daylight. The bank disappeared in a tangle of ground shrubs and bromeliads and he was forced into the stream.

The water pressed him back but David moved ahead steadily, climbing through the stream. The jungle grew dense around him, the double canopy blotting out the sky. The ascent grew steeper and a break came overhead as the stream split around a stone outcropping. He paused and looked up the hill.

He thought he could see even denser woods at the summit, recognizing mahogany trees topping the endless green, turning the heights into a cloud forest. The stream veered off now, avoiding a confrontation with the peak of the hill. David began to move again, the stream came together, and after a stretch of bamboo thicket, the forest closed overhead once more.

His breathing grew cramped and painful as he pushed up the hill against the stream. He felt suddenly weak. Tuyen was in bad shape, physically, when he escaped. Could he come this far? Would he think of the stream as the escape route? And to where? To the airstrip eventually; to the sea. David shook the doubts out of his head. The light was dim. He looked at his watch and the forests wheeled: the time had passed with no sense of its touching him. The time specified in the agreement with the pilot was very near. The man would leave the island in a little over an hour. David had to find Tuyen soon.

David took some solace from the stream's persistence. It was still strong, and it was flowing, he thought, down a shoulder of the hill. He moved again, up the stream, cautiously now, stopping before each turning to check the newly revealed stretch of water. Tuyen would be alert to his pursuers, would be ready to vanish back into the forest.

Again and again David crouched low in the stream and looked carefully ahead for any movement. Once, a splash quickened his breath, pushed him deeper into his crouch, nearly submerged into the water, but there was no further sound, nothing visible, and he moved on.

The time was growing very short. But David was determined not to go back unless he found Tuyen. If he was stranded here it would be better than to abandon Tuyen at the last moment, he thought. The stream turned once more. David reflexively assumed his position close to the water and near to the thick undergrowth on his left. The turn was gradual and he would add only a few yards to his view with the next several steps. But when he moved and looked upstream, he saw Tuyen.

Tuyen had his back to David. He was leaning against a tree and urinating into the stream. He did not move. After a long moment he finished, straightened up slightly, then sank down onto a wide flat root at the water's edge. He sat in profile to David, not twenty yards away. David watched him closely and he pitied his obliviousness. Tuyen's head drooped wearily, his eyes were closed, his mouth hung slack, his head was shaved, his prison uniform was in tatters, his forearms lay along his thighs, his hands dangled as if without feeling over the rushing water. David straightened up and began slowly to wade toward him.

It was not until he drew nearly within arm's length of him that Tuyen knew anyone was there. But Tuyen did not start. He opened his eyes and lifted his face calmly and the two men stared at each other. At last Tuyen's actual face filled David's vision: a squared jaw, a large mole high on his right cheek, the sharp-cut eyes of a Vietnamese with no French blood at all. And those eyes, though steady, seemed veiled, seemed to speak of his ordeal. It occurred to David that Tuyen did not start because he did not see, did not comprehend. But he escaped, David told himself. He had found his way to the stream, following the very logic that David anticipated. Then David saw Tuyen's calmness as resignation. He'd given it up, let his life go at last.

"Tuyen," David said. No trace of comprehension showed on the face. The white spots of the electrodes were vivid on his throat even in the gloom of the forest.

"I am not here to take you back to the prison," David said in Vietnamese. Tuyen's face turned away almost idly.

"Do you understand what I'm saying?" David said, fighting back panic. How could Tuyen come this far if his mind had been damaged? He couldn't, David told himself. He couldn't. But he didn't understand. David saw a spot of drool forming at the corner of his mouth. David panted in fear: have I been mistaken? Is he the man I thought he was? David felt suddenly alone. He said, "Tuyen." He paused. He had no more words. "Tuyen," he repeated and then just the facts: "I came here to help you. I can take you from here. I have a helicopter." There was no movement in the man. David felt himself trembling now. He turned. He began to wade downstream. He had to go. He had to get away from this stranger.

Then there was a voice behind him. "Wait."

David turned around. Tuyen was looking at him steadily. They faced each other with no sound, no movement in the world. Then Tuyen laughed. The laugh began as a low, broken cough but gained strength as it grew, and he shook his head slowly. "I have suffered many things," he said. "The pain in my body was very great and I had to be very strong to try to keep my mind whole. But this moment of my insanity has been the most bizarre of all. By a jungle stream an American suddenly appears speaking precise Vietnamese and saying he would rescue me and then when I don't leap at this suggestion he just turns his back and walks away." Tuyen laughed again and David laughed with him.

"Come quickly," David said. "My pilot is under instructions to take off in less than thirty minutes."

"I don't believe in you," Tuyen said.

"I'm real," David said.

"Why are you doing this?"

Tuyen was the first to ask this. David had no answer. Because I read what you wrote on your cell wall: David could offer this as an explanation, but it sounded meaningless now and so he said, "It's too complicated to explain. Our time is running out."

"I don't trust you."

"What reason would I have to act like this so far if I was a threat to you? If you had reason to fear me, I'd draw a weapon on you or I'd be here with a squad of soldiers . . . Come on now. We have to hurry."

"I'm afraid I don't have the physical strength."

"I'm strong enough to help you."

"Where will you take me?"

David hesitated only a moment. He knew where the VC were the strongest in Phuoc Thuy province. "To the Long Khanh Mountains. You have people there."

Tuyen closely studied David's face. Then he smiled faintly. "I'd already set my mind to dying here," he said.

"I don't truly have to reason you into living," David said, returning the smile. "And we have no time for the sport of it."

Tuyen tried to rise and David went to him. "I am stronger than I appear," Tuyen said.

David counted on the downhill passage with the current to make up for some of their lost time, but Tuyen fell repeatedly. He came to rely more and more on David's support to move down the hill. Tuyen's legs buckled and he fell face forward into the water, dragging David to his knees. David pulled Tuyen's head clear of the water, for when he fell, all of the man's strength disappeared for a time and he seemed incapable of even lifting his head from the current.

The two said nothing in their flight, their breath coming heavily, the water roaring in their ears, the passage of time crying out even louder, declaring their fading hopes for escape. They paused at a stone outcropping and Tuyen swooned. David held him tightly about the shoulders and splashed water into his face and onto the back of his neck. He was a small man. David was aware of that as he supported him, but the quality seemed detached from Tuyen himself. David felt the man's mind and will struggling beside him and these were Tuyen.

David helped Tuyen to his feet and began to despair of their chances. He did not look at his watch again until they stumbled and splashed their way to what he recognized as the final turn in the stream. Then he found that they had five minutes to get to the airstrip.

"Trust me," David said to Tuyen as they emerged from the forest. The jeep still sat at the road. Lieutenant Quoc saw them and leaped up and began to run toward them.

"You did it," Quoc said as he approached.

"Yes," David said. "Help me into the jeep with him."

When Tuyen was in the back seat of the jeep, David pulled his .38 on Quoc. "Drive us to the airport, lieutenant. Fast."

Quoc looked at the .38, then at David's face. He nodded and drove off at high speed. David kept the pistol on him as they passed down the foot of the hill and into the village. Quoc swerved to avoid a goat in the road but David kept control of the weapon. As the airport terminal came into sight, there was a sharp discharge as an engine began to turn over. The pilot was about to take off.

"Faster," David said, thrusting the pistol at the lieutenant. He complied and the jeep raced past the fields and onto a service road. It rounded the terminal as the chopper's blades reached their highest pitch and the craft began to shake. David reached across and honked the jeep's horn. The lieutenant showed restraint, did not grab at the gun, and the jeep pulled alongside the helicopter and stopped. David honked the horn again as Tuyen climbed out of the back seat but the sound vanished in the pounding of the chopper's engines. The pilot didn't hear. David jumped out of the jeep and then he felt a movement behind him and turned. Quoc grasped at his shoulder and David struck his arm away. He pointed the pistol at Quoc's face and the man recoiled. David backed away as the helicopter shook violently in its preparation to ascend. Tuyen's torso was in the open side door and David pushed at him. The chopper began to lift off and David gasped, his arms jumped. He felt Tuyen's hand on his shoulder. David leaped and was inside and the chopper veered and rose rapidly. Tuyen, clutching one of the seats, held David under the arm as the helicopter banked and David felt a pull from the doorway. But the chopper leveled off, the pull ceased, and David got to his feet.

He found the .38 still in his hand, though he didn't remember holding it in the final leap for the plane. He went forward to the cockpit and when the pilot protested landing in the Long Khanhs David pointed the pistol at him and the man nodded his assent without the need for any complicated explanations about when the pistol might be used on him.

David went back and sat down across from Tuyen. They did not speak as the South China Sea passed beneath them, the sea stretching as far as the horizon, containing in its curve the silence of their last minutes together. The wind beat at their chests, battered their eyes, but they sat perfectly still, looking at each other. A pain somewhere in Tuyen's body cut sharply into his face. He closed his eyes, turned away, and when he turned back he both acknowledged David's concern and reassured him with a minute nod. The delta passed now beneath them, and David felt the chopper swing northeast as the pilot complied with the order.

Tuyen slept and David was glad, though he missed the man's consciousness. Tuyen's head nodded in sleep and each nod sent a pulse of calmness through David. The wind clutched at David's shoulders, beat at his legs, and he did not move. He watched the hot, empty sky, watched the sharp line of the now distant sea. He, too, slept for a time, waking easily, refreshed, as the Long Khanhs appeared ahead.

He leaned forward and touched Tuyen on the shoulder and the man woke easily. David motioned to the mountains and Tuyen looked at them and then pointed to a plain at the southern edge of a large peak. David went forward to the pilot and pointed to the spot. The pilot nodded and the helicopter began to descend.

David returned to Tuyen. They still did not speak, never spoke again to each other. The helicopter descended; the mountain reared above them; the chopper hovered and settled. Tuyen eased himself down from the door and turned. David grasped Tuyen's hand for a brief moment and then the helicopter rose. David watched Tuyen standing below, his face upturned, his eyes steady, as if he understood. David watched until the man's features grew dim, his body small. And Tuyen did not move from where he stood, had not moved even when he disappeared in the distance of the plain.

In his inward courtroom, David as prosecutor and David as defendant blinked at each other. Very few words had passed between himself and Tuyen. Nor did he ever feel a regret at that. Enough had been said to confirm that Tuyen was the man he had thought him to be and then David set him free and that was enough. David as prosecutor sat and folded his hands on the table before him and he would say nothing about the events on Con Son Island. This was someone else's grudge being played out: Hedberg's voice swooped past and the one-legged man loped by, his testimony ended. All that David knew from his own reliving of those events in Vietnam was that the single-mindedness and the scorn for risk that took him to Con Son were needed again to take him back to Vietnam in search of his son.

He looked about himself. He had already begun to do what needed to be done beyond this courtroom. But here he was still passive. For valid reasons. But he stirred now, wanted to act. Something had struck him in his memory of Con Son. He had told the commandant that he was seeking Tuyen for questioning on a case. And he'd said nothing to the contrary to Quoc. David could have been snatching Tuyen to interrogate him further, even to take him away and kill him. Maybe there was a lie to tell after all. David was rising, Carl was rising beside him, the colonel was gone and they were leaving the courtroom and David wondered if he could construct a lie that would at least get him his ticket to Saigon. But in his mind he heard Hedberg beginning to probe: Lieutenant Quoc said that you and Pham Van Tuyen worked together in the escape. Isn't this true? Isn't it true that you covered Quoc with your pistol while this VC official boarded the helicopter—*eagerly* boarded the helicopter? Were these the actions of a man conducting an enemy to an interrogation?

David staggered in the hallway. He could not answer Hedberg even in his mind. He looked at Carl and the man's face was unsmiling, rigid. "It's going bad," David said.

"Yes."

Up ahead were reporters. They'd left the courtroom before David, waited for him just outside the front door, following the colonel's restrictions.

"David," Carl said, "you have to go on the stand."

"I know."

Carl glanced at him in surprise at this ready assent. "Do you have a story?" Carl asked.

"I've tried to find one but it's too complex to lie. There's no one to back me up."

They reached the door and the gabble of reporters.

David blinked at the blurring of his vision as camera lights went on, microphones sprouted, lenses leaned toward him, notebooks bobbed, and the voices pitched high until one emerged. David shrank back, considered turning and escaping back into the court building, but Carl inserted himself now between David and the questions and David knew from the panic in himself that he'd been wise to decide not to lie.

"Captain Fleming," a voice said. "You seem super straight, if anything. How do you see yourself?"

Only curses shaped in David's mind in response. But Carl spoke instead. "David loves his country very much. You'll be hearing his testimony soon. He will take the stand. And when he does, you're going to have to look elsewhere for the reasons behind his extraordinary act. You're going to have to look at the compassion of the human heart."

When David returned from his run the next morning, he found Jennifer at the kitchen table. The newspaper was spread out before her. "You're in here," she said.

"I don't want to see it."

"They call you a paradox. They call you a man deeply divided, just like the country was."

David stood in the kitchen door, still sweating, poised between anger and curiosity over the story. He was divided in the news story between what and what? Super straight soldier and peacenik, probably.

"Your picture's here," she said.

"Stop it, Jennifer. I really don't want to know."

"I'm sorry." She turned her face to him and smiled. "It's a nice picture. I think you're very cute." Then her smile faded at once; she looked as if she would cry; but she stiffened, held back the tears, closed the newspaper.

David saw her intense concern for him. He knew she loved him, wanted him to be safe from harm, and David moved across the kitchen. When he touched her hair he was seized by the urge to tell her the truth, tell her about Suong, his certainty about the existence of another son. Tell her now. His hand trembled very slightly as he stroked her hair and as she clutched the hand. He almost spoke then. Almost said, There was a woman . . . But he held back.

"What's going to happen to us?" she said.

"I don't know," he said, his voice very low. The truth would be academic at this point, his mind insisted. Perhaps he wouldn't have the opportunity to go back to Vietnam. The chances were slim that he'd be acquitted. And the things they might convict him of could easily carry prison sentences. Long ones. Maybe worse. Why tell Jennifer now? If he never had a chance to go back, there would be no reason for her to know, to carry that burden too. That made sense. But perhaps they could flee before the verdict. Run to Canada. But not until Trask had given him his passport, his ticket. He had to wait for Trask. He had to wait. Then it struck him: why couldn't he run now and have Trask get him his passport and ticket in Canada? That was simple. But he couldn't call Trask to suggest this. He'd said that if David called, the deal was off, and David knew the man meant it. He would be uncompromising. Why hadn't David thought to suggest this when he was with Trask? It just hadn't occurred to him. He didn't think of it. "Damn," he said aloud.

"What is it?" Jennifer said.

Now I have to wait, David cried out to himself.

"David," Jennifer said, her voice insistent.

He looked at his wife. He'd alarmed her. How could he explain his curse?

"What *is* it, David?"

"Nothing."

"I want to know."

He could think of no lie. Why was he always under pressure to think of lies? He was tired of this.

Jennifer rose from the kitchen table. She squared off before him, angry now. "I'm tired of this," she said.

Her words repeating his thought, as if mocking him,

made him angry. He was living with a perpetual lie; not to tell Jennifer of this central fact about himself was to lie.

"I'm supposed to be your wife." Her voice vibrated, though she kept it low. "Remember? You used to talk to me a little, at least. I used to think I at least knew the important things."

"All right, dammit," David said. "Sit down."

Jennifer recoiled as if he'd hit her. She sat. He sat down beside her, leaned to her. He said, "Please understand that what I'm going to tell you about happened before I met you."

"Yes," she said softly. Her face sagged and again he was asked to lie. To speak this truth in the kitchen, in his sweat clothes, goaded by a trivial event, a few angry words: this was madness, impulsive madness. But he spoke.

"In Saigon I knew a woman," he said. "She meant nothing to me, though that wasn't clear at first. We had a brief time together."

"An affair," Jennifer said, though without any harshness. Her tone said she was acting mature, strong, she was helping him out, suggesting that he didn't have to be circumspect.

"Brief," he said. "Only three months or so. She broke it off, though I was certainly ready for that. It meant nothing."

David paused. Jennifer waited. He knew this much was relatively easy for her to bear—a brief, long-finished affair with a woman on the other side of the world. David thought to simply stop at that. He'd been thinking of this woman and he felt guilty. That's why he'd been silent. Jennifer even began to take this as the full story, for she said, "It's done. I'm glad." She spoke gently.

But now that David had begun to tell the story, he could not bear to keep part of it back. And if he found a way to return to Vietnam, the rest would have to come out eventually anyway. "There's more," he said. "At the time, I didn't know why she broke it off, really. Not the exact reason. But in the past few days a couple of things have been said and I saw those baby-lift scenes on TV and I began to think about it."

This pause made Jennifer stir. David felt short of breath. He was afraid of this part, but he said, "For the first time since I last saw her I figured out what had happened. I think —I feel certain now—that she was pregnant."

After only a pulse beat of silence Jennifer said, "By you?"

"She was no whore," David said.

"I'm sure she wasn't." Her voice was hard.

The little escalation of anger between them brought on another silence. She was fighting him already and the worst for her was yet to come—his having to go back. He couldn't say that now, not while she was like this.

"Why the hell are you telling me about this?" she said.

"You wanted to know why I was quiet."

"You've been thinking about your family in Vietnam, have you?"

He wanted her anger to stop. He touched her arm and she jerked it away.

He said, "You don't have to feel threatened."

"Don't throw your damn clichés at me," she said and she stood up, moved away, without a clear direction at first, just around the table; then she moved toward the doorway and disappeared into the next room.

David sat at the table; his shoulders sagged. He regretted saying anything. But even as he did, a stronger feeling came: he regretted not going all the way, getting this over with, telling her what he had to do next.

He rose and went into the living room. She was sitting on a chair. He sat down across from her, on the couch, and she immediately said, "I'm sorry." But her voice was full of strain and she wasn't looking at him. This apology was an act of her will, he knew.

"I'm sorry too," he said. "I'm not inflicting this on you idly. There's a reason."

She turned her face to him and moved her shoulders as

if to say, What next? David's will faltered again. He did not speak. Finally Jennifer said, very softly but with an angry precision, "And what is the reason?"

"Please, Jen. I'm sorry I'm doing this. Please don't be hurt, please don't be angry. I'm not doing this because I want to. I'm not interested in any woman but you. Believe that."

Jennifer angled her face away and closed her eyes. "These are tough times," she said. "Too much is going on."

"I'm sorry."

"Please stop saying that." All that was in Jennifer's tone now was a weariness. "Just tell me what you have to tell me."

"I'm certain I have a son in Vietnam. He's maybe four years old. I guess it's David Junior who's made me so sensitive to this. I don't know why I should be, exactly. But I see Vietnam falling and all those children on TV with American fathers, and I know I have to find out for sure about my own child. That country's going down, Jen, and something of mine is there."

"And what does this mean—you have to find out for sure?"

"I mean I have to go back there. Just to . . ." He found he had no completion for this sentence. "Just for a brief time."

"How do you expect to do that when you're locked up in jail?" She rose up to shout this.

"I don't know that just yet."

"Don't know what? Don't know you're going to jail? Of course you're going to jail. You're not doing a damn thing to defend yourself."

"Maybe we can still . . . escape."

"Escape? We rejected that the last time all this came up . . . But that was before this woman entered the picture. I see. You want our son and me to be forced into exile so that you can have a chance to fly off to this Saigon dolly of yours."

"Dammit, Jennifer." David stood up, matched her anger at last. "I don't care about the woman. It's the boy."

"How do you know there's a boy?"

"I know. Don't ask me how. I figured it out."

"She's not going to let you have him."

"Look. I just have to *know*. I'm not trying to . . . trying to do anything more. I'm not." In fact, David didn't know what he wanted. Not specifically. He watched Jennifer's eyes narrow at his stammering.

"You're talking like a fool," she said.

"I know."

"A damn fool."

"It's not something that I *chose* to want . . . I *have* to go . . ."

"I don't even know who you are sometimes."

"Please, Jen."

"This was probably how you took out after that Vietcong who put us in this mess." Then she put a schoolgirl mockery in her voice. "You just *had* to go." The taunt rang in the room and her face changed; she grew sullen; she seemed to be conscious of her tone; she turned away. "I'm not up to this," she said. "Not all your problems."

"I understand."

Her face snapped back to him. Her anger had grown reasonable—hard, but reasonable. "You feel this allegiance to a presumed son in Vietnam . . . a responsibility of some kind."

"Yes . . . something like that."

"Well, what about David Junior? What about me? We're here in front of you. You're responsible for us. What about that?"

"That's just it, " David said. "I know where the two of you are. But this other son is lost to me. He exists—I know he does—and I can't reach him. I'm not abandoning you. I just want to go and locate this child so I can *know* where he is. I want to see that he's all right. He's something I made happen back there. He's something of *mine*, something of me, and I have to go to him. Can't you see that, Jen?"

Jennifer wagged her head slowly, squeezed her eyes shut for a moment. "David, David," she said without any sentence intended to follow. Just his name, as if that was all she knew.

"Please," he said and he stepped to her, cupped her shoulders in his palms.

"You won't have a chance anyway," she said softly, sadly now. "The Army won't let you."

David considered very briefly telling her about Trask. She was softening and he could say it but he held back. She didn't have to know the details. She'd worry about a CIA connection with all this. He said nothing, but drew her to him.

She sniffed a laugh. "We don't have the money to buy you a plane ticket anyway."

She let him hold her, and finally she put her arms around him.

"Just don't think about it," he said.

That day there was the deposition of Lieutenant Quoc, and there was a thin-lipped American MP sergeant who testified that David said "They're gonna win" when he was picked up; and while David wondered why this man would lie or what might actually have been said that could have been misconstrued in this way, the sergeant stepped down from the stand and Hedberg rested the prosecution's case. Court was adjourned and then there were voices at the end of the hall, more clamor outside, words to the press, an NBC network news mobile-unit truck, Carl's car—they could no longer walk off the base without the press in pursuit—and Carl started the engine and drove away.

They turned onto Holabird's main street and as they passed a corner, a newspaper vending machine snagged

David, made him say, "Wait. Stop." Carl stopped the car and David got out. Only when he walked back along the street did David consciously realize that it was the front page of today's paper he wanted to see: the news on Vietnam, on the fall. His time was growing short, but now his realization of this stopped him. He was still several yards from the machine; the headlines were large; a hundred miles from Saigon, the words said; the North's main force; David did not come any nearer; he turned and went back to the car.

Carl said, "What was it?"

"Nothing."

Carl looked briefly concerned, but then he changed the subject. "Tomorrow I'll have Wilson Hand testify."

"He doesn't really know me."

"I've got some bad news."

"What's that?"

"Major Dole is dead."

"Dole?" David tried to shape a picture in his mind of his first commanding officer in Vietnam, but he could not. "Dead?"

"Cancer, I'm told."

"Of the stomach?"

"I don't know."

"He always had a bad stomach in Vietnam. He thought it was just the tropics. He was a gourmet. Loved the French restaurants in Saigon and loved the hooch maids' soup. His stomach problems were the worst thing about his tour over there." David spoke matter-of-factly. He did not have the strong feeling for Dole that his speaking like this had apparently led Carl—who was quiet now, grim-faced—to infer.

"I'm sorry," Carl finally said.

"So it's Wilson Hand and then what?"

"And then you."

"Good." David felt a little surge of strength. "Get on with it." A hundred miles: the phrase slithered through him, sucking away his strength as it went. "Get on with it," he repeated, but this time animated by panic.

When David entered the apartment he found Jennifer
sitting in the living room in silence, in the dark, her arms
lying on the arms of the easy chair, her palms up, as if in
weariness, her legs on a footstool. He stood before her and
they did not speak and the silence buzzed around him and
he was conscious of the telephone, its implacability; the
silence of the room seemed to flow from the phone, from
Trask.

"Were there any calls?" he said.

"No."

He stood for a moment more, waiting for the phone to
ring.

"Not even a hello when you come in?" she said, though
the rebuke was not stressed; it seemed that she would sound
wry, playful even, if she weren't so tired.

The silence still swarmed in him but he suddenly felt it
insisting on a new meaning, a new response: Jennifer did
not have the TV on, in accordance with his wishes, and this
made him feel guilty.

"Hello," he said and he bent to her and kissed her, the
gesture prompted at that moment by his guilt more than
anything else. She did not lift her face to return the kiss but
let it land on her brow. "I thought you'd still be upset with
me," he said.

She did not reply and David moved off, passed out of the
room, through the hallway, and into his son's room. He went
to the crib and the boy was sleeping on his stomach, his
hands lying on each side of his head, his face turned toward
the wall. The back of his head had a swirl of yellow down
and David bent and kissed his son there. He straightened
up and watched the boy, watched his body swell and dimin-
ish in a deep breath, watched him sucking with his mouth
in his sleep for a moment and then stop. The silence hissed
again in David and he gripped the bars of the crib and
squeezed tightly, thinking, Trask you son-of-a-bitch call me,
and then the breathing of his son in this room shaped another room in his head, the breath of another child, a four-

year-old boy curled on a pallet in an alley room in Saigon, the silence there fissured with distant gunfire, artillery rounds falling closer and closer. David's hands let go of the crib, they rose up in the desire to pick up his Vietnamese son, carry him out of the room, quickly, the artillery was walking across the city, growing louder with each step and David ran, ran with the sleeping child. David found himself panting here, in this room in Baltimore, not Saigon, in Baltimore where he could not run. Dammit, Trask, now, phone now. David turned and he found Jennifer standing in the doorway, watching him.

He crossed the floor to her. She turned and they went out to the living room and sat down beside each other on the couch, but with half an arm's length of space between them. David felt keenly that too much was unresolved in his life, too much was important to him and it was unresolved and he leaned his head back and closed his eyes and he tried to go blank. He found he could remove Vietnam and his son and Jennifer and Suong and the trial, but when he did this, there was still the silence. This circle could not be broken; he could quiet the silence but only with the thought of these things; he could put aside these things but then there would be the silence; and the silence spoke of David's suspension, of his helplessness.

Then Jennifer spoke. "When you look at our son, do you think of this other child?"

"I don't want to argue with you."

"I'm not arguing," she said with a little surge of anger in her voice. She seemed to be instantly aware of this paradox, for she drastically softened her tone to say, "I'm just trying to feel what you're feeling. I think I can. I'm trying to see how difficult a notion like that would be for you."

"It's not a notion."

"I didn't mean it that way," she said with an eagerness that sounded like sincerity and David opened his eyes and turned his head toward her. Her face hovered close to him now. "I didn't mean to trivialize it," she said.

He didn't want to talk about this subject with her. In this suspension, depending on Kenneth Trask, he could not even bear to think about his Vietnam son and so he tried to guide her away. "The prosecution rested its case today," he said.

Jennifer's chin rose slightly and for a moment David expected her to press him further on his thoughts of his other child, with anger perhaps, given this tilt of her head. But she said, "That's good timing."

"Are you feeling strong enough to come watch again?"

"Yes."

"Good," he said, and he realized he meant it.

Jennifer's head dipped. "Actually I think I could have done all right the last couple of sessions, but I couldn't stand to hear them talk against you."

David took Jennifer's hand and she squared around to sit shoulder to shoulder beside him. They both put their heads back against the crest of the couch.

David said, "It'll be just as bad with our own case. Hedberg will cross-examine."

"I'm out of excuses. The birthing's over."

"You don't need an excuse except the pain of seeing all this," David said. "I'd understand."

"I know you would." She looked at him.

David felt her scrutiny and he turned to her. He sensed that what had started in Jennifer as appreciation of his understanding had been transformed into some sort of criticism of him. "What is it?" he said.

"Maybe you're so understanding because you'd *prefer* me not to be there."

"Jen," he said with nothing to follow. Maybe she was right.

"You'd rather be alone," she said.

"The birthing's *not* over."

"Don't give me any postpartum crap. Maybe I *did* change when I went through all that. Maybe I did learn a few things."

David had no answers about himself for Jennifer. He looked away from her, closed his eyes, waited for Jennifer's anger to roll past.

She said, "Maybe it's *her* you see when you look at David Junior."

David thought surely this was just the opening statement in a long line of angry reasoning, but Jennifer said no more. David waited, but the silence persisted and after a time he opened his eyes and looked at her and her head, too, was resting, her face was inclined to the ceiling, but her eyes were open and they were filled with tears.

"It's not true, Jen," he whispered.

Wilson Hand looked prosperous. He smiled and nodded almost imperceptibly at David when he first took the stand. The acknowledgment was no doubt against Carl's wishes, for this was to be objective, no coziness between the two men should even be hinted at. And indeed David had no feelings about Wilson except that he seemed to have put on some weight, he wasn't as thin as he'd remembered him; Wilson had put on weight with the freedom of mind of being out of the Army and under no legal jeopardy for anything. David found himself feeling faintly resentful. Wilson wore his hair much longer than in his Army days and he was heavier and he was free to come and go. Wilson had his own private investigating business in New York, advising mostly corporations on industrial security.

Carl walked Wilson through his recollections of Vietnam and of David, carefully constructing a Captain David Fleming who was fiercely loyal to both his men and his country. Carl was expansive, puffing and gyring before the witness box in a way he had never quite done in his cross-examination of Hedberg's witnesses. His only awkwardness was with his hands. His thumbs seemed to want to tuck themselves into the pockets of a vest, but the Army coat frustrated that, allowed no refuge for thumbs, and so in between dramatic gestures Carl's hands seemed out of place, sometimes diffident, sometimes fearful, clutching at each other or clinging to the rail of the witness box.

"He struck me as very straight," Wilson was saying. "Army-straight."

Wilson seemed to have recovered now from the trauma of his capture. When David last saw him—shortly following the rescue—he was only just beginning to feel the effects. David had heard that Wilson's state had grown much worse soon after.

Wilson had spent a week as a VC prisoner. He'd been snatched from an orphanage where he and David had gone to give a donation collected at payday at Homestead. They'd been very foolish for a long time and it had finally caught up with them: they went every payday at the same time; the VC saw the pattern and they took Wilson. David escaped and then he had no thought but to get Wilson back. And he finally did it. That's where Carl was heading—the daring rescue of this man by superpatriot Captain David Fleming. Scourging the Vietcong even as he was becoming obsessed with Pham Van Tuyen.

"Captain Fleming," Wilson was saying, "had a very strict Army bearing and that showed itself in his concern for his men."

Concern seemed the right word to David, though not with the connotation of sincere regard that Wilson was giving it. David felt nothing like that for Wilson and for Clifford Wilkes. But he was concerned about the responsibility he had for them as their officer-in-charge. And he got Wilson back. One of their local agent handlers, a Vietnamese man they called Seymour, gave David an urgent piece of information, urgent enough that David acted at once, alone—part of the tip was that they were going to move Wilson out of the area very soon, perhaps that very day.

They were holding Wilson in a dark-stained wood shanty in a crowded corner of the village of Honai. David parked his jeep at one end of the dirt road; the shack was at the other end. It was just past one and the road was quiet except for the clucking of a few chickens. The village was sleeping now in the midday heat and David approached the shack carefully, moving from the cover of house to house in his approach. Then there was an open stretch before him. He watched the black gape of the shanty's window and there was no face, no movement. Maybe this was a bad tip; maybe they'd taken Wilson away already. But David had to treat this seriously, nonetheless.

He looked back down the street. It was deserted still. He turned to the shack and its rough facade remained inscrutable. He had no alternative but to act.

He ran low through the space, cutting across the yard, heading for the side of the shack farthest from the window and closest to the door. Then he was there, pushing flat against the wall. The door was around the corner, and at arm's length was another window. He crouched and moved to the far side of it.

David carefully raised his head till his eyes were on a level with the lowest corner of the window. He moved cautiously to the left and pulled back quickly. In the dim room he had seen two Vietnamese. One sat beside the door with an AK47 across his lap. His head was turned, looking away from David. The second man was lying on the other side of the door, asleep. David saw no weapon near him. He thought, At least I've found some VC. But Wilson was not in this part of the room.

He moved to the other side of the window and again prepared to take the necessary chance. He flashed his face into a corner of the opening and drew back. He stifled a gasp. Wilson was lying against a back wall. He had looked gaunt in the frozen frame of David's glance, but he was there. A third VC sat near Wilson, dozing, his arm wrapped around a carbine.

David waited until his breath slowed, then he moved to the corner of the shack. He looked down the street. There was no one. The jeep struck him as being very far away, but it may have been no more than fifty yards. He looked at the M16 in his hands. Its lines were suddenly vivid to him, as if he were seeing it for the first time. He put the selector on automatic and went to the door.

The door hinged on David's right. The one VC who would be awake was sitting to his left. The dozing man would be almost directly in front of him, with Wilson maybe six feet to the left. The sleeping man would be blocked by the opening of the door.

David took one deep breath and kicked the door in. He stepped into the room shooting one burst into the man to the left. David was blinded by the move from sun into dark. He aimed straight forward and fired another burst. His eyes cleared. Wilson was rolling away, a body beside him. David turned to the left again but the man was sprawled in blood. He turned to the right. The door was moving toward him. He went to his left and crouched. The third man loomed. David saw wide eyes, an open mouth, a pistol rising. Another burst and the man leaped backwards, his white shirt scrawled in red. David swiveled. The room was still. Wilson's eyes were wide, his mouth was open, but there was no sound.

In the courtroom David's heart raced, his arms felt strong, he was conscious of the width of his shoulders, he was panting in completion of his task, and Wilson said, "He told me to relax, it was over."

Carl said, "So he burst into this shack and . . ."

"Yes. And he killed the three VC."

"Did he show any remorse over this afterwards?"

"No."

"What did his emotional state seem to be at that point?"

"Relief, I'd say. He was glad to get me back, I guess."

"Did he express any sympathy at all for the three men he'd just killed?"

"No, he did not."

"And these men were Communists? Vietcong?"

"Yes."

"What did you think when he rescued you?"

Wilson laughed. "When he first came in I didn't know who it was. I couldn't see him. He was just a shape in the door. I thought he was after me. He scared me more than the VC did."

"How would you describe his . . . ah . . . bearing?"

"Fierce."

"Fierce."

"Yes. But I thought I was the target. I thought it was all over. They were done with me. I thought I was dead."

"But Captain Fleming had another mission."

"That's right. I didn't feel any pain. I didn't die. And the VC were flying around the room. I still thought he was one of them, but he was just the worst fucking shot in the whole fucking world."

The courtroom swelled in laughter, a large sound: David was reminded with a little shock of all the people behind him packed into the room. This made him uneasy. Wilson was probably doing him some good, but he too was beginning to make David uneasy. Yes, he'd killed those three men without remorse. He'd never given them a second thought. They could each of them have been a close personal friend of Tuyen's, a brother even, a kindred spirit with a cool mind and courage and a keen sense of irony. But David hadn't given a damn about any of them. And yet he had already begun to care deeply about Tuyen, a man who at that moment had been only a few words on a wall.

Carl was soon finished with Wilson, and Hedberg rose and tried to lead him into criticizing David for letting him be captured in the first place. Carl objected that this was irrelevant, that David was not on trial for his operational competence, and the judge sustained him. Wilson stepped down and Carl rose again and asked for a recess until tomorrow.

David had known the recess was coming, he knew Carl wanted the specialness of his appearance on the stand to be preserved, but the move still dismayed David. He wanted to testify now; another day would pass and the North's forces would move to within ninety miles, or eighty, of Saigon or the South would collapse suddenly, the doors would all slam shut. He leaned to Carl and whispered to him, "Now. Can't I do it now?"

Carl squinted at him in concern. "You've got to get hold of yourself, David."

People were moving around him, there were widespread scraping and scuffling sounds from the gallery; it was too late anyway. "Forget it," David said and he dragged his wrist across his forehead before standing up. He turned and Jennifer was in the front row of the gallery waiting for him. She smiled at him faintly, clearly an act of her will, but David could not return the smile. He knew she was trying hard but he himself had no strength.

Jennifer took David's hand in the back seat of Carl's car and they held hands tightly up the sidewalk and into their apartment. Once the babysitter—an elderly woman from the apartment building—was gone and the door was shut, Jennifer and David found themselves in the center of the living room floor and she embraced him and he held her tightly in return and he had a vision of himself over the past few weeks. He had grown very quiet around Jennifer, irritable, and then he had forced her to consider his distant child, another woman's child. He realized that he had been acting as if he'd never encountered Tuyen. He had always felt that finding and freeing Tuyen had opened him, had made his marriage to Jennifer possible. But he'd closed up again in these recent weeks. The more he'd heard about what he'd done, the more he'd closed up. So he held Jennifer and he said, "I'm sorry."

"What for?"

"For being so . . . difficult . . . I haven't been able to give . . . I haven't been able to . . ." The word that began to shape in his mouth was love, he hadn't been able to love; as soon as he realized this, he gritted at the word, forced it back. But he'd heard the word himself, in his own mind, and he knew it was true and he closed his eyes, he felt very weak, his face burned. My sons, he cried to himself. I do love my sons.

"I understand," Jennifer said softly.

David drew her more tightly against him. "I love you," he said.

She pulled back slightly so she could look at him. Her eyes were full of tears but they were eager, happy even. "I know you do," she said.

David stroked her hair, tried to bring her head against his chest again but she resisted. She smiled at him and said, "I discovered something in the courtroom today." She paused.

"What is it?"

"If I'm ever angry at you I'm going to try to catch you unawares and watch the back of your head . . . I was watching the back of your head all through the trial today and I was filled with this tender feeling for you. The back of your head seems so vulnerable somehow, pitiable. Your ears stick out and that seems to me so . . . childlike, no matter how old you are . . . How could I not understand your moods, all the things that trouble you and make you act the way you do, when I'm looking at the back of your head? . . . I must sound crazy."

"Who am I to say that's crazy? Me with my handful of words from a cell wall."

"You're as crazy as I am."

Now he was able to press her head against his chest once more.

"Are you going to be all right tomorrow?" she said.

"I don't know."

"Are you afraid?"

He hesitated only briefly. "Yes," he said.

They spoke no more for a long while and then Jennifer

said, "I'll check on little David." She slowly broke their embrace and disappeared into the other room.

David looked about him. He looked at the phone—as still as Trask's eyes—and he looked at the television. He went to the set and switched it on—serious faces, a dramatic organ arpeggio—and he turned away, crossed the floor, entered the bedroom and he lay down. Just to rest for a few minutes; his fear had turned suddenly to weariness.

When he woke, it was dark. He rose and went into the hall. He stood in the doorway and Jennifer sat on the couch, the evening news shuffling images before her. He glanced to his left and saw the kitchen table set with their good china and a candle. He crossed to the couch and sat beside her. She started and began to rise to turn off the TV.

"It's all right," he said and she sat back down, moving close to him; he put his arm around her and nestled her against him.

She said, "I thought, since you turned it on . . ."

"That's why I did it. Yes."

The face on the screen was President Thieu's, the round, slick face with its odd, curled-up earlobes. David could not concentrate on the voices on the TV. "What is it?" he asked.

"He resigned," Jennifer said.

"Thieu?"

"Yes. Day before yesterday. He went out blaming America for the whole damn thing."

"Thieu's gone."

"Yes."

There was a shot of a very old Vietnamese man. Ailing Tran Van Huong, the TV said. Huong had his hand in the air. The new president.

"Can we turn if off now, Jen?" David said quietly, working hard to keep his voice steady.

Jennifer rose up and switched off the set.

"Thanks," he said and his voice was so small he could hardly make it out in the silent room.

. . .

On the stand the next day, with Carl carefully drawing out the story, David told of the words on the wall of the interrogation cell, of his image of Tuyen, of his compassion for this man he'd never seen. He told of his inquiries after Tuyen, incidental at first, as David worked on other cases; deliberate later on as he feared for Tuyen's life as the man was tortured in the prisons of South Vietnam. Carl leaned heavily on the indications of Tuyen's torture. He explored David's firsthand knowledge of the South's severe interrogation techniques. David heard himself coming across as if he were driven by a strong moral aversion to these techniques. David had perceived in Tuyen a brave man who was being illegally tortured and he acted to put an end to it: this was the Captain David Fleming on trial here. And David marveled at this image of himself, at the irony of the other incident in Vietnam, the death of the prisoner by the stream in the woods, the prisoner with the bad heart who might have known something of Wilson Hand's capture. David himself had overseen a kind of torture and it had led to the death of a man. But now he was a crusader against the dirtiness of the Vietnam war and the faces stuffed tight in the gallery leaned forward and they shouted the silence of an indignant sympathy. David tried not to look at the faces arrayed there, in spite of his clear sense of their feeling for him. And he looked not at all at the men who would judge him. Instead he concentrated on Carl and on his own voice which still sounded small to him, as small as it did last night, but the words were coming out, Carl was strumming him like a guitar, an old guitar—forgotten in the closet of some ex-hippie with this tune of moral indignation left in it—and though the sound was thin, all the right notes were coming out.

And then Carl sat down and Hedberg stood up. He gripped his glasses with both hands, but the adjustment that was apparently made was so slight that it was undetectable.

The hands fell and Hedberg approached the witness box and David knew that he had better ignore all the little physical tricks of the man. He had to focus on the words.

"Captain Fleming," Hedberg said, drawing the name out, "let's talk a little bit more about your deep moral concern over these interrogation techniques. When did you first learn that this sort of thing went on in Vietnam?"

David's breath was yanked from him, his face grew very hot. He could not understand how he could pass through the next few minutes of his life, he could not even understand how to make his mouth move, make words come out. He struggled to shape a thought.

"Was it back in the States?" Hedberg said.

David didn't give a damn about interrogation techniques. This was the only thought clear in his mind. Nothing else. And he knew this could never be spoken.

"How about it, Captain Fleming? Did you have a strong moral revulsion over what those South Vietnamese were doing when you were in the States? Or did you develop it in Vietnam?"

David knew Hedberg understood what was in David's thoughts. This was how Hedberg would prevent David from ever seeing his child in Vietnam. David straightened up in anger and this cleared his mind. He said, "A feeling like that evolves. It probably started in the States. I read things about what was happening . . ."

"What things?"

"A lot of things."

"Can you give me one example from this reading?"

"Articles on Thieu's prisons, for instance. Not one specific article. That's not how I form ideas. I'm not swayed by just one thing. It was a number of them."

"What were these articles saying that troubled you so much?"

"The tiger cages, for example. I'd read about the tiger cages. How the prisoners were kept in holes in the ground and the guards would throw lye on them and piss on them."

"Did you believe all these things you were reading?"

"Yes."

"Didn't you find a general bias in what you were reading? An overall bias against what your commander-in-chief was trying to accomplish in Vietnam?"

David's little surge of strength ebbed. He wanted to be away from here. He couldn't play this game. But his sons cried out in his mind. Two sons. "I accounted for the bias," he said.

"So you had a strong feeling about these interrogation techniques before you ever went to Vietnam?"

David had no basis from which to speak and he tried to construct one quickly. What would be best for his case? "Not strong, exactly. Not then. The feeling was beginning, certainly, but not . . . ah . . . it wasn't strong."

"When you got your orders to go to Vietnam. Were you aware at that time that these feelings in you might affect your ability to do your duty?"

Carl leaped up with an objection. Hedberg said something, the judge said something, David felt a panting in his chest, he wondered if it was audible.

"Now Captain Fleming, how long have you been in intelligence?"

David answered and Hedberg's questions turned seemingly bland, biographical; David described his college career, Hedberg occasionally fishing for leftist politics, but David could turn those questions aside with the truth, he had no politics, and then they were talking about his Army career and the questions were still bland and David's breathing slowed a bit. He heard the dry smack of his own words, his mouth felt anesthetized, juiceless as the soles of his shoes. Then Hedberg brought David to Vietnam and when he began to ask about the office at Homestead, its mission, a stroke of insight cracked through David's mind: Hedberg knew about the prisoner David had tortured. That's where he was heading. And that would be the end. David's image of moral indignation would vanish, his compassion for the Vietnamese would vanish, and he would drift motiveless off to an Army jail for the rest of his life. All this struck him even as he gave his bland answers to the bland questions: how big was the office, how were reports generated, what kinds of field operations did the office run; all leading, David knew, to the stream where the prisoner had died.

But Hedberg asked an unexpected question. "Now, this man Wilson Hand, Sergeant Wilson Hand, was here to testify. What about the other man who served under you in Vietnam? Sergeant Clifford Wilkes? Where is he now?"

"I don't know."

"Didn't he do something in Vietnam that was . . . unusual?"

"He deserted."

"Is that so? A man under your command deserted?"

"Yes."

"Why?"

"I don't know."

"Did you ever have any conversations with Clifford Wilkes about politics?"

Carl was on his feet again and while the two lawyers bounced angry comments to each other off the judge, David puffed and closed his eyes tightly and wiped his forehead with his wrist. He knew the jury would watch this gesture and read guilt into it—Carl had told him to keep his hands on the arms of his chair or in his lap no matter what happened—but David didn't care now, he had a more serious display of nerves to fight back and he spread his thumb and forefinger from temple to temple and pressed hard.

Hedberg was facing him again. And now came a question David had expected. "Did you interrogate prisoners in Vietnam, Captain Fleming?"

David knew he dared not seem evasive. "Yes," he said firmly.

"And what techniques did you use?"

A hissing rose in David's head. Hedberg knew. Hedberg knew and David would be lost. "The standard techniques . . ."

"And what seemed to be the standard in Vietnam?"

"I didn't torture anyone," David said and the hissing moved from his head, through his throat, wrapped up his words. He knew he sounded defensive, he sounded like a liar, his mind thrashed around for more words. "I pitied the man. I pitied Tuyen. I didn't want him to be tortured. It was an act of compassion, dammit."

Hedberg spoke, the judge spoke, but David could clearly hear only the echo of his own words, and he heard the panic that had been in his voice, the desperateness, the anger.

". . . no further questions." Hedberg's voice.

David wondered at this. Didn't Hedberg know about the man he had killed? There were no more questions. Hedberg was a damn fool. The judge spoke, telling David he could step down, recessing the court, and David rose from his chair and he was struck by the way this had all gone. Though he'd resisted Carl so adamantly, he'd lied after all. His larger moral concern: that was a lie. And now in the end he'd declared his compassion, his pity, for Tuyen. But even that felt like a lie. Even that. And David wondered if indeed he was mad.

In the afternoon the closing arguments were made. David was a covert radical acting in concert with his deep sympathy for the Communist cause, freeing a very important VC official to continue his fight against the United States and its ally. David was a man of compassion acting to preserve one human being from a torture that violated both the Geneva convention and a higher moral law. Afterwards, in the first moments alone with Jennifer in their apartment, David stopped just inside the door and he began to tremble. "Jennifer," he said, low.

She turned to him, her expression dilated in fear, and

she came to him quickly. He didn't want her to see him like this, but he could not control the trembling. As if he were very cold, his chest, his arms trembled, his legs. Jennifer held him and then he began to weep. His eyes filled in a rush and he gasped—mostly in surprise at all of this, he thought—but then he knew it was a sound of crying and he was weeping and he held Jennifer against him. "I'm sorry," he said, the words fracturing. She shushed him, patted him. "I'm all right," he said, trying to pull away from her, but he did not try hard and he let her stop him and he wept now in silence and he was conscious of no feeling in himself. The tears knew something he didn't; they knew something and he wanted to know it too. He wept and he concentrated, he listened for the source of the tears as if it were an unseen stream off somewhere in the woods.

"It's all right," Jennifer was saying. She said it over and over and he was saying it to himself, I'm all right, I'm all right, and Jennifer's voice sounded very fragile as she reassured him and he felt a pity roll through him; he pitied Jennifer and he felt angry at himself.

"I'm sorry," he said.

"It's all right," she said again. "It's all right to cry."

"I'm sorry I can't understand what's going on in me. I'm sorry because I know that means I hurt you."

"Stop. Please." She pulled back slightly and patted at his lips with the tips of her fingers. He took her hand but kept it near his mouth. He kissed her fingers and his tears began to flow again.

He let go of her, turned away. "Dammit," he said.

"No," she said firmly. "Please don't ruin this."

It seemed an odd thing for her to say. But then he knew what she meant. Crying, he was accessible to her in a way he hadn't been for a long time. He drew her to him and they embraced once more. He said, "I was thinking not so long ago of how I'd changed since Vietnam . . . I want you to be close to me, Jen. But lately I've messed it up again. I'm like I was before I met you. Before I . . ." He paused.

"Yes?"

"Before Tuyen."

"Did all that really change you?"

"I don't know. I thought so. But now I'm scared it didn't. Maybe I'm just the same."

Jennifer puffed, as if in exasperation. Then she bowed her head against his chest. "It wasn't as bad today as I thought it would be," she said.

"Hedberg."

"Yes."

"Carl said that Hedberg was caught off guard a little bit, that he was ill-prepared and arrogant."

"I thought he'd do more."

"But thinking back on it, it felt bad enough. He didn't have to do any more than that. The act was there, undeniable. He made me look desperate. Made me look like a liar about my motives. Don't forget the kind of people who are sitting on the jury."

David felt Jennifer shudder. "Don't talk about it," she said.

"We have to face it," David said, but gently. "They're going to find me guilty of *something*."

"Something *less* . . . something . . ."

David felt a burning begin in his face. "You were right. We shouldn't talk about it. There's nothing to be done now, anyway."

Jennifer looked at him closely and she smiled at him and rubbed at his cheek with the tip of her forefinger, rubbed at a place that David realized had felt tight from dried tears. Then Jennifer began to kiss him and they kissed until the kisses grew deep and they went off to the bedroom and they began to make love. David was glad for the chance to clear his mind and this he did; he found the grace of forgetfulness by projecting his mind into the surface of his skin and he made love to his wife and he kept his head back to watch Jennifer's face, her eyes closed, her brow creasing and smoothing and creasing again as he moved inside her, and he kept his mind in the place where their skin touched and there was nothing else and at the moment of his release he asked her to open her eyes, he tried to do more, to concentrate on her patient love for him, but he tried too hard and at the end he felt awkward, self-absorbed. Still, he'd had a few moments with Jennifer and it struck him that he might have very few more. The men who would judge him were deliberating even then.

When they were lying side by side, Jennifer said, "That was wonderful, David."

It took him a moment to realize she meant making love.

"Yes," he said.

"I've been wanting to do that very badly from the moment I saw you cry."

David felt drained. He put his hands behind his head and stared at the ceiling. The room was dim. Through the window he heard the network evening news, Walter Cronkite speaking from the next patio about Vietnam. The panic began to nibble its way back into the center of David's chest.

"I believe you," Jennifer said. She paused.

David wondered if he'd missed something she'd been saying.

Then she said, "About your . . . interest in Vietnam. I could sense you were thinking of me when we made love just now . . . You *were*, weren't you?"

He turned to her. "Yes," he said and he was glad he didn't have to lie.

"You don't love anyone else, do you? Any other woman?"

"No, Jen. Believe me."

"Not the woman in Vietnam?"

"No. Not her. Not anyone else."

"I believe you. I do."

"Good."

Jennifer looked at his face closely for a moment, then made a quick, knowing smile, and she rose up from the bed and crossed to the dresser. She opened a drawer and pulled out an envelope and she returned to the bed and sat beside him. She handed him the envelope and he propped himself up.

"What is it?" he said, even as he turned it over in his hand and saw the embossed logo and return address of Jennifer's father's company. The envelope was addressed to Jennifer in a neat script that David recognized as belonging to the man himself. David opened the flap and inside was a check. He took the check out and looked inside the envelope again, but it was empty. David held up the check and it was made out to him and the amount was four thousand dollars. David felt himself gape at the numbers. "What the hell . . . ?" He stared hard at the numbers and they remained the same.

Jennifer said, "Now . . . if you just get the chance . . . at least you can buy a ticket to go to Vietnam . . ."

David took a deep breath. He could think only of what Jennifer had to do to herself to come to ask for this money.

"He said he'd put in some extra in case you had to bribe somebody or something."

"Jen . . ." David couldn't think how to finish the sentence.

"I know. I know. Please don't talk about it."

Not being able to express his feeling for this act of hers, he shifted his attention to the father. "He didn't even put in a note."

"I didn't ask him to write to me," Jennifer said, her voice flat. "I asked him for money."

"At least he put his own hand to the envelope."

"I think that was just so his secretary wouldn't get involved in this transaction."

David briefly had the impulse to give the check back. He could tell Jennifer about Trask and then they could return the money to the father. But Jennifer had already paid the emotional price for the check. And she would worry about the CIA. He said, "I know what you went through . . ."

"I just want you to find what you're looking for."

"There's a child, Jen."

"I want you to do what you have to do." Her eyes had filled with tears.

Then David heard his own name spoken from outside. He knew this was real because Jennifer's face instantly turned toward the window. As the voice that spoke his name spoke on, David realized it was Cronkite. Then there was another voice and then Carl's voice and then David's own voice.

"God help us," Jennifer said.

Early the next afternoon, the telephone rang and David leaped from the chair where he sat in the living room. He was certain it was Trask. He would see Trask in fifteen minutes somewhere in Baltimore and he would fly to Vietnam only hours before a judgment was rendered against him. Jennifer was in the kitchen, near the phone, and she answered it. She did not call him immediately but it took a long moment for him to put aside the last bit of hope that Trask would preempt the verdict. Jennifer spoke a word, and she hung up. She entered the living room. "It was Carl," she said. "They've reached a verdict. He'll be by for you in about twenty minutes."

David rose up. He was in jeans and a sweat shirt. He had to put his uniform on. He went out of the living room. He entered the bedroom and went to the closet. He bent and picked up his shoes. Before him the shoes reflected the light. His face bulged there in the toe. He bent again and pulled out the box of polish and rags and brushes and he sat on the chair by the dresser. He placed the shoes on the floor before him and he pried off the top to the black polish, pausing to look at the kiwi bird, as bulbous as the reflection of his face in his shoe. He took up a cloth and doubled it so as not to make a polish stain on his finger and he ran the cloth around the indented track of polish and he picked up one of his shoes and Jennifer was beside him. She touched his shoulder. He looked up at her.

"You don't have to do that," she whispered.

David looked down at the shoe. She was right. It was as shiny as it could possibly be. He looked at the black-tipped cloth. He smelled the black smell of the polish. He grew slightly alarmed at this state of his mind, but as soon as he became conscious of it, it changed, he felt like a sleepwalker who'd awakened to find himself standing in another room. He looked up again at Jennifer. "Don't be alarmed," he said. "I'm all right."

And so he dressed and Carl picked him up and at the courthouse Jennifer went ahead into the gallery and shortly after three o'clock by David's watch he and Carl entered the clogged and quiet courtroom, the faces squeezing together beyond the railing, the eyes following him. David turned his back on all of that and sat at the defense table, Carl sitting beside him.

Soon the colonel and the jury filed in and David rose. When the colonel was sitting, David marched the few paces to the bench as Carl had instructed him to do, and he stood at attention and saluted the gray, implacable face and he waited.

The colonel cleared his throat and he lifted a piece of paper and the numbness that David realized he had been feeling began to ebb, a prickling began in his limbs, in his face. The colonel read: "Captain Fleming, it is my duty as president of this court to inform you that the court, in closed session and upon secret ballot, all of the members present at the time the vote was taken concurring in the finding, finds you, of the specifications of the charge, guilty of aiding the enemy."

David heard a swirl of sound behind him, a distant sound, a crowd milling at a great distance. He knew he was supposed to salute now and return to the defense table, but he could not raise his arm. The colonel was banging his gavel for silence and David focused on his right arm, focused on raising his right arm and he did, he raised his arm and he stiffened his hand and he saluted and turned and crossed the space to the table and he saw Jennifer in the front row and her face was in her hands and she was trembling. David passed the defense table and went to the gallery rail and he reached across and touched Jennifer's bowed head. She opened her hands, lifted her stricken face, and behind David the colonel was speaking his name. Carl was beside him now and had his arm around him and was saying something about sitting, about adjourning, and David tried to think of what to say to Jennifer but no words came. He yielded to Carl, he turned away and went back to the table and he sat to hear the colonel speak of a sentencing tomorrow, and the court was rising again and David rose too, rose with no volition in the act. Then manacles were on his wrists and two MPs were beside him and only their military bearing kept him from falling down.

That night David was put in a cell to wait for tomorrow and the sentencing. He lay on the bunk and focused hard on the ceiling. The ceiling was neutral; it held no clear sign of his imprisonment; it was gray and dim and David clung to it and there were two prongs of pain sunk deep into his chest. At first one prong burned much hotter than the other: he could see Jennifer with her head bowed, her hands over her face. He could not move in the courtroom. He stood there and watched Jennifer's despair and he could not move from where he stood, he could not reach her to touch her, to comfort her. Nor could he escape. And he saw now the pain he'd caused her. How had he been drawn into this? He'd once known not to get too close to people; this pain he saw before him was the outcome. But to withdraw again would cause even more pain; that's what Jennifer's tears said to him. He cursed himself softly in his cell. He'd hurt her; he'd always hurt her. But he could not regret, she could not regret, for from them came a child.

Then he felt the second pain. David Junior was sleeping now in his crib. The child was tiny and fragile and alone in his room and David could not go to him, could not touch him, hold him, protect him. The child's life had been seized along with David's. They were both imprisoned, father and son. But separately. David Junior was as distant now, as lost, as the boy in Vietnam. The boys were twins, the boys were David's two hands extended and shackled. Worse than that. For one of his sons would never know his attachment to him. Vietnam would fall and David would never find his first-born son.

The ceiling blurred and he closed his eyes and he tried to see his son in Vietnam. Four years old, but much larger than the other children. David's son. The boy stood beside the inlet in Nha Be and he turned to his father and smiled and the child's hair was dark and fine, the one trace of Suong in him, her dark, fine hair, but the boy's face and body were from David, with his thin, stretched mouth, his wide nose, with his thick neck and arms and legs. The boy's skin was darkened slightly and his hair was black, but in all other respects he was clearly David's son. The dark twin to David Junior.

This vision asserted its own will as David's mind modulated into sleep. A hot wind blew through Nha Be. Silver fish leaped in the inlet and disappeared without rippling the surface and David crossed to his son.

Father, the boy said in perfect English.

Yes, David replied.

I'm all right, the boy said. I've been waiting for you.

You know me?

Of course I know you. Isn't it clear who I am? Who you are?

Very clear.

Why does it surprise you then, that I should see you and know you?

Did your mother tell you about me?

No.

Then how . . . ?

It's in my face and in the shape of my mind.

David didn't know what to do next. The child began to smile as David's silence persisted. The child began to laugh.

What is it? David said.

What is it? the boy said, laughing.

Why are you laughing? David said.

Why are you laughing? the boy said.

Tell me.

Tell me.

The child laughed louder, his face wrinkling around the eyes just the way Jennifer had once said David's face wrinkled. David understood the children's game that was being played. It made him uneasy, made him cry out with pain: Don't do this.

Don't do this, the child mimicked.

David thought: What can I do to make him speak for himself? And even as this thought formed in his mind, the child said: What can I do to make him speak for himself?

Please, David said.

Please, the child said, his voice deep, his eyes pleading just as David's must have pleaded, with this desperate longing shaping in him.

Don't you love me? David said.

Don't you love me?

Yes, David said. Yes.

And the boy vanished. The fish leaped and the boy was gone and David awoke and he was sitting on his cot. Before him were iron bars running up and down in the dark.

David lay back and he turned his face to the cell wall and he was conscious that this was the very gesture he'd imagined Tuyen making in one of his cells. Where are you tonight, Tuyen? Do you sense that it is I who am now a prisoner?

. . .

Gerald Ford's goofy smile had turned sinister. The face hung behind the colonel's empty chair and it fixed David with a smile that was shrewder than David had given it credit for; Gerald Ford knew exactly what was happening here; it was obvious from that smile. The flags were limp on either side and the court was very still as it waited and David could hear the faint slip of his own breath, fragile, easily cut off. Carl shifted in his chair, then his voice came in a whisper: "Are you all right?"

David could not answer him. No. He wasn't all right. No. The room felt very tight, as tight as the cell he'd spent the night in, as tight as Tuyen's cell, the six-foot-square cubicle that began all of this. David stared at the wall behind the colonel's desk. Below the picture of Ford was a large blank space. He wondered what he might write on it if he were alone here. The first thing he thought of was: I'm all right. But this phrase repulsed him. It was whining, fearful: it didn't reflect anything of what David felt was his own strength; he would not even be able to recognize such a phrase as his. He tried to think of something else. An eye for an eye. But the comment on the court's venging spirit was too direct. Perhaps: an arm and a leg. He imagined it written across the wall, scratched there with the shiny buckle from his belt. No. It conceded too much power to the court. Ford smirked above, vapid, foolish. Then David decided what he would write. He'd scrawl it up higher, closer to the picture: *a man after my own heart.* David smiled at this but he was having trouble drawing a breath. Then a door opened, the bailiff was speaking, David was trying to move his legs and finally he was able to stand. More words, a touch on his elbow from Carl, and David moved around the table and out into the open space before the colonel. He saluted and waited.

The colonel lifted a piece of paper and he read: "Captain David B. Fleming, it is my duty as president of this court to inform you that the court in closed session and upon secret written ballot, two-thirds of the members present at the time the vote was taken concurring, sentences you to a reduction to the lowest enlisted rank, the forfeiture of all pay and allowances, and a dishonorable discharge from the Armed Forces of the United States of America." The colonel's voice ceased and David scrambled through these words in his mind, clutched them, felt them hastily, put them aside temporarily, as if he were looking for a lost object in a pile of rubble, the words not quite coming together. There was a moment of stillness in the courtroom and then a burst of sound and with it the words cohered and David understood, there were gasps, applause, tears, behind him. The colonel banged his gavel for silence. David played the sentencing over and over: busted and discharged, busted and discharged. There was no prison term. None.

The colonel was speaking: "I'd like to comment on the sentence, since the attention of the country has been brought to bear on this trial and I don't want this to be misunderstood. I have good reason to assume that the very visible presence of the press at this trial may have had an influence on the sentencing. Even without a jury knowing directly what's being said in the media on the outside, it is easy to extrapolate by just observing and listening to reactions inside the courtroom. I can say this freely because I'm certain the defense is satisfied with this resolution. But as president of this trial, I feel it is my duty to make one thing clear." The gray face hardened further, the words became as overprecise as they would be if David were a Vietnamese. "Captain Fleming, by this sentence the Army is showing you it has no intention of making you the national martyr that you obviously wish to become. And if this country ever gets its values right again, you will be adequately punished by the stigma of what you've done and by the penalties of this sentence." The colonel straightened up and his lips pursed in satisfaction and he dismissed the court.

David turned and Carl was upon him, hugging him, then

letting him go and David saw Jennifer standing at the gallery rail. He moved to her and they embraced, Jennifer's body quaking against him. They held each other and bulbs flashed, voices approached. David closed his eyes and he held Jennifer closer and he whispered to her, "Now I can go find him."

That night David and Jennifer sat on the living room couch and she was curled up against him and they didn't speak; the holding was sufficient, thrillingly sufficient for a time, as if they were a junior high school couple in their first embrace in an empty house. David felt no impatience for now. He knew that Trask had been watching, that the call would soon come. David understood that the circle around Saigon was growing tighter, that the Americans were coming out. But he would go in. Within twenty-four hours he'd be there. Or forty-eight. But thinking of the passing of hours made the fears begin to stir and he focused on his freedom. He could sit here on the couch and embrace Jennifer and he would not be put in another cell. He could walk into the next room and hold his son. Now this, too, breathed on his fear, quickened its latent fire. There was still a son he could not hold.

The phone rang.

"I'll get it," David said, and he eased away from Jennifer.

"Be quick," she said.

David strode to the kitchen phone and snatched up the receiver and said, "Hello."

"Captain Fleming?"

The voice was not Trask's. Maybe it was another CIA man. Trask had delegated this operation to someone else. "Yes," David said.

"My name is Lionel Metzger."

"Who?"

"Lionel Metzger. You don't know me. I'm calling from

Portland. I own a chain of health food stores in Oregon and Northern California."

David said, "Listen, if you're working for Trask, cut the spy crap. Just tell me what I'm supposed to do."

There was silence on the other end of the phone. The line crackled and hissed, confirming the long distance. David realized that this man was who he said he was.

"How did you get my number?" David asked.

"Ah . . . from a friend," Metzger said. "Listen, Captain Fleming, I don't want to intrude or bother you or anything. I just respect you, you know. For what you did. And I wanted you to know that a D.D. means nothing to me, so if you ever need a job or something, there's always the health food business. I'd be happy to give you a store to manage. Really. Maybe I'd even need an executive someday. A partner. I'm a rich man. This isn't a scam. I just want to help you."

David listened to these words with a compulsive attentiveness. He was filled with astonishment at them, a surreal astonishment that quickly made him feel quite mad. Then the fear came back as the quotidian clutched him: he could never hope to fly to Vietnam, to find his son, in a world like this.

"Health food," the voice on the phone was saying. "There's a humanity to the business that you don't find very often . . ."

David looked around him. The faucet was dripping. The electric clock hummed faintly over the stove. The phone was off the hook.

"I appreciate all this," David said, cutting the voice off. "But it's a little too soon."

"I understand," the voice said.

"I'm expecting an important call," David said. "I have to stop this now." And he hung up the phone.

He returned to the living room and he sat beside Jennifer on the couch and he knew his time of patience and confidence was over.

"Who was it?" Jennifer said.

"A job offer."

"Really? What kind?"

"Health foods."

Jennifer laughed. David was afraid she would ask more questions, but she didn't. She curled up against him where he sat and she said no more and he was very thankful for this; he kissed her hair in appreciation.

A long time passed before the phone rang again. This time it was Trask's voice. "Congratulations," he said, instead of hello.

"Thanks."

"Are you jogging tonight, David?"

"Yes."

"Usual route. I'll find you."

"Okay."

"Pack your bag," Trask said and he was gone.

This time Trask's car was farther down the hill, closer to the steel mill, in a dark stretch of the street where the air smelled strongly of naphtha.

"The Army thinks it's being smart with you," Trask said.

"It worked out okay for you guys, too."

Trask laughed at this, a single bark of a laugh, and he said no more.

David waited and Trask pulled an envelope out of the briefcase leaning against him. "You'll find three things in here," he said. "There's your plane ticket. You'll fly to Bangkok out of Toronto, then to Saigon on Air France."

"When?"

"Your hop to Toronto leaves Friendship in eight hours."

David's breath caught. "Okay," he said. "Okay."

"The second item is a passport. Canadian. The picture I had of you from Vietnam was a little severe, but Canadian leftists tend to look like that anyway."

David had no patience for Trask's professional small

talk, but it reminded him of the man's allegiance. David said, "Is the plane ticket round-trip?"

Trask laughed again, identical in cadence to the earlier laugh. "The date is left open. But it'll bring you back, if Air France is still flying."

"What am I supposed to do for you?"

"Don't worry about that for now," Trask said. "It's not going to be very exciting, whatever it is. Our needs will be basic. When the country goes down our expectations won't be very great. Somebody will find you at the hotel. He may be Vietnamese. He'll ask if you know if La Pagode Restaurant is still open for business."

Trask's voice moved very slowly in the dark. When he paused, David pressed him. "What else do you have to tell me?"

"You'll find another name on the passport. We had to choose one."

"What is it?"

"Crowley. David Crowley."

"Crowley. Okay." David's feet stirred. He had to run soon. Back up the hill. He would leave in eight hours. "What else?"

"There's a third item. Very useful." Trask opened the envelope, felt inside, his hand came out, his other hand put the envelope down and reached across David into the glove compartment and he removed something—a penlight, which shot its beam now from his hand. He shined it on an identification card. David looked. His own face was there— a little younger, his hair trimmed to echo the moon curve of his head—and the name was David Crowley. The card had two thin red vertical stripes at the right edge and the lettering above said International Peace-Workers Congress. "Extremely useful," Trask cooed, his voice very proud of this little card. "It's a good group," he said. "Commie through and through and we've got our people in key places. This will give you some real credibility, Dave, if you get trapped after the fall. You're in Saigon trying to find the remaining

US deserters in the back alleys. That's your cover. You're there to give them a socialist highway back to the West." Trask paused, brought his face closer to the card. "This is a really fine piece of work, this little group," he said. "Keep your cool if you're picked up. Okay?"

"I won't blow your cover."

Trask looked at David. In the dark, David couldn't make out his features. Trask seemed to be aware of this. He turned the penlight on his own face, knifing it with Halloween shadows. He was smiling. "See?" he said, and his voice was very soft. "Here comes another burst of sincerity . . . I know you won't blow our little cover. You're a good man, Dave. You got off pretty easy and I'm glad. If you ever need a permanent job . . . out of the country somewhere . . ."

"I already got a job offer today."

"Keep us in mind."

"Anything else before I run up this hill?"

Trask flicked off the penlight. "When you get to Saigon, take a room at the Hotel Regard. You remember the Regard?"

"Across from the Majestic at the end of Tu Do."

"That's right . . . And, oh yes, you'll find some money in the envelope. Not a lot. Not for the whole stay. You've got some of your own money for over there?"

"Yes."

"Take some greenbacks. But don't forget to take at least as much in Canadian currency."

"Okay."

"The money inside the envelope is to bribe your way into the country. Use your story about helping the deserters. But you're going to need a bribe, as well."

"Ken."

"Yes?"

"How long till it falls?"

"Saigon?"

"Yes."

"Three days, maximum."

. . .

The apartment was quiet when David returned. He passed through the living room, dark except for a small table lamp, and into the bedroom. Jennifer lay sleeping beneath the covers, her hair splayed against the pillow, one arm thrown over her head. David withdrew, he went down the hall and stepped into his son's room. He, too, slept, his arms stretched straight to the side, his mouth half open and twisted against the mattress. David felt a spreading aptness in his chest, in his arms, like the feeling after making undistracted love. This was precisely how he wanted his family to be for the next few weeks, for himself and for them: They were sleeping; a deep, safe sleep; and he would do what he had to do to resolve his yearning and when he returned they would still be like this, unaware even that he'd been away.

David returned to his bedroom and undressed very quietly and he slipped into the bed beside Jennifer. She awoke at once. This made his chest tighten, stripped away his ease, but he knew what he must do now to make this all tolerable for her. He began to make love to her. She wept in assent at his professions of love as they touched. And at each vision of airplanes, of Saigon, of the streets, the Hotel Regard, his Vietnamese son, he forced himself again to speak to Jennifer, to tell her that he loved her.

When they were quiet once more, spent, holding each other in the dark, in the silence, in the sixth hour before his departure, Jennifer said, very softly, the questioning straining to be rhetorical, "You're coming back?"

"Yes."

"If the Communists start to come in . . . get out of there. Okay?"

"Yes," he said, but he knew it might be a lie; he wondered what he would indeed do if it was clear the country was done for and he hadn't found his son and he had to choose whether to remain and look or to leave. Even without resolving this question for himself, he knew he had to lessen Jennifer's worry if in fact he had no choice when the time came. "If something does happen," he said, "if you see the country fall and I'm not out . . ."

"Please . . . don't let that happen."

"If it does, I'm going to be all right . . . I've got papers. A passport. Other things. I'm going in as a Canadian."

She pulled away from his embrace slightly to look at him. "Where did you . . . ?" She didn't finish the question and he waited. She shifted her eyes away, squeezed them shut, she put her face against him. Clearly she didn't want to know. She let a deep breath out.

"I'll be back," he said.

Jennifer did not speak.

"Soon," he said.

He felt a trembling rise in her. He held her close. "Trust me," he said, and the words sounded ridiculous to him: the sense of control that his detachment gave him was a lie, had always been a lie; for the second time in his life he was in the grip of an obsession he did not clearly understand; he was rushing into a country full of panic and bloodshed and the inexorable advance of an enemy that he had been taught for a decade to fear and hate; and he did not deserve the trust of his wife; from this danger he sought so eagerly, he knew he could not even trust himself. So he said the words again, "Trust me," and Jennifer's trembling stopped.

David sat in a molded plastic chair at his departure gate in the Toronto airport. A man in the opposite row flipped his newspaper, folded it back for compact reading, and there was David's face, staring from the page, another story on his trial. David looked away. He placed his hands on his knees and he shut down his mind and he waited. For a time—from the sentencing to his arrival an hour ago from Baltimore— he had had a sense of great speed in his life, events crowding together, carrying him along. Now the world was moving slowly and he was very anxious; but he shut his eyes, not expecting to sleep, expecting only to concentrate on the darkness, the shapeless phosphenes floating there. After a long while a woman's voice said, "Aren't you that Army captain?"

David opened his eyes and a young woman, an eager smile, was beside him. "You're David Fleming, aren't you?" she said.

"No," he said and he turned his face away, shut his eyes again.

Then at last he was on the plane and it was high over Canadian tundra and he knew he was going very fast but to look around him suggested he was not moving at all. And David finally slept. He woke once and there was a landscape of clouds beneath him, stretching out to the horizon. He woke again and there was a vinyl sea. Too far from Thailand he woke for good and he thumbed sightlessly through magazines and listened to a stereo track of Wagner and Ravel till his head ached and his ears were numb and then he struggled with his arms and legs for a long time, keeping them still, keeping them from carrying him suddenly into the aisle to leap and flail. Once he went to a lavatory and locked the door and put the top lid down and he sat there for a long time, the air nozzle blowing on him, and it was here that he finally felt the plane draw itself back and begin to fall. A woman's voice came into the lavatory announcing their descent for Bangkok and David got up, pushed past the body pressing forward into the vacant lavatory. He went by faces in a line, bored faces, necks stretching and bending to remove cricks, and he buckled himself into his seat. Below were paddies and then tracks of water and then Bangkok, webbed with its canals and glittering with pagoda roofs. The plane circled, it fell, it ran along the runway.

The airbridge came to the door of their plane and he went from the casing of jet to more molded plastic and air-conditioning and he stopped at the window. He looked back out, across the runways, to a distant stand of palm trees, the hot tropical sky. He felt now as if he had made progress; he felt nearer his son.

Signs were posted at the departure gate explaining in French, English, Thai, and Vietnamese the risks, given the current political situation, of entry into Saigon. This flight could be canceled at any moment, the signs said.

The plane was virtually empty when David boarded. He had a sudden fear that this very flight would be canceled. "Are we going to fly?" he asked a stewardess.

"Do you mean . . . ?" she said with a French accent.

"Will we be canceled?"

"No," she said, "we will fly. It is to bring people out that we will fly this time."

When the jet rose from the runway, David felt the lift in a personal way. The plane was in the air: at least he would have a chance.

He waited for landfall as they flew over the Gulf of Thailand, waited as he'd waited over the South China Sea as he'd flown to Con Son Island, but instead of the pounding of air through the open helicopter, he was much higher, above the sea in the stillness of a jet, in the stillness of memory. But his anticipation was the same and finally they were over Vietnam, the rivers scrolling there, then a thickening of jungle that was all of a scabrous green piece, seeming from this height to be lichen on a broad, flat rock. Then there were scars, wide stretches of ravaged ground, the defoliated zones. This image of the war plucked at his eyes, made him turn away. He tried to think what he would do. David Crowley. He was Canadian. "David Crowley, eh?" He said it softly and smiled. He recognized a hope in himself. His son was nearby. He would check into the Hotel Regard. He'd occasionally had drinks in the bar there with Trask. He could picture the hotel—small and ornate in a faintly seedy way, with a balding young French owner, Georges—and the

Regard's familiarity made him a little calmer. He would check into the hotel and then go to the house of Suong's family, where he'd sat on the roof and held her and they'd listened to the bombs on the horizon. That was simple enough. He'd go to her house.

He rested then, until the plane began to descend. He looked out the window, but Saigon's sprawl seemed at once so vast and so dense that he could not look at it for fear that his quest here was futile. The plane landed and there was no airbridge. David went down the steps and onto the apron and he felt the suck of tropical heat for the first time in over three years. He paused and there was a sound of small arms fire off to the east, a clustering of sounds as dense as the low-slung Saigon shacks he'd seen from the air. Two helicopters hammered by overhead, a jeep raced past, the stewardess was behind him saying, "Please, monsieur, we are going to load soon," and David walked toward the terminal, people moving in the periphery of his sight, Vietnamese army men running, mechanics arguing, screaming in Vietnamese words that David couldn't understand. And there was a faint background din now, a complex but vaguely cohesive sound that he did not identify until he drew nearer to the terminal. The soldiers were running to reinforce the gate. The sound grew louder, voices, hundreds of voices, a thousand voices beseeching. David passed through a phalanx of ARVN soldiers and the voices had faces. There was a barricade; he was directed in a sharp left turn down a corridor, but he had a glimpse of the broad, open space of the terminal writhing with people, faces squeezing together like the gallery at his trial, but these with voices that cried out in panic, the voices clustering like small arms fire, like the hovels of Saigon which could hide a million orphaned children.

David went quickly down the hall toward a baggage dump and customs. David Crowley. The fighting was very near. A sharper sound. Metallic thunder. A rocket outside, out no farther than the edge of the airport, he decided. The voices, which had cohered again in their cry, fragmented at this rocket blast; the voices cried louder, individually, and receded.

David took his bag off a cart. He approached a government official beside a low table. The din of David's heart obscured even the sound of the crowd down the corridor as he approached this middle-aged Vietnamese man in his official white shirt, his peaked cap.

David placed his bag on the table and handed the man his passport. There was an odd stillness around them; the entry room was empty. David wondered why this man was still here, still going through the motions. Even as he thought this, David saw the man's hands quaking slightly as he stared at the passport, saw a haggardness in the man's face, saw the eyes—which rose now to look at David—saw a desperation in these eyes. He wondered how many people this man had challenged for much fainter traces of these very same signals of anxiety. "Mr. Crowley?" the man said.

"Yes."

"Why do you want to come to Vietnam?"

"I work for a group that is interested in the American deserters in Saigon. I want to . . ."

"What do you have so that I will let you into Vietnam?" The man's voice was pinched with the same panic that roiled down the corridor. Only the volume was controlled.

David took from his pocket the roll of American currency still wrapped in a rubber band, probably from Trask's desk drawer. The customs official took the money, thumbed it, put it in his pocket, and jerked his head toward the door in dismissal.

David picked up his bag and began to go, but he stopped and came back. "How long is left for Saigon?" he asked in Vietnamese.

The official's face wrinkled in surprise, then he smiled faintly. The Vietnamese were always delighted at a Westerner knowing their language: David gauged the seriousness of the situation from the faintness of this smile. The man said in Vietnamese, "There were four rockets at the airport just past midnight. You can hear the fighting now very close. We will fall maybe tomorrow. Maybe the next day."

David did not move at once. His worst fear was confirmed and it held him fast for a moment. Then he gripped hard at the handle of his bag and he turned and moved away, deliberately at first, then quickly.

Outside there was a flow of vehicles, people, rushing toward the front doors of the terminal: a Honda with five on it—a family from father to infant—a jeep full of Chinese vases driven by a Vietnamese army officer, people with suitcases, bundles, babies. The cry out here was replaced by the silent final push to the terminal. And in the distance was still the gunfire. But no cabs. David looked for the tiny cream and blue Renault taxicabs of Saigon but he saw none.

"Damn," he said aloud. And again, "Damn." Then he saw a xich-lo. It sat empty across the street; its lines—its wide, open seat on two wheels set before the back half of a motorized bicycle—were so familiar, so strongly associated with his time in Saigon, that it calmed him a bit. He was here. He was in Saigon. And the xich-lo was empty.

David dashed through the traffic, Hondas veered, and he put his bag on the seat of the vehicle. A man crouched nearby, pinching his forehead over and over with his fingers. "Is this your xich-lo?" David asked in Vietnamese.

The man's face jerked up. "Yes," he said.

"I want to go downtown. To the Hotel Regard."

The man looked at David for a moment and then he shrugged and rose. David sat on the seat, the familiar mutter began of the one-stroke engine, and the xich-lo edged out and moved against all the traffic, out of the airport—the garbage dumps high in the street, the banners still draped on walls bristling at compromise with the North— past the US military assistance headquarters and into Cach Mang.

The trees began here, the tall trees of Saigon, the tamarind and the chestnut, and the opposite flow of people thinned slightly, the street gave the brief illusion of a normal Saigon. The xich-lo ran fast beneath the trees and David was on the open seat with nothing in front of him but this Saigon boulevard and its trees and pastel walls and flickers of people all peeling past and there was no awareness of the machine, the sense of speed that in a car was in the cheeks and back of the head was now suddenly in David's chest. He was moving fast, clearly so, and purposefully, and then a vast sound battered him, and another, from behind, his head was filled with sound, rang with sound, he doubled up, his eyes closed, but he felt no pain; it was reflex, the sound was not meant for him. He straightened and turned around to look. A broad column of smoke was rising back down Cach Mang. The xich-lo driver did not look, did not slow down. They sped away from all that. Another hammer of sound, a billow of flame from the smoke. David judged the distance, the angle: this one was at the airport. From the size of the explosion it must be an ammunition dump, David thought. He glanced at the face of the xich-lo driver: impassive, the eyes fixed ahead. David nodded at the face, as if the man had given him a piece of good advice. David faced forward and let the speed absorb him.

But soon the streets grew crowded again and when they hit Cong Ly the flow was in the same direction as they were heading. And again there were families rushing together, clinging to parcels of clothes, suitcases, a man staggered along with a mattress on his back, another with a small, draped table clutched in his arms—a domestic shrine to an ancestor, David knew—this man was running, the shrine held close, like a child.

The xich-lo was going very slowly now in the crowd. In some odd way the city in its panic seemed to David more self-controlled than before, when the streets were full of impromptu commerce and intensely personal coming and going. Now there was a presiding intent. He wondered where this group was heading. Escaping by the river? Then he thought of the US Embassy. Of course: now that the enemy was coming in, the Americans would take everyone out; that was the reasoning.

The xich-lo bumped up onto a shoulder of the street where it could bully the pedestrians out of the way and at a side street—Yen Do—the driver took a right turn and the traffic was lighter and most of it was heading the other way. The xich-lo ran along Yen Do, giving way only to an ARVN deuce-and-a-half full of frightened faces.

David knew that his driver was working his way to the west of the center of the city to approach the hotel from a direction that would not be seen as an escape route.

Down Yen Do a Vietnamese army captain was standing in the middle of the street firing his pistol straight up into the air. The xich-lo arced around him and the man did not even seem to notice. Soon after, the driver turned to the south and David watched the trees moving above him; he put a hand on his bag to steady it and he watched the trees, the sky; he let his mind skim along up there where the madness of Saigon was not visible.

Then they were running along the river, going east again. The river was crowded but it did not convey a sense of panic. Sampans, an oil tanker moving out, patrol boats— the xich-lo ran past them and finally turned up Bach Dang, still skirting the river, but there was a brief glimpse down the wide, straight stretch of Nguyen Du to the circular fountain at Le Loi in the distance and the cupola of City Hall beyond.

At last they passed the familiar wedge of the Majestic Hotel on the corner of Tu Do—the bland facade of this more famous Saigon hotel always struck him in its contrast to the Regard on the opposite corner, where they now stopped. The hotel was small and French in a translated way, as if its architect had deduced a French style from a visit to New Orleans: it was low—three stories—and its balconies looking onto Tu Do had filigreed ironwork.

David stepped down from the xich-lo. He paid the driver and tipped him well for extricating them from the panic of his countrymen and for his impassive face at the airport explosions. The man took the money with a curt thanks and he sped off. David looked up Tu Do and not far away was a man putting boxes into the back of a black Citröen; a stereo, a fan, a vase were at his feet, a woman appeared from a storefront and she laid another box beside him. Beyond that, the street seemed calm. A bar across the way was shuttered, closed up; but a woman's voice nearby said, "You like a Vietnam girl friend make you happy forever?"

David looked and in the doorway of the Flowers Bar was a young Vietnamese woman in a miniskirt. David picked up his bag and went through the front doors of the Regard.

The lobby was small and dark with a cut-glass chandelier. To the right, through a wide archway into the bar, David could see the faintly wavy glass of the windows looking onto the river. He stopped. He'd always expected a terrorist bomb to crash through those windows, a bomb large enough to bring down the chandelier as well. But they'd miraculously survived. All those years of the French and the Americans and these glass statements of bourgeois impudence remained, spared no doubt by the more obvious target across the street; the Majestic had been bombed several times. David looked up at the chandelier which quaked faintly in the dim light. Like the driver's impassive face, it encouraged him.

At the front desk David had to tap the bell many times before a young Vietnamese woman in an ao dai appeared. "I'm sorry, monsieur," she said. "We have very little help now."

"That's all right," David said. "I'd like a room."

As he went through the registration procedure, the woman's remark on having little help lingered in David. He thought of the Regard's owner, Georges, a balding young Frenchman who was very friendly with Trask. "And where's Georges?" David finally asked.

The woman shrugged but her voice grew faint. "I do not know, monsieur."

David felt a thin trickle of fear at the back of his throat. But he thrust Georges out of his mind. He resolved not to permit himself another thought of the old Saigon unless it was directly connected to finding Suong and the boy. He took his key and moved away and he was conscious of the trembling glass above him.

David did no more in his room than leave his bag and he went back out into the street. He walked up Tu Do, looking again for a cab or xich-lo, ignoring the nervous whores before the quiet bars, and he was stopped by barbed wire and ARVN troops at Le Loi. The square before the National Assembly Building was blocked off. Surely the old man Huong was no longer president, although David didn't know for sure; he imagined phony government after phony government traipsing in and out of the Assembly building—with its scooped front making it look like a band shell—as the South searched frantically for the right combination of officials to placate the rage of the North. David retreated back down Tu Do and he found a xich-lo at last and as it rushed through the streets he watched the sky or veiled his eyes in thoughtless anticipation of Suong's house, ignoring Saigon the way he'd ignored the whores on Tu Do; then he was conscious of the chestnut trees along Tran Hung Dao and a movie house with a billboard advertising a Run Run Shaw film, then the Metropole, where David had lived for a time. The street turned residential, David's mouth was dry, his heart raced as fast as the xich-lo, he leaned into the rush of air and at last the five-story building approached, the house of Suong's family. The xich-lo came to a stop.

David paid the driver, not letting himself look closely yet, not until he was alone. As the xich-lo receded, he became conscious of the silence in the street. There was no panic here. At least not outward. David turned to face the house, expecting to see the Rouge et Jaune nightclub on the ground floor. But there was no canopy, no stained-glass door, no trace of the club. Only scraps of lumber cluttered against the house, and the frame of an old motorcycle beside the fence. David wondered if this was the right house. He looked at the other houses around him. He looked at the number over the door. Yes. He looked up toward the roof. He'd sat with Suong beyond the balustrade. His hands jumped up. Something was wrong here.

He went to the door, began to knock, but it was ajar. He pushed the door open and he stepped in. The baby-faced Vietnamese officers danced in this space in a color wheel on the night he visited Suong's club. Now the room was dim and full of trash—scattered clothes, mattresses, bicycle frames and parts—and there were people. David strained to look into the dimness as the people finally registered on his sight; there were people on the mattresses, thin covers pulled over them, old people, the cragged Vietnamese faces of the very old, their eyes turning slowly toward him. A sound now. A child began to cry nearby. Not just the old; a naked child, too, a little girl, fell into a woman's arms, a strange woman to David, a stranger. The child was less than two years old.

David thought to step back through the door. Suong could not be here. But how could he be sure? He moved through the room. The faces angled away; no one clutched at him; no one begged him for help in getting out of the country: and that made David sad, sad and frightened. The despair hung thick as the mildew in this room, this room that was connected to Suong. He looked for someone to ask about the family that had once owned the house, but there was no one he felt he could speak to.

He was at the stairs leading to the upper floors. From above he heard garbled sounds, back alley sounds, children crying, a sharp scolding woman's voice, the lurching of a blues harmonica. Behind him was silence and David shuddered at it and he climbed the steps.

On the second floor he became aware of the smell of the house: urine and marijuana and sour milk. He moved down

the hallway toward the front room. The sound of a brass
mobile filled his mind: memory. Now he heard a child
crying; someone's else's child, David knew. Suong was
gone. And there was the background strum of a guitar, then
an American voice singing, a jagged voice.

David passed a door on the corridor and within was a
family—a man, barebacked, with only the stump of a left
arm, a woman with the black pantaloons of an ao dai and a
New York Yankees T-shirt, two small children, all crouched
flat-footed around an upturned helmet liner. They held
chopsticks, but David could not see what was in the liner.
The four faces looked at him and the smaller child—a boy—
said, "Fuck you, GI." Only the boy laughed.

David moved on. He approached a second room off the
corridor and inside Bob Dylan was singing: "Hey, Mr. Tam-
bourine Man, play a song for me." Before the record stood a
young Vietnamese man wearing wire-rim sunglasses and a
watch cap. He was pantomiming the song. A candle burned
on a table. David moved along the hall, approached the living room, and he stopped in the doorway. The room was
almost bare, as if this were the surface of a dirty stream and
the detritus had all settled to the bottom, the floor below.
David saw an elderly man and woman sitting on a mat in the
center of the room, a family shrine behind them, with faded
pictures and incense smoking. The incense and the smell of
pot burned in David's lungs. The old man passed a joint to
the woman.

David stepped farther into the room, looking at the pho-
tos on the shrine. Neither was of Suong's father. David became aware of something in his periphery. He looked and
saw mats with pillows and in a corner a middle-aged woman
crouched near boxes of Tide. The boxes were stacked neatly
against the wall, dozens of them, a hundred of them, and she
drew nearer the boxes as he watched her, her eyes shading
in suspicion at him. Dylan was singing that his weariness
amazed him, he had no one to meet. David turned his head
to the voice—"My ancient empty streets too dead for dream-

ing"—and the smell of incense and marijuana was making him dizzy.

He stepped to the old man, who looked up at him; the man seemed alert. David said slowly, in Vietnamese, "Where is the family that used to own this house?"

The old man laughed. "You speak very good Vietnamese."

"Yes. Do you know about the family who . . ."

"The family of Mr. Thanh."

"Yes. He was an important man under Diem."

"Oh yes. Everyone knew Thanh."

"Where is he?"

"He died long ago."

"I meant his family. Are they still here?"

The woman spoke. "If they were here, we wouldn't be."

David crouched beside the two old people. "Where did they go?"

"No one knows," the man said. "They didn't like Thieu."

"Thanh's wife is *somewhere*," the woman said.

"And what about the daughter? Nguyen Thi Tuyet Suong?"

The man shrugged. The woman shook her head and said, "They all left. Then no one came in here so other people did."

"You said something about Thanh's wife . . ."

"They're all dead," the woman said with a wave of her hand, a dismissal.

"All dead," the man repeated. He sucked deep at the joint and David rose.

He backed away, turned, went out into the hall. Dylan sang, "To dance beneath the diamond sky with one hand waving free." David expected when he glanced into the passing room to see the young Vietnamese man pantomiming, with his hand waving, playing at being this American singer. But instead he was sitting on the floor, his head bared now and bowed, nodding faintly. "With all memory and fate driven deep beneath the waves."

David went down the stairs, through the ground floor room, out into the street. The sky was bruised with twilight. The horizon crackled with gunfire, thumped with rockets, but David did not even look over his shoulder at the house where these had once been the sounds of romance.

There was only silence from Tu Do Street. David lay on his bed in the dark and though the rockets were falling now to the west in salvos of four and five, David felt insulated from the outside because the street was quiet. The bars of Tu Do were shuttered and the drunken soldiers and squabbling whores and Saigon cowboys and hustlers and beggars were hiding or had fled. A space had been cleared for David and he lay in it and he found he was very weary. He had returned to his hotel and eaten a dinner in the bar with his back to the river and he had come to his room and had lain down on the bed without considering the blind alley that Suong's house had become, an alley filled with strangers. Now, in his recollection, he could not look away from the faces that had turned blankly on him. They knew nothing. But there was one more place to go: the place where Suong's family had always gone in troubled times; the place where David's son was conceived. His son. He had to keep all his thoughts, all his energy, focused on his son. At the house on Tran Hung Dao the boy felt very distant. Suong was there, the spoor of her in David's memory, but in fact she was gone. Dead? Was she dead as the old woman had asserted? Was the whole family dead? But that remark had come just moments after the woman said that Thanh's wife—Suong's mother—was known to be somewhere. David had learned nothing except that his son wasn't at the house on Tran Hung Dao. Tomorrow, he thought, as his mind blurred. Tomorrow he'd go to Nha Be.

A clap of sound yanked David up by the chest. A rocket had fallen nearby. He groped, still rising from sleep, for Jennifer next to him. "Little David," he said aloud, meaning it to rouse Jennifer to go with him to see if the child was all right, if this sound had disturbed him. David found the bed empty and he was sweating; a paddle fan was beating softly above him in the dark, moving the air. He was in Saigon. Jennifer and little David were sleeping, just as he'd left them. And his other son: it was he whose sleep was troubled by rockets. Was he within the sound of that explosion? When the country fell, there would be no way to get to Nha Be. He thought of going now, at night. But his chances of making it were worse in the dark. He had to wait.

He lay back down. He opened with the suspension of a full-body tropical sweat and he yearned for sleep, for the burden of thought to be lifted from him till he was able to act. The faces of the Vietnamese in Suong's house stared at him from the shadows as he strove to release his mind. Quiet Vietnamese: he thought of the first night after his transfer to Saigon. He returned to the Metropole after dark in a closed taxi. Only jukebox music came from the bars across the street —the Okay Lounge, the San Francisco Bar—and that seemed like a kind of silence. Just a few bar girls—fat or old —remained in the doors and the mothers and children of the girls were outside now, crouching on the sidewalk. Milling nearby were half a dozen Vietnamese boys, teenagers, the Saigon cowboys who would make trouble later, rolling the drunk GIs, selling drugs to the half sober ones. David stood there, knowing he should go upstairs to sleep. But he looked down the street that ran in front of the Metropole and he began to walk. In his new assignment in Saigon he was determined to operate freely and effectively, but even as he asserted this to himself, he knew there was more than defiance in his evening stroll. The city that had wheedled and begged and clutched in the day began to withdraw at night; it allowed David his distance and he felt a kind of comfort here at last. He slipped past the evenness of the security floodlight and into the humid dark of Saigon. Like the day, the night stank of dead fish and grease and kerosene and garbage. The people who had earlier crowded the sidewalks crouched in invisible doorways or gathered on stools at the food stands. The dark was unremitting, the isolated light of paraffin lamps near the stands staining the night rather than illuminating it. David passed by, and through the gridwork of a closed shop he saw a family sitting among motor parts, rice bowls raised to their chins, watching ARVN troops firing mortars on a TV screen. On a corner were tables under umbrellas and the stools held mothers in loose blouses, children clinging to their arms—David lingered now as he lay in his hotel, adjusting the memory; he looked at a child in its mother's arms but saw not even a trace of a Western feature in its face—and he let himself move on, in the memory, he passed the soldiers growing expansive, drinking the Vietnamese beer, but ignoring David. They all ignored David. He turned the corner and the side street was black. There were no food stands and there was only a tiny fan of fluorescence from an opening in a storefront mid-block. But the people were there, David knew. His vision dilated and he could see some of them dimly, their shapes, and he sensed the others, silent in the darkness, sitting unseen in the doorways, on balconies, in the gutters. And as he stood there, had he felt this silence as the doomed sadness of the Vietnamese? Probably not. But he felt that now: this voluble people silent in the dark, silent like those whose eyes had turned on him today; and then there was another silence in him, more demanding: the silence of egg and seed joining, the silence of separation.

David woke to the sound of small arms fire. There was light in the room and he arose and dressed quickly. Downstairs there was no one at the front desk, no one tending the bar either. There was a small group of Westerners hunched together at a table far from the window. The faces, forms, didn't register in David. He wondered if all the hotel's staff had fled. A voice with an English accent stopped David as he turned to leave. "Hello? Do you want to join us?" There was a distant booming. A ripple of rifle fire.

David paused. All he wanted to do was go out the door and head for Nha Be. But he wondered what the situation was outside the city. Even inside the city. He realized that so far he'd purposely remained ignorant of the big events; events, though, that could affect his search. He approached the table.

The Englishman, younger than his voice, not much older than David, spoke his own name—he worked for the BBC, he said—and began to speak the names of the half dozen others, each face nodding in turn.

David said, "My name is David Crowley. I'm Canadian. I'm sorry I can't be more sociable at this time, but I have to find someone south of the city. Can you tell me what the word is on when Saigon will fall?"

"Certainly very soon," the Englishman said. "They've begun their attack on the airport."

"And south? I have to go southeast to Nha Be."

"There are Communist soldiers south, too," said one of the others.

"In Nha Be?"

"I don't know."

"The Swiss came round this morning," the Englishman said. "They're offering all the foreign guests at all the hotels refuge at the Red Cross Headquarters on Hong Tap Tu. It's been declared a neutral zone. We're just sort of getting together now to go round . . ."

"Perhaps later for me," David said. "I've got to go to Nha Be . . . Does one of you know where I can get a car . . . or maybe better, a . . ."

There was a rushing of footsteps outside, in Tu Do. Gunfire.

"You'd best not try to go anywhere," said another voice

from the table. "The ARVNs are starting to go crazy with fear. They're looting. And worse."

"I need a vehicle," David said. "Can one of you help me?"

"We're all going over in a car," said another of the voices. "How long will you be gone?"

"It's a little over six miles to Nha Be," David said.

"The roads may be cut off."

"This is very important. Life and death," David said and he decided not to waste any more time here. He'd hire somebody in the street, one of those who was not running, one of the quietly desperate.

But the voice that asked how long he'd be gone said, "Listen. I've a little scooter. A Vespa out back. You can take that."

"Thanks very much."

"Just return it to the Red Cross HQ when you're done. You'd be going there anyway, wouldn't you?"

"Yes. Of course. Thanks."

David went down the corridor toward the exit to Ngo Duc Ke. Just inside the back door was a lime-colored Vespa.

Out in the street David saw a thick column of black smoke rising to the west and a rumbling came from there, secondary explosions—the airport—a salvo of rockets, then three closely clumped cracks of sound. David started the Vespa and rolled to the corner of Bach Dang.

People were running. Over the sidewalks, down the center of the street, out along the quays, men, women, children in arms, larger children running with parents, all silent in their flight, with no clear direction in this street—there were almost as many running south as north. The street was wide and the conflicting flows had room to pass, though even as David watched, two women ran headlong into each other and fell hard, a man running behind stepped on an outstretched arm and stumbled. David found his chest beginning to tighten, his head growing light; the panic was like exhaled pot in a closed room—it hung, expelled from the lungs of others, affecting even an observer passing through. But David knew that he was not as much an outsider in all this as he wanted to believe. Time was running out for him as well.

He accelerated into the street, going south on Bach Dang, weaving through the running figures, swerving as an ARVN deuce-and-a-half careened out of a side street. The truck was full of household goods and four children's faces peeking out the back. It roared south and David followed it closely, letting it clear the way and it crossed the Ben Nghe Canal, David right behind, the children not moving, not smiling, not waving, a startling sight, Vietnamese children so frightened now that they wouldn't smile even going fast in an open truck.

The deuce-and-a-half turned off into a side street and David continued south, through District Four, the shops all closed up, and in the runs of shanties, families were dragging their bedding and clothes out into the street, others were standing in their doorways, very still, and the street was growing full of people. Not running here, as they'd been in Bach Dang. And in Bach Dang they'd been running with nothing in their hands, fleeing only with skin and bone and blood. This flow was slower and it was laden with goods—pots and chickens and children and lamps and hoes—and the people were all of a mind now in the direction for their flight, they were all heading into Saigon, away from the place where David had to go, their diligent, unanimous flight speaking to David, saying that he would never find his son.

He squeezed this thought out of his mind. He concentrated on the narrow margin of road that he could slip along in his race to the south. When he reached the bridge over the Kinh Te, it was packed from guard rail to guard rail. He stopped as the refugees stumbled off the bridge, swarmed down an incline and pressed on north toward Saigon. David walked the Vespa up to the bridge, tried to wedge his way along the right guard rail, but the people were compressing and stumbling, a pot handle hit him in the face, a chicken pecked at his eyes. He pulled back and looked at the Kinh Te. The water was brackish and it swirled. None of the refugees were trying to ford it.

He waited, craning his neck, looking for an opening. He saw a large green provincial bus packed high with bundles and stuffed with people, boys clinging to the side windows and to the roof racks. The bus was blowing its horn, approaching the bridge from the south. There was a sudden surge in the crowd, the bus came up, someone went over the rail and into the river. No one stopped, no one looked. The person in the river was swimming. David watched the bus asserting itself, cutting a wide swath. It rolled past and its wake was filling but there was still a looseness to the crowd behind and David pushed forward, started his engine, and pressed on across. A woman was slumped against a railing, crying, clothes were scattered, people eddied, the crowd was tightening again and David edged through, revved the engine and finally he broke free and onto Highway 15 and the refugees there were strung out into a thinner line; there was a narrow lane for him, on the margin of the pavement. The line of refugees, with the peasant women's conical straw hats, stretched along the highway like a giant mythical millipede, horn-backed, with a million legs; and the creature implied, as well, some vast bird that would fall from the empty sky to prey on this long, fragile body. Behind, in the distance, there were still explosions. Ahead: David strained to hear the sounds of war, but there was only the roar of the scooter's engine and then the air horn of an ARVN truck, the refugees scattering as the truck raced this way. David slowed, eased off the road, the truck looming. David preferred to risk his life rather than risk the Vespa that had to carry him still farther. He felt the slippery wet of the paddy as the swirl and roar of the truck rushed past.

He wrenched the Vespa from the suck of earth and back onto the surface of the road. He raced now for a time without hindrance as the line of refugees only slowly linked itself after being thrown aside. The rush of air against David pumped up his sense of hope—wildly—all out of proportion, he knew, to the reality. He saw thin wisps of smoke on the horizon—a firefight somewhere—but he was entering Nha Be at last and he watched closely for the cutoff to Suong's house. He recalled it coming almost immediately after entering the district and then he saw a dusty lane ahead.

David turned there. On the corner was a mieu—one of the little shrines on a post placed to mark the scene of an accident, to honor the souls of the victims. The road looked familiar, but he didn't remember the mieu from before. He knew he had to fight the urge to read significance or foreboding into small things. Just wait, he cried to himself. Wait, dammit. You're almost there.

Ahead was the high gray wall, the house hidden behind. David turned in and the iron gate was open—off its upper hinge, he noticed as he went through. He stopped before the house.

The grounds were shaggy, overgrown, flies swirled up from a coconut bleeding its milk in rocks beneath a tree. But for a moment, as he sat before this place where he knew his son was conceived, there was a silence, a hot tropical silence, that drew his eyes to the front door. It stood open. He waited for Suong to appear there, her hair curving down a shoulder, her feet bare, the child in her arms, an infant still; she smiled and raised the boy to him. But the child was older, David knew. He tried to adjust the vision and then it was too much an act of the will and there was only the open door.

David approached the house. He did not pause at the door but entered, the dim familiarity prickling his skin, then the differences inside instantly scraping him with doubt. Only the Roman feeling of stone was left: the vases and the lacquerware, all the touches of wealth, were gone; even the chandelier in the front room was gone, though the chain still hung from the ceiling, link by link descending to nothing, to empty suspension. There was furniture in the front room, but broken sets, worn, with spindly walnut legs; the wealth had been stripped some time ago. As with the house in Tran Hung Dao, David's first impulse was to withdraw at once. But he had nothing else. This house was the end for him. The furniture was ragged. The gate was off the hinge. He sensed the empty chain dangling over him. He barked in fear now, a low popping negative; he said it more clearly in his mind, then aloud, "No," meaning he couldn't accept this as the end. There was someone here with information. He stepped back out into the foyer and he moved through the dining room, pausing briefly at the staircase which had led to the bed where his son began. He did not go up the stairs but went on through the sitting room, into the kitchen, and he drew back.

There was a figure on a chair by the window, featureless in the glint from the sun, its shoulders rounded, a woman. David began to tremble. He struggled to draw a breath. He stepped forward and he said, barely audibly, "Suong."

The figure turned, the face rose, and it had a white scar running from the right ear, across the cheek, and down to the jaw. A young woman. Suong's servant; David remembered her at once from the day here. Not Suong. Her servant. He was panting in release.

"Where's Suong?" he asked.

The woman said nothing. He realized he'd spoken in English. "Where's Suong?" he repeated in Vietnamese.

The woman moved her shoulders. "I don't know," she said.

David took a step forward. He was angry at her seeming indifference. But he made his voice gentle. "Do you remember me?"

The woman peered at him. "No."

"I came here one Sunday afternoon with Suong. Several years ago."

The woman shrugged again. "Yes. All right."

"Where has Suong gone?" he said.

"I don't know."

"I want to help her. I can . . . help her to get out."

"She's been gone for a long time."

"How long?"

"A year perhaps."

David pulled the back of his hand across his forehead. "Do you know where she went?"

"No."

"Do you know anything at all about her?"

"No. Not for a year or more. She just didn't show up."

"Who took all the furnishings from the house?"

"She did."

"Over a year ago?"

"She sold them."

David turned away, wandered around the kitchen, stopped at the window; his mind dipped and dipped, like the palm frond over the roof of the tiny pagoda out back. "Don't you have any idea where she might be?"

"No. Thieu hated her. I don't know where she is."

"President Thieu?"

"She hated him too. His government."

David could see beyond the pagoda, beyond the gazebo, to the inlet from the Nha Be River. As richly evocative as the place was in his memories, in his dreams, now the place seemed barren. He heard gunfire across the paddies. Not thunder, not the bombs of the B-52s, but small arms fire. Personal, messy, and nearby.

David turned to the woman with a question that he was tempted not to ask, since he no longer knew what to do to find Suong. But he had to ask: "Did Suong have a child?" he said. "Born about four years ago?"

The face turned to him. The scar was on the cheek away from the window, but it was very white in spite of the shadow. "I don't know exactly when the child was born," she said. "But yes. There was a child."

"Tell me about him." David knew at once that the Vietnamese word he used—the proper word—expressed the family status of the child by age and implied nothing of sex.

"I don't know anything," she said. "I saw the child only once. Suong's mother cared for it."

"Do you know where her mother is?"

"No."

"Did her mother go with Suong, wherever she went?"

"I don't know. I almost never saw her out here. Please, I don't know anything."

"One question more," David said. "Was the child a boy?"

"Yes."

David did not remain at the Red Cross Headquarters but left the Vespa and returned to the Regard. Not quite all the staff of the hotel had fled, and he ate dinner in the bar. He went to his room and locked the door and he lay down. He had traveled from Nha Be to this bed in a suspension between two powerful and inimical facts: his boy existed and there was no way to find him. The refugees, the crazed soldiers, the gunfire, the abandoned cars, the running, running, bodies hurtling, panting—he had traveled through all of this and he was as remote from it as if he'd been in a jet passing through a cloud.

He wondered—almost idly—if the city would fall tonight. He supposed it would. He tried to remember what day it was, but he didn't know. Either the twenty-ninth or thirtieth of April. It occurred to him that he should try to escape now, to leave the country. The airport was under attack, but surely there was an American evacuation underway somewhere. He could go to the US Embassy. But he'd been prepared from the first for this possibility. He hadn't really expected to find his son instantly. He knew he might have to let the South fall around him while he continued his search. But at this he felt a quaver of fear begin. Inevitably. There were the Communists coming in, the vast faceless horde of the VC ready to find its revenge. Remember Hue. Someone had said that. It had been today, but he couldn't recall who or when or even in what language. But the VC massacre of civilians in Hue during Tet of '68 was on someone's mind.

"I'm a Canadian." David said it aloud. There was a burst of automatic rifle fire down the street. An ARVN looting a bar, David decided.

And then in his mind he replied to his spoken words: As David Crowley caught after the fall of Saigon you'll be hearing from the CIA. What will you do then?

I don't know, he answered himself.

They'll give you some damn fool mission that will only serve to put you in jeopardy.

I don't know what to think about this now.

You have to face it.

There's worse than that to face.

He fell silent before his own challenge. Then he said, aloud, "My son." He didn't know how to find his son and his eyes filled, his tears were quick as blood, he heard the rockets falling out on the edge of the city, then a distant hollow voice speaking on a loudspeaker, and small arms fire calling like a whore in Tu Do.

David rubbed hard at his eyes with the heels of his hands. He wanted to sleep. He hung in another suspension: he did not know where to turn next but he could not yet abandon his search. He needed to sleep. "Sleep," he said, as if he were speaking to a restless child. Then his Vietnamese son suddenly shaped in his mind: David's own face and form in miniature, but with the black hair of his mother. David did not want any dreams now. Not of this son. He could not bear to look at the child's face, clearly shaped by his own seed, without knowing what to do next to find him.

Go away, David said in his mind to the image of the boy, but gently.

The boy slowly shook his head no.

Please, David said.

"Find me," the boy said, but it was David's voice, speaking aloud in his hotel room.

There was no more to say. The eyes of the boy and David's eyes—the same eyes—did not blink, did not turn away until sleep darkened their sight and then finally there was nothing to see.

When David woke, there was sunlight and there was silence. He knew the city had fallen. And he found his mind held the same silence; his plan had fallen, like Saigon; and as with everyone else in the city, there was nothing he could do, nothing to decide except whether to remain where he was or go out into the street.

He heard no gunfire, so he went out. Tu Do was nearly empty. In the door of the Flowers Bar a young woman peeked out. She was of a bar girl's age and figure, but her face was wiped plain—she had no makeup at all—and she wore a loose, shapeless blouse, black pantaloons. She looked at David and her face disappeared from the doorway.

He moved along the street and mid-block he saw a street vendor with a small table before him. As David approached, there was a flash of a familiar color—an array of flags on a table, red flags each with a gold star—the North Vietnamese flag.

The old man smiled at David. "You buy?" he said. "Very good. New flag. Special price."

And then the red and gold were repeated at the end of the block. A green truck with the North's flag painted on it turned into Tu Do Street, heading this way. David stopped. He could see the heads of troops in the back, rifle barrels, then he heard the deep grind of an engine—odd sound for a truck, David thought—but turning into Tu Do behind the truck was a tank, following closely, the red flag with the gold star waving this time on a thin metal antenna sticking up from the turret. The truck, the tank were moving toward David, another tank turned the corner now—all from Le Loi

—all rolling down Tu Do and David had the impulse to bolt, to run. He looked around him and even the flag seller was stirring nervously, was grasping for a flag to wave. David wanted to run, but he had no direction and the truck was almost upon him.

He straightened up, squared around to face the street, and the truck passed. The old man waved a flag, David stood at attention, and the row of North Vietnamese faces, soldiers with green pith helmets, smiled. Every face opened in a smile and the first tank grumbled past and the North Vietnamese soldier sitting in the turret hatch laughed and waved. David smiled; not to return the smiles of these North Vietnamese but at the irony of all this; it struck him that these Northerners the US fought and feared for a decade were really the charming, friendly people that many Americans in Saigon had learned were typical of the South Vietnamese. The Vietnamese soldier in the turret of the second tank flipped the old man a snappy salute. David almost laughed aloud. These were just a bunch of friendly country boys on the town. Another troop truck came by and there were Saigon children hitching a ride on the sides, on the bumper, and there was an old woman clinging to one of the soldiers; a reunion, David knew, a family split by the war reunited now.

Seeing this old woman made David think of Suong's mother. He began to walk along the street, his head down, focused now on the old woman. At both places where he'd known to look, he'd gotten an impression that the mother— the grandmother—might still be around. And she had taken care of the boy before. The servant at Nha Be said so. Maybe he was with her now, he was with his grandmother. When the family was forced out of the house on Tran Hung Dao, whoever was left among them went somewhere else. The ones in the house itself, the squatters, seemed to know nothing. But maybe there were friends of the family still living nearby. He'd canvass the street. He'd focus on the old woman this time. Start with her.

In a side street off Tu Do he found a xich-lo at the curb and the driver in a doorway. The man nodded tensely at David's approach, but once they were on their way there was no sign of the conquering army. The city seemed very quiet, almost deserted. The North had apparently just arrived. It would take a while for them to occupy streets like this one—Tran Hung Dao, with its houses and shops shuttered, holding the city's fear behind a placid facade. David thought: at least Suong's neighbors will be at home when I call.

He got down from the xich-lo in front of Suong's house but he never gave the place a glance. He went next door to a smaller house, two stories with a flat roof and a balcony. He knocked at the front door. There was no answer. He knocked again, trying to look through the gauzy curtains in the front window, but he could see nothing. No one answered the door. He backed away, looked up at the balcony. A paper lantern hung over the railing and it lifted and turned in a gust of breeze. But there were no faces in the windows. The people inside were refusing to answer and this made David curse softly. Then he thought of an alternative— they'd fled. They'd bought their way out of the country. This made him stagger. Suong sold her furnishings at Nha Be a year ago. Now he knew why. She'd left the country. She'd seen what was going to happen and she took the child and she fled. She was somewhere else. In Paris or in Tokyo or in Seattle or in Vancouver. Somewhere else. The child was lost now to him forever. She'd fled.

David moved his legs. This thought had come to him so abruptly that it seemed to be true. Automatically true. But he slowed down his mind. He moved to the next house and he tried to hold back the rush of his fears. It need not be true. There could have been some other reason for Suong to turn her possessions into cash. She sold the furnishings at Nha Be, but why didn't she sell the house? The two houses were the most obvious assets the family had. She sold neither of them. Thieu hated her. That's what they said. David stopped. Now his concern swung the other way. The family was taken off to prison, to Con Son Island. His child was in a cell, in the same cell that had held Tuyen. David fought off this madness, these mad connections. The child was somewhere nearby, he cried to himself. The child was with his grandmother and they were somewhere nearby.

David knocked at the door of the next house. No one came. He knocked again, he pounded hard at the door until his hand ached and as soon as he stopped, his arm throbbing up to his elbow, the door opened a crack. A face appeared. A middle-aged man. The door opened wider. "Yessir?" the man said in English.

David took a deep breath, tried to seem calm. He knew he had one clear bit of leverage along this street—he was a Westerner. It was a knock from a Vietnamese that these people feared. "Good morning," David said in Vietnamese.

The man smiled, but his eyes scanned the street.

David said, "The city is calm. There's nothing to fear."

The man nodded and his smile stretched wider. "Please come in."

"Thank you." David stepped into the dim light of the room. The man's wife and several children edged out of the shadows. David focused on him as he began to chatter in relief. David gently interrupted. "My name is David Crowley. I'm a Canadian. I'm looking for someone and perhaps you can help me find her."

The man's face grew instantly solemn. The wife's face drew near.

David said, "I want to help this person . . . I'm looking for Nguyen Van Thanh's wife."

"Thanh's wife?" the man said.

"I want to find his family. Do you know them?"

"Of course. They were our neighbors for many years."

"Where is . . . do you know where the daughter is? Tuyet Suong?"

"No."

"The mother then."

"Madame Trung." The wife spoke.

"Trung. Yes," David said. Now that he remembered her name, he began to remember her face. She was named after the two first-century warrior sisters who had briefly thrown out the Chinese. But Suong's mother looked more like a mandarin's daughter, too delicate to speak loudly, much less make war. "Do you know where she is?"

"No," the man said. "They left suddenly."

"Do you think . . ." The words snagged in David. He squeezed them out. "Do you think they left the country?"

"No. Not at that time, at least."

"Are you sure?"

"I'm not sure, but there was some trouble."

"The daughter," the woman said.

"Suong."

"Yes. She was active politically against Thieu. There was some trouble. But we never learned what happened."

The man turned to his wife with a thoughtful nod and it was to her that he spoke. "Mr. Chau may know where Madame Trung is."

"Yes." The woman nodded at her husband. "He may."

"Where is Mr. Chau?" David asked.

The man looked back to David. "He's across the street from the house where Thanh's family lived. The small villa behind the wall."

David started to turn but the man stopped him. "Wait. I'll phone him. I'll tell him you're coming so that he'll open the door." The man moved into the shadows and David felt fidgety. He pulled the bamboo shade slightly back from the window on the door and looked out into the street. There was no one there; David felt comfortable with his attention in the empty street. He was still conscious, though, of the phone call and he heard no sound. The phone clacked back into its cradle. David turned to find the man's face constricted now in fear.

"The phone's dead," the man said.

"I knew it," the wife said.

"They've got the list."

"What list?" David said.

The man shook his head slowly and then his hand rose and he made the sign of the cross. "The phone book," he said. "The list of private citizens who have phones. All of us are automatically the enemies, the exploiters. Our telephones will betray us."

"I must go now," David said.

"I hope you can help Madame Trung," the woman said.

David went out quickly. He crossed the street and saw a high, lichen-stained wall opposite Suong's house. He went through the gate and up to the door. He knocked loudly. He expected trouble in rousing Mr. Chau and his family. He thought to call out the man's name but the door opened abruptly, fully, and an old man stood there wearing a brimless mandarin hat and dressed in a robe with a golden dragon rising on the chest. The man had clearly prepared for this moment of defiance. He was ready to be arrested. David thought he saw a flicker of disappointment on the man's face at the sight of a Westerner.

"Mr. Chau?"

"Yes."

"My name is David Crowley. I need your help."

"My help?"

"I'm looking for Madame Trung."

"She's your friend." Chau did not speak this as a question. He said it in a flat voice, almost sadly.

"Yes," David said.

"I had some American friends. They could not do anything for me in the end."

"I'm Canadian."

Then Chau seemed to shake off the sadness. His voice surged. "But is there time? Hasn't the city fallen?"

"I . . . don't know for sure. I think I can still do something for Madame Trung. But I have to find her."

"I've been listening to the radio, but there is nothing yet. There's nothing at all."

"Do you know where she is?"

"Do you want to come in? I've suddenly forgotten where I am, it seems."

"It's all right, Mr. Chau. I just need to find Madame Trung. Time is very important now."

"Of course. If you can help her . . . yes. Well, I think I have the address of the place where she went." The man opened the door but David barely crossed the threshold before he stopped. He could not step inside this house. His focus was very narrow now. He waited as Mr. Chau went off. David tried to stand still, tried to control the rushing inside him. The mother was alive. She was in Saigon. He would find her this very morning.

Chau came back. He had an address that he explained to David; the place was down a little passageway off Pho Duc Chinh Street. Not far from the river.

"How far from Tu Do Street?" David asked.

"Some blocks. Not too far. Closer to the Central Market."

David took the address and thanked the man and he left the house, left Chau to prepare himself again to defy the new regime with his mandarin dress, to face his enemy with an ancient gold dragon rising on his chest.

Out in Tran Hung Dao there was no traffic. David began to walk east on the street, watching over his shoulder, waiting for a taxi to pass. But none did. He walked on in the thickening heat of morning and it wasn't until he reached the Metropole, his old hotel, that he found a xich-lo. The driver wanted payment with a greenback and David consented.

In Pho Duc Chinh there were people in the street. Girls in ao dais and boys in sport shirts were gathering on the sidewalk. David saw some of the red and gold flags scattered in the crowd. Two older men in the same civilian dress— plaid sport shirts, chinos, sneakers—were shouting polite orders to the small crowd, organizing them. Cadres out of hiding, David assumed. He passed the group and turned into the passageway.

It was a narrow walk between buildings, with tiny apartments opening into the passage. These windows were not shuttered and there were faces, waiting, some instinctive adult smiles, children with eyes widening, one woman in a doorway distracted by a fit of sneezing. David looked at the numbers over the doors and approached the one he wanted and the passage was very tight, he felt as if he were in a tunnel in a cave, the weight of eons of rock squeezing down on him. He moved and then he was at the door. He knocked.

The door opened and Suong's mother stood before him. David laid a hand on the doorjamb. Something steady. The woman was very familiar now. He'd seen her only a few times and always in the background, in a passing room, lingering in the hallway, though he'd met her once, he'd returned her bow once, just such a bow as she now performed, as if she remembered him too, but without any surprise that he should be here years later.

"Do you know who I am?" he said.

She did not answer instantly; she looked at him carefully for a moment and then said, "Of course."

Madame Trung opened the door and he stepped inside. His eyes leaped around the room, expecting now to see his son, but he was wrong. The room was stark: a large straw rug, a couch, a chair, a hot plate against one wall, a few bowls stacked nearby; against the opposite wall was a shrine. Here was the picture of Suong's father, the picture David remembered. The man's face was long-jawed, almost Western; Suong had her father's face, not her mother's; this woman who was motioning for him to sit was from the world of golden dragons, mandarin robes, her face was round, finely etched, the delight of emperors, not businessmen.

David sat. His eyes jumped from object to object in the room. A rug, a hot plate, a shrine, a chair. Nothing of a child. There was a doorway into a back room that seemed, from this angle, utterly bare. He could see only a part of this other room, but there was nothing in it but the blank floor and wall. Still, the grandmother was here. She would know the answer to the most critical questions. Questions, as he looked back to her, that he was suddenly afraid to ask. He almost rose. He wanted to rise, to walk out the door, run down the passageway, out into the street, escape now, go back to his son, to David Junior, the child that he'd been given with certainty. But there were no Americans in this country now. This was no longer South Vietnam. He was in another country. The wench was dead, he thought. He was guilty of fornication and this was another country.

Madame Trung said nothing. She waited, watching him.

"Do you really remember me?" David said.

"I do."

David wanted to press her, cross-examine her; he almost demanded that she tell him his name, but he held back.

"Where is Suong?" he asked, the question willing itself from him, surprising him a little. He didn't want to know.

Madame Trung's face did not change. She was as implacable as a Buddha. Her voice, though, was softly sad. "She is in prison."

"Where?"

"In Saigon."

"Who put her there?"

"Thieu."

"When?"

"Almost a year ago."

"Have you heard anything about her?" David was acutely conscious of the questions he was failing to ask. He found that he was interested in Suong's fate, distressed certainly that she'd been imprisoned; the details of all this were important. But the questions that wanted to come out first were the ones about the boy.

"I've heard nothing," Madame Trung said.

"What did she do?" he said.

"She worked against him."

"How?"

"I don't know."

This answer stopped David. It suggested Madame

Trung's insularity, her disconnection from Suong. The old woman was on her own. His attention slid from her, tumbled around the room again. There was nothing here. The rug, the hot plate, the shrine. A small shape at the base of a wall, a shape like a pear, though the outline was too symmetrical, too perfect for a pear. But Madame Trung *knows* about the boy, he thought. She knows. She sat waiting. David looked at her. Her gaze was steady. Why didn't she ask why he was here? Did that confirm that she knew him? Or belie it?

"Do you really know who I am?" David asked.

"Of course I know."

David grew angry at the woman's reserve. "Who am I, then? Tell me."

Madame Trung's brow wrinkled. David was sorry for his sharpness and now he recognized the real impetus for his frustration. He'd held all this in for too long. As soon as he realized that, other words rushed out of him. "There was a child. Suong had a son. I'm the father. I'm David Fleming."

Madame Trung's face changed in some subtle way that struck David without his being able to identify what the change was. There was a very slight pause and then she said, "I know who you are, Captain Fleming. I know you are the father of my grandson." The voice was as small and as steady as it had been from the first. The sense of her independence was very strong. This small, hard nut of a voice had nothing but itself to reveal. But that was unlike the Vietnamese; the old people were never alone.

David looked away from her. His eyes fell once more on the object, pear-shaped, across the room. It was the only thing intrusive in this plain room, the object small enough that it had escaped his notice for a time. Then he knew what it was: a top.

"Why did you come here?" Madame Trung said.

David looked at her. He looked at the top. A child's toy. He looked at the doorway to the other room. A child was standing there. A boy. As soon as David saw him, the boy backed away, disappeared. David jumped up, gaping at the now empty doorway. What had he seen? A boy. About four years old. But the face was all wrong.

"Yes, Captain," Madame Trung said. "That's your son."

David cocked his head. He felt he was truly mad. The child he'd seen was not his son. The face was surely not the face of his son. David crossed the room, his legs straining to hold him up. He paused at the doorway. He stepped in and turned and on a straw mat, crouching there in the flat-footed Vietnamese way, was the child. At David's glance the boy scooted farther away, pressed against the wall, his face turned a bit; he looked at David from the corner of his eye, as if protecting himself by not exposing his full face to the intruder. The face. It was very round, evenly sallowed with the Orient; the nose was snubbed and wide-nostriled; the eyes showed their lids when open, almost Western eyes, but no more so than Suong's own eyes. There was nothing of David in this face at all. Nothing. The boy tried to compress himself under David's gaze; he pulled his arms tight against himself. He was large, this boy. His body was certainly larger and thicker than a typical Vietnamese four-year-old, but that could be the vagaries of early growth or the effects of someone else's genes. This stature could be from David, but it was a vague link on its own, inconclusive, meaningless. The face was utterly different and the child was frightened of him, shrinking against the wall, and David could not shape a thought, could not speak a word. His only feeling was the urge to escape, to run. He was moving now. He was backing out of the inner room, he moved across the floor, past the rising Madame Trung, out the door, into the passageway, into the street full of strangers speaking in a strange tongue.

He walked, without letting himself think, without letting himself see, he walked. First to the river, then away from the river, then up Le Loi and there were crowds along the sidewalk, expectant crowds, tanks rolled by, troop trucks, the crowds cheered. David turned off Le Loi and sat in a doorway and he wondered if Madame Trung had lied. David remembered her little pause when he asked her if she knew him. Even worse: he'd been the first to mention his connection to Suong, to the child. "Damn," he said aloud. He punched his fist into his palm. People slowed as they passed him, women in ao dais, faces looked at him where he sat in the doorway which was full of the ammoniac smell of old piss. "Damn," he said again. He could never know the truth now. He'd told the old woman that he was the father and there'd been another pause—that subtle change in her face—and at that moment she could have decided to lie. She knew the boy was in the next room; she had the boy; she saw someone who might help the boy; she lied for the boy's sake. David leaned his head against the cool concrete of the doorway. It was a lie. There was no son. But why should that bother him? If the boy wasn't his, then nothing existed to keep him here. He should feel relieved. But he didn't. Was it the possibility that she was telling the truth? It registered now that she'd called him *Captain* Fleming. So it was not a lie that she remembered him. After more than four years why should she remember him if there weren't some significance given to him during that time? Otherwise he would have been in her eyes a very brief, very casual suitor for her daughter—there surely had been many others—and she would have never remembered a detail like his rank. But she'd called him Captain Fleming.

"It's all right," a voice said.

"What?" David looked up into the face of a Vietnamese man. A round, dusky foreign face.

"It's all right," the man repeated in flawless English. "They're not hurting anyone caught behind. Or anyone else."

David gaped—stupidly, he realized—and the face disappeared. David looked about him. He was sitting in a doorway like a street beggar. He knew his face must be speaking of his turmoil, a street beggar's face, a face of sadness. Still, he did not move at once. His mind tried to keep its distance, but it slid back into the reasoning of all this. This persistent ravishment: it was from the possibility that Madame Trung had not lied. The boy's body was husky. Like David's own. Like David's American son. It was still possibly true that this child was his. But that was academic. The fact was that this possibility had no emotional truth. The child had been terrified of David. David had felt no trace of a connection to the child. There was nothing. Nothing at all between them. The biology of it was a lie, a shallow lie.

David forced himself to stand. He heard the crowd on Le Loi cheering and he was drawn to the noise. He moved toward it. He sought this mindless, alien noise just as he'd once sought the needle-pricked silence of the Cascades.

There were soldiers among the crowd, soldiers of the North. They were smiling, but their rifles were held across their chests. The green pith helmets looked too big on their heads, looked, in their hard, down-turned brim and central knob, too casual, too much like ceremonial gear, looked colonial even. The vehicles with the red and gold flags flowed past to cheering. David walked on up Le Loi, skirting the crowd, letting the noise fill his head.

He passed the circular fountain at Nguyen Hue and ahead was the band-shell National Assembly Building. The blockades were gone. The people of Saigon were flowing through the streets, across the grassy square where the Vietnamese Unknown Soldier's monument lay in rubble. The people seemed giddy in relief that they weren't being shot.

At Tu Do David began to turn south to go back to his hotel, but a loudspeaker voice told the people to make a space please before the Assembly building, to line up in an orderly way please so that they could see the new Saigon– Gia Dinh Military Management Committee that would soon be arriving.

David crossed the street, cutting diagonally in front of the Caravelle Hotel, and he was in the middle of Vietnamese bodies that shifted and eddied and he pushed on forward and found himself against a rope that was rising waist-high. With this rope as a clear boundary, the Vietnamese bodies crowded around and spread out down to the street; but David was at the front of the crowd, near the steps of the Assembly building, within arm's reach of the path that the new leaders would follow from the street as they arrived.

He looked at a similar packing of people on the opposite side of the path. Every twenty feet, standing before the crowd but outside the rope, were soldiers, the ammo clips of their AK47s cutting a swooping curve against their chests. But David was still surprised at the laxity in security. The North seemed determined—even at this risk—to let the people of Saigon join the happy proletariat.

Then the jeeps began to arrive and the officials, in green slacks and shirts, most of them bareheaded, most of them wearing rubber sandals, came through the pathway and up the stairs. Voices carried along their identifications as they approached. David did not listen to most of the names; he looked at the passing faces with an ironic detachment. These men were very casual, as bland as barbers. "Huyen Tan Phat." The name came from down the line and the title of president of the Provisional Revolutionary Government. He'd been one of the biggest targets for David's operations. The leader of the PRG. The man who followed the name had a striking face, dark eyebrows, looking rather like Chou En-lai. More officials and then Tran Van Tra, the head of the Military Management Committee, a thin man with glasses, a little bookish-looking but with a smooth smile. He nodded at the smattering of applause.

David realized he'd been standing here too long; the distraction had faded with the repetition of faces and he was beginning to think of the boy again. Tra had not built the arrivals to his own climactic entry. Like a good Communist ideologue, he allowed others to follow him, lesser officials, and David began to think of how to wedge his way out of this crowd. But as he was about to turn, a name was spoken down the line. He turned back almost calmly, the name not quite consciously registering, but holding him already. The title of this man was spoken: Director of Security for Saigon– Gia Dinh. And then the name again. Pham Van Tuyen.

David looked down the pathway and he saw Tuyen approaching. The man's head was angled slightly toward the opposite crowd, but David saw the square jaw, the sharp-cut eyes, even the mole on his cheek. It was Tuyen. And the man's face was turning now as he approached, turning slowly, a faint smile on the face; the eyes turned and David was very still inside, very still as the eyes moved; as this face approached, David could anticipate the timing. Tuyen's gaze fell on the crowd just a few yards before passing David and the eyes tracked along. David waited and then Tuyen was opposite him and for a brief moment the two men looked at each other, each face still; David did not see any sign of recognition in Tuyen but the moment was gone instantly and David knew that his own face, too, had been blank. Tuyen was up the steps of the Assembly building now, not looking back. He was through the doors and gone.

David lay on his bed on this third night in Saigon and the welter of his thoughts filled the room, filled the silence beyond the room. But there was so much inside him that for a long time he could focus on nothing. The paddle fan moved in the dark and he was sweating and faces swirled in him, riding the soft spirals of air. Jennifer and David Junior and the boy—he still did not know the child's name—the boy who might not even be his son, who was as much a stranger as the other faces crowding into this room—Phat of the PRG and the xich-lo driver from the airport and the man who tried to console David in the doorway and the woman weeping against the guard rail on the bridge over the Kinh Te and the servant with the scar and Suong, Suong imprisoned, and Madame Trung, her face very still, inscrutable—lying to him or not lying, he could not even say—and he could not understand why all these Vietnamese faces were moving in him when he came here to find only one, only the boy. But in the end the boy was like all these others. Perhaps that was why they were cluttered together, the ones who should be part of him and the ones who were strangers. None of them truly engaged him. None of them moved him. Not even his son. He wanted only to go away. He wanted to go and he realized he had the rationale: the boy in fact might not be his son. Indeed, it sometimes seemed truly clear that he wasn't. The boy had Vietnamese parents and he bore only the distant image of the French that was passed through his mother. Trung had lied. For obvious reasons and through the opportunity stupidly given her by David himself. All David had to do now was to accept this and he could go. He could turn his mind to leaving the country and that would be the end of this madness. This time there'd be no extraordinary rescue, nothing like a confrontation by a jungle stream, or a commandeered helicopter. Had Tuyen recognized him today? And what did David feel about Tuyen? Tuyen's was a Vietnamese face that had not entered the swirl in his mind, that had watched from a distance, detached. David had felt a clear sense of recognition when he'd seen Tuyen, a clear link to their one meeting. But he could not concentrate on Tuyen. The others kept crowding David, jostling him, all these strangers; in spite of his alienation from them, they kept pawing at him.

There was a knock at the door. David leaped up. The first thing in his mind was Tuyen's title. It had been passed along from down the line today just moments before his name registered. He was Director of Security for Saigon–Gia Dinh. Now he'd sent for David. That was David's first thought. He crossed to the door and he opened it and a Vietnamese man in a white waiter's coat was standing there. The man was old, his cheeks sunken from bad teeth. David had seen him once behind the hotel bar and again, briefly, yesterday at the front desk.

"What is it?" David said in Vietnamese.

"Mr. Crowley, you went out today?"

"Yes."

"I wanted to know if La Pagode Restaurant is still open for business."

David felt relieved. He observed this reaction in himself, thinking it a little odd. He would have expected himself to curse the CIA for showing up now. But he didn't. He was relieved to have a duty to carry out. Something clear and external that did not require him to create his own personal connections with others. The room was suddenly empty. The faces were gone. There was only David and this link to Trask and soon a job to accomplish. "Come in," David said.

The old man stepped inside quickly and closed the door and took David to the chairs by the balcony. They sat.

"Mr. Crowley," the man said, "you are aware that there no longer is a Republic of South Vietnam."

"Of course."

"With your identity as a Canadian you will have a freedom for a time. Freedom to move around. Make certain—"

"What is it they want?"

"There were several of your colleagues who were operating in Saigon under a cover. They posed as US Army deserters, living in the alleys."

"Not bad." David smiled at Trask's little game. David's cover ID was set up specifically to help these agents out. "Not bad," he said, thinking about how they would operate. They would be radical in politics, vehemently anti-American; they would win the interest and confidence of the local VC cadre. Then David thought of Clifford Wilkes. Maybe Cliff had gone off to be one of Trask's boys. The CIA would not think that David had a need-to-know in that matter and so it had seemed to him, as it did to the world, as if it were a real desertion. And that had just made things hotter for David at the trial. He wondered if Trask's reason for coming to him in Baltimore had been tinged with guilt over the phony desertion being used by the prosecution. "Who am I supposed to find?" he said.

The old man told David a name—Carl Thornman—and

explained an address in an alley in District Three, near the Xa Loi Shrine. "Find this man," he said. "See what he needs. He may also have information for you."

"What then?"

"I'll be here tomorrow night. We'll talk again."

"All right."

The old man rose. "Good night, Mr. Crowley."

"One other thing," David said.

"Yes?"

"When I want to get out of here . . . I take it you can arrange something."

"I have no instructions on that."

David jumped up. "You tell your contact to let them know back across the pond that I may need some help."

"I'll ask them. I'll see you tomorrow night," he said. "No later than nine."

The old man went out the door and David was alone again. The old man was well trained. He had an arrogance of reticence about him that reminded David of Trask. But that was all right. David could at least focus his mind now. An alley address, an agent to contact, Trask running the show. That was all right. There was no other demand on him. Just his duty.

When David went out the next morning, he heard a scream of jets overhead. He looked up and in the slice of sky over Tu Do three jets went by in tight formation. He recognized the high tails of Russian-built MIGs. They stopped him with a chill. The CIA had no power here anymore. Three jets told him that. Saigon women in ao dais cheering the arrival of that string of bland little men yesterday told him that. Tuyen told him that. David tried to walk, but his thoughts stopped him. Tuyen was in charge of security. David was here on a CIA passport. Phony name. Phony nationality. On paper Tuyen would be his enemy. And the man seemed not even to recognize him. David walked on and slowed to another stop. The Americans were gone. Trask was sitting in an office in Virginia. The Canadians were never really here and whatever had been their diplomatic presence, they would have left when the government they recognized fell. David had been a Canadian to get into Vietnam; it would not help him to get out.

He thought to turn around, return to the hotel. But that wouldn't help him either. And there were the faces in his room. He walked on. He found a taxi easily this morning. Business again as usual. He went to the address in District Three, stepping out of the cab at the mouth of the alley. The taxi sped away and David looked around. He'd not been followed. There were no troops in the street. There were tamarind trees on the thoroughfare, but the alley was pinched by tall, tropic-blasted plaster buildings, layered with long balconies, fluttering with laundry, clucking with chickens, stinking of fish oil and garbage, scattered with more faces, children running, and old women, red-mouthed from betel nuts, washing in basins or cooking, men shrinking in doorways; the women were bold still, aggressively casual; the men seemed shy, almost coy.

David walked down the alley, puddled with oily rainwater and slippery with old fruit skins, vegetable parings, chicken gristle. David counted the buildings on the right and entered a staircase. He went up three flights—the stairwell was clean, only the streets were dirty—and he walked down a long, communal balcony, past the nods of the women, the eddies of children, clutter of voices, dishes, flapping clothes, the twang—almost Appalachian—of some ancient Vietnamese instrument coming from a PX cassette player sitting in a doorway. As David counted the apartments, he wondered at this American whom he sought. The man had made a life here; a double life, but still he lived here, slept here, among these sounds, with nowhere to escape.

David found the apartment. There was a blue tile on the doorstep, the final little mark of identification, and he knocked at the open doorway. A young woman appeared. She was very pretty, Vietnamese but with a thin nose and a long swooping curl to her black hair. David said, in Vietnamese, "I'm looking for Carl Thornman."

Tears instantly came to the woman's eyes and began to roll down her cheeks. She did not brush them away but said, "He's gone."

"Where?

"I don't know."

"I'm a friend. I want to help."

"Then give him back to me."

"Someone took him?"

"Your country took him . . . maybe yours. Maybe some other country. Maybe North Vietnam took him. He left. That's all. And there was no promise to me."

"When did he leave?"

"Two nights ago. He said he had business up-country, but I know what that means."

"What?"

The woman moved her head slightly, not understanding his question. The tears still flowed freely, but she did not lift her hand, did not acknowledge them.

David said, "*What* does it mean, his going up-country?"

"It means Xa is the unhappiest girl in Saigon. I know this time he's never coming back. I know things have changed in Vietnam forever."

David felt uneasy. He felt he was expected to do something, say something, not for Trask but for this woman, Xa, who still refused to wipe the tears from her face. David heard himself say, "Did Carl leave any message behind?" It was not what he wanted to say, but there were no other words in him, only these.

"No," Xa said, "there were no promises to me."

"Anyone else?"

"For . . ." David could not bear Xa's tears any longer, her stricken face. But he thought of one more possibility. His little mission here still tugged at him. "Did Carl leave any of his things behind?"

"A radio. A few clothes."

"Anything else?"

"I don't know. He took most of his things in a duffel bag. I knew he wouldn't be back."

"Any papers? Did he leave any papers?"

"Maybe. There were a few things, maybe." Xa moved back into the apartment. David stepped in. The room was tiny and on a mat a child was sleeping, a child with his black Vietnamese hair blended into dark brown, with his skin almost pale, his chin cleft, a little boy whose eyes fluttered open now. David drew back.

The boy made a sound, seeing David, the eyes were opening and Xa was there, crouching beside the boy, picking him up. Carl Thornman's son. The child's eyes were wide open and they were very pale, the eyes were not brown but pale, Xa and the boy were standing in the light from the window and the eyes were almost blue, the face of this man Thornman, the face of Thornman's son.

David backed out of the apartment. He turned and rushed along the balcony, down the stairs, cursing this man he did not know, cursing him in anger for leaving his son behind; cursing him, too, in envy, that his son should have his face.

He still felt the anger, the impulse to flee, when he emerged from the alley. He stopped then and tried to calm himself and think what to do. The clear choice was to go back to Trung and the boy. At once some other voice in him cried: this isn't clear because it's right, this is just a reflex of your anger at Thornman. A great reluctance seized David, but he fought it; he felt like a hypocrite in his anger at Thornman, even though his own case was different, obviously different, the child might not even be his own.

He walked down the street to the intersection. On the

opposite corner was a trio of North Vietnamese soldiers, seemingly idle, but armed, one of them chatting with a man sitting on a Honda, another of them glancing across at David but not moving. David forced a smile and he nodded at the soldier. The soldier smiled back, broadly, and waved. A cab approached and David hailed it and he got in and under the continued gaze of the soldier, he gave the address of the passageway where Trung and the boy lived.

When Madame Trung answered his knock, she showed no surprise, no anger either, she simply opened the door to him and he stepped in. The boy was squatting beside the hot plate with a bowl in his hand, shoveling rice into his mouth with a pair of chopsticks. He looked at David and turned his body away. But he did not stop eating. David watched the child's flat, dark profile, the chopsticks drawn so close that they seemed to be a part of the face, moving like insect mandibles. David shivered. It was a mistake for him to come here again. The boy was no longer terrified of David, but this vaguely hostile indifference, the intense focus on the food, was worse. He was no longer a terrified child to David, but an animal, a small, scavenging alley animal. David turned to Trung. She was watching him. He said, "Have you said anything to him about me?"

"No."

"He's not as frightened."

"I told him that much."

"What did you say?"

"I said if the American man returns, you should not be frightened of him. He won't hurt you."

"Is that all?"

"I said no more than that."

"Nothing about . . ." David could not speak it. He sensed the child listening.

"Nothing," Madame Trung said.

David looked at the boy. He stopped eating briefly and shot David a quick, sideways glance. David turned back to Trung. "Is he . . . normal? Is his mind . . . ?"

"Of course he's normal. He's just not used to being around a man. It's very sad. Our family was once very large and close. No longer. We are not really Vietnamese any longer."

"There's just you?"

"For this child, yes. There are others in the family, but they've disappeared or been scattered away. I worry for your child. I'm an old woman. When I die, I don't know what will happen to him."

"You say he's my child."

"You knew that yourself."

"No. Not for certain."

"He is your son."

"How do you know? When were you told I'm the father?"

"Soon after Suong learned she was pregnant."

"What did she say?"

"She said that you and she were lovers."

"When? What did she say exactly?"

"Why do you need me to answer these questions?"

"Because you could be lying to me. You could be trying to help your grandchild by telling me these things so that I'd help him."

With her same even calmness, Madame Trung said, "I did not summon you, Captain Fleming. You suddenly showed up here, even after our country had fallen. What is it you want with me? Did you come for a Vietnamese child or did you not?"

"Were you just trying to give me what you thought I wanted?"

Madame Trung said nothing but her eyes held steadily on him.

David tried to wait her out, force her to speak, but he couldn't; the alternative insisted on finding words. "Or did you tell me the truth?" He regretted this at once.

"I told you the truth."

"I put those words into your mouth just now."

"Do you think I couldn't have invented those words for myself if I'd wished?"

David was sweating. Was she toying with him? But why? Couldn't he just believe her? "The boy does not look like me," he said.

"He is your son."

"Didn't you hear me?"

"You underestimate the Vietnamese genes, Captain Fleming. He looks like his Vietnamese ancestors. You have to accept that."

"I saw a child today . . . I've seen many children . . . There'd be something clear in the face to tell me . . . Surely there'd be. I can't believe you, Madame Trung. Suong had other lovers. She and I came together too easily."

"Please, Captain Fleming. If you think I am lying, then just go. I didn't ask you to come here."

"You say you don't know what will happen to him when you die. What about Suong?"

"She's in prison."

"Thieu's prison. His prisons will be flung open now."

"She's been gone for a very long time. She may no longer be alive."

"Do you know that? Have you heard something?"

Madame Trung's eyes finally let go their hold on him. Their gaze slowly moved out the window. "I've heard what happens in there. A year is too long. For a beautiful woman especially."

"Where is the prison?"

She looked back to him with the same slow movement. "The old Vietnamese-French Cultural Society building on Hong Thap Tu."

"The Communists will let her out."

She smiled faintly, a patronizing smile. For this bland assertion. He briefly felt that he deserved it. But then he insisted on the hope to himself again: she's alive; she will return to her child; the child will be all right. He looked over to the boy. He was putting his bowl down. David said, "What's his name?"

"Ask him."

He looked at Trung.

"Go on," she said.

David struggled with the suspension that held him. Just as he was caught now in Saigon, he was caught where he stood. He could not go to the boy; he could not leave. Both Trung and the child were watching him now, the child with his full face toward him.

David moved. He took a step toward the boy, who waited without stirring, then another step, and another, and he stopped before him. The boy held his position, did not even turn his body away this time. He lifted his eyes and David felt a little twist of pleasure that the child had not yielded, that he had overcome his fear of this tall stranger, this man who bore so little resemblance to anyone he could recognize as his own.

David said, "What's your name?"

The boy glanced across the room, toward Trung, then looked back up at David. "Khai," he said, in a bent little sliver of a voice, broken off from the tin gong of all the Vietnamese children, their metallic twanging voices from all the Saigon streets David had been in.

Now the boy holding his ground seemed alien to David, this very act that had given him a brief pleasure seemed alien; the child seemed to be watching David from a place so distant that there could never be any threat. The child's round face was upturned, the eyes were as still as Trung's. The boy waited and David had nothing more to say.

"Tell him," Trung said.

This challenge made David turn, moved him across the room, out the door. He was leaving the child for a second time. Or is this the third time? he demanded of himself. Did he first leave the child in Suong's womb? He had no answer for that. And so as David went down the stairs, he thought of Suong imprisoned in this city. She might tell him the truth, and if not, or if the truth could not touch him, at least he'd try to give the mother back to the boy. Maybe that would let David go.

Out on Pho Duc Chinh there was a patrol of three soldiers on foot, the pith helmets bobbing this way; David turned and walked in the opposite direction, toward the river. There were more soldiers visible in Saigon now. David suspected that the mood would begin to change in the city. All the charm may have been a strategy. Guerrilla tactics. He walked a little faster, waiting to be hailed. But he reached Chuong Duong. The river was before him and a row of taxis.

He entered the first cab and gave the driver an intersection of Hong Thap Tu near the prison. The cab started and they turned up a street and there was another little patrol. Yes. There were more soldiers now. David stopped watching. He leaned his head back against the seat. Finding Suong would be enough, he thought, to free him. Then he could go home. If he could just locate her, make sure she was all right. An enemy of Thieu would be seen as no enemy of North Vietnam.

David got out of the cab and the street was deep in tamarind shade. There were high walls, villas, but the rich were gone or hiding. David walked up the street and one of the walls ahead had barbed wire on the top, a double-lane iron door leading into large grounds. He approached and even the VIET-PHAP nameplate was still on the wall. Two North Vietnamese soldiers guarded the gate. David stopped a few yards from them. He had no clear plan, beyond direct inquiry. He felt a crawling on his skin: it was madness to force the new government to notice him. He could still turn around and walk away. But whoever the boy was, he deserved an inquiry about his mother. And David had to do something to complete all this in his own mind. The expiation was worth the risk.

David approached the soldiers who were already watching him. He smiled. They smiled. He felt Vietnamese words shaping in his mouth but he blocked them. He was Canadian. He said, in English, "I want to ask . . ."

The soldiers wagged their heads at once and said they couldn't understand him. David knew a little French and he asked if they spoke that language. One of them said yes, a little, and David explained he was inquiring after a woman who was put in this prison by Nguyen Van Thieu.

"May I see your passport?" the soldier replied.

David pulled the passport from his pocket. The man took it and looked at it and then pardoned himself and stepped inside the gate to a telephone. David waited, keeping his hands still, his face calm. The remaining guard smiled and nodded each time David glanced at him. The guard with David's passport was talking on the phone, but David could not hear any of the words. Finally the man hung up. He looked into the grounds of the prison and David followed the man's gaze, up the driveway, to the side of the large, rambling house, and a jeep emerged, moving this way. There were two soldiers in the jeep and David's throat, his chest, clenched; he thought to run. But the gate was opening, the jeep approached, he didn't have his passport, there were long stretches of street on either side, nowhere to run, and he stood very still as the jeep came up. The first guard handed David's passport to the driver and the other man in the jeep said in English, "Please to come with us."

They brought David to City Hall, where Morello's office had been, where David had reported on his first day in his Saigon assignment. There was a North Vietnamese flag draped from the front balcony and David tried to calm his fears. He knew these fears themselves—the outward effect of them—would betray him faster than anything else. But even though he told himself it was natural for this building to be used by the new government in an official way, it still seemed an unnerving coincidence, it seemed as if they knew every-

thing about him already, they were returning him to the
scene of his crimes against the North; or if they didn't know,
then at least the building would cry out his name as soon as
he entered.

They drove the jeep into the courtyard behind the building and took him in through the back door. The soldiers
were courteous; they smiled and they didn't touch him; but
they walked on either side and again David thought—knowing it was foolish—of running. They passed into the main
hall. The front doors were before him and he could see
down Nguyen Hue, along a skimpy park to the circular fountain at Le Loi, and beyond, to the river far down at the end
of the street. The river called him to run, but he did not. He
knew it was crazy—dangerous, even—to think like this. He
lowered his eyes to the floor where the light from the doors
glinted gray on swirls of dust and scuffs.

They went up the broad stairway, its banisters and new-
els darkly ornate, like the walls, enameled in brown and
gold. The stairs doubled back toward the front of the building and opened onto a vast ballroom with the balcony that
overlooked the street. Beneath fading French cherubs in the
domed ceiling, shirt-sleeved officials worked with soldiers
at unfolding tables and setting them up in a row. They were
preparing, it seemed, for some large-scale registration. This
made David feel a little easier. And then it even seemed
logical to have no serious concern. There was no way for
this government suddenly emerging from the jungles and
alleys to be able to disprove his identity as a Canadian national.

He was guided into an antechamber off the ballroom.
Behind a desk was a middle-aged Vietnamese man perhaps
a head shorter than Jennifer and with what seemed to be, in
its uneven bristliness, a self-inflicted crew cut. He rose with
only a quick, neutral glance at David and he took the passport and nodded the two soldiers out of the room. The door
clicked shut. A Panasonic fan slowly scanned the room from
the desk top. The man finally looked squarely at David and

then, in formal coordination, he smiled and offered to shake David's hand.

The handshake surprised David in its limp passivity. This was not the spirit of the revolution, surely. David sat down and he felt confident now. This was routine.

The man spoke in very slow English. "Mr. Crowley, what is your language?"

"English."

"Do you speak more language?"

"A little French." David held up his thumb and forefinger indicating a very small amount.

The man nodded. "Canada citizen?"

"Yes."

The man paused and he stared at the open passport, lifting his eyes once, as if to verify that the face in the photo was the same as the face in the chair. But David had the impression—he could not say how—that the man was waiting for something. Then the door clicked and opened, the echoes of the ballroom entered, a press of air; David turned to look and in the doorway stood Tuyen.

As on the morning he'd seen Tuyen entering the Assembly building, the man's eyes fixed on David without apparent recognition. David realized the same look was on his own face, and indeed the first rush he felt at seeing Tuyen was an oddly dispassionate one. His curiosity was stirred, but nothing more. Then David grew fearful. This was the one man in the new government who could know that David was lying.

The first man said in Vietnamese: "He speaks only English very well." Tuyen looked at the speaker. The man continued, "I'll get an interpreter."

Tuyen turned back to David and his face showed perhaps a brief trace of puzzlement. Perhaps. Was he remembering David's fluent Vietnamese from the stream on Con Son? David watched closely but he could not be sure. Tuyen said, "Good. Go on and get one."

The other man rose, moved past Tuyen, and out the

door. Tuyen crossed to the desk. The door remained open. Shadows flashed there, tables scraped, there were voices. Tuyen picked up the passport and looked at it. He glanced briefly at David. There was nothing in his face, nothing to tell David what he was thinking. Nothing to tell David whether he dared to speak. This was the security director for Saigon. One of his clearest enemies would be a US CIA operative in Vietnam with a false identity. Perhaps he did not even remember David, did not recognize him. Maybe he'd been too groggy from his torture and from his escape to have formed a clear memory of David. Or else he was trying to decide on his own response, trying, himself, to figure out what to feel, what to do. And of course he would do this without letting any of it show. That would be the Tuyen David had come to know so well, even from the first, even from his few words scrawled on the wall of his cell.

But David wanted desperately to speak to him. Tuyen was turning the pages of the passport, looking now at the International Peace-Workers Congress ID, and David wanted to say: Tuyen, it's me; it's me and we can talk now; you will know what's in my mind.

But a man entered the room. Tuyen looked up at him and said, "Good. I need you to translate for me. He speaks only English." At this, Tuyen glanced at David, but it was not clear what the look meant. It could have been a simple referential glance, or it could have meant: I know who you are but we must go through this charade.

David knew that whatever Tuyen's intent might be, he himself had to stay with the cover story. He turned to the interpreter as if to wait for the translation of what Tuyen had just said. The interpreter was young and wearing civilian clothes—a plaid shirt and jeans. Behind him was the short man, the official who'd first talked to David. The tiny room was crowded. David crossed his legs. He laid his hands on his lap and concentrated on keeping them still. The desk fan scanned to him, then away.

"Why are you still in Saigon?" Tuyen asked in Vietnamese. The interpreter, whom David still watched, spoke the words in English, though instead of Saigon he said Ho Chi Minh City with a brief nod at Tuyen.

David looked at Tuyen. The man had a faint smile on his face. David knew it was a smile of irony, an aloof smile at this young man's zeal. David felt absolutely certain he understood the smile. This was Tuyen, after all. David did not take his eyes from him and he said, "My country has never been at war with yours. I didn't think it necessary to run."

While the young man translated, Tuyen realized that David was watching him and he met his gaze, evenly, frankly, still without recognition, without warmth—David did not expect these things—but the two men did not relinquish this connection; watching each other, they waited for the interpreter to do his job.

Tuyen said, "That's right. You're Canadian, aren't you."

The translator spoke in English and David listened instead to the echo of Tuyen's Vietnamese words. Was there a tone of irony, as there'd been with the faint smile? David strained to hear it, but he could not. Tuyen's face did not flicker. There was no smile.

"Yes. I'm Canadian."

The translator's voice was only a buzz to David now, a little pause to weigh tones and words.

"What are you doing here?" Tuyen said. Any suspicion was masked. But there was no warmth. This was Tuyen, after all. He was detached.

"You have my identification card with my passport. I'm a member of the International Peace-Workers Congress. Perhaps you've heard of it?" David had trouble getting these words out, surprising trouble. The kind of trouble he'd anticipated having on the witness stand. He tried to see this interrogation as part of Trask's games. This should be like old times, the times of operation by a military intelligence agent in command of whatever words served his purpose. But he could not play the role: he was too much present in this room.

"Is this an organization that I should know?" Tuyen said.

David felt motiveless again. He could not make sense of his own actions again. Why was he still in Vietnam? "It's a Communist youth group," he said—lamely, he knew. How could he lie to Tuyen? Tuyen knew the truth. Surely he knew the truth.

Tuyen said, "I'm afraid we're not yet a progressive Communist country. These organizations are a bit of a luxury here." Was he speaking with some complex irony? Was David supposed to understand?

David could not respond, but Tuyen did not let him dangle. As soon as the interpreter finished the previous statement, Tuyen spoke again. "What is your purpose in Vietnam, Mr. Crowley?"

David heard no irony in the use of the name. None. Suddenly he had the impression that Tuyen was taking him at his word. David Crowley. Tuyen now invited another lie. This should be simple. This was the same kind of lie, an operational lie, that he'd always worked with. But the words came hard. "I'm in Vietnam to try and track down American Army deserters." It wasn't convincing, what he was saying. David wanted to survive. He wanted to get out of this place. Tuyen didn't know him and David couldn't tell him the truth, not in front of these two strangers; Tuyen could do nothing but perform his revolutionary duty.

"Deserters?" Tuyen said.

"Yes." David cleared his throat, angled his face slightly to the sweep of the fan. The sweat on his face turned chill. "These deserters have awakened to the . . . reality of their . . . imperialist government." David's voice had grown very small in his head, though he knew he was speaking loudly. Too loudly even. "My organization wants to offer them a way back to the West that will not . . . subject them . . ." David broke off. He could say no more. Tuyen's face was the same as it was. Yes. Even as David lied, the face stayed the same. If Tuyen did not have a special feeling for David —if he did not know the truth about David's connection to him—then the face would be changing before David's obvious lies. But it was the same—cool, distant, alert. He must know.

Tuyen said, "And the prison on Hong Thap Tu? What took you there?"

David realized he'd be able to answer this question with something close to the truth. He let out a breath—he'd been holding more air inside him than he'd realized—he heard himself sigh, as if in great emotion. He lowered his eyes briefly. "I was in love with a Vietnamese woman." David's voice broke. "She hated President Thieu. She worked against him and she was thrown into that prison a year ago. I went to find her."

The interpreter did not translate immediately. David looked up at him and the young man's eyes were wide in pity. At David's glance, he turned sharply away, translated the statement.

David looked at Tuyen, whose eyes had not left him. Tuyen lifted his head slightly—a vague gesture—and he said, "What is her name?"

David did not even try to interpret the gesture. He waited for the words in English and said, "Nguyen Thi Tuyet Suong."

"She went into the prison a year ago?" Tuyen's voice was flat.

The interpreter's translation was spoken warmly, solicitously. David squeezed his mind shut. He could not accept the pity of the stranger and the indifference of Tuyen. "Yes," he answered. "A year ago."

Tuyen picked up David's passport and ID card and handed them to him. "We'll try to find an answer for you."

David took the documents, rose to his feet. He grew shaky inside. Not from fear, or the release from fear, but from distress at leaving Tuyen without speaking of their bond.

He might never see the man again. This was madness, to meet like this and talk as if they were strangers. But the interpreter and the other official stepped to Tuyen's side. There would be no private word. And Tuyen showed no sign of concern about this. He had the power to clear the room but he did not do it. David was indeed a stranger to him.

Tuyen said, "Before you leave, you will register outside, please. We'll give you identification papers that you must keep with you at all times."

As the interpreter translated, David knew that his last moments with Tuyen were passing. He groped for words, something to delay his departure, and finally there was silence and he knew he was dismissed. Then David said to Tuyen, "I saw you yesterday when you entered the Assembly building. I know you're in charge of all Saigon–Gia Dinh security. You're an important man. Why should you have taken a personal interest in this interview with me?"

The interpreter answered, "We have no 'important men' in our society, except for Papa Ho. We are all equal in—"

David cut him off. "Ask the question, please."

The interpreter repeated David's question in Vietnamese. Tuyen's face seemed not to change, his voice was steady and passionless, but David sensed him grow more serious. He said, "There are very few Westerners now in our country. These are a special concern to me. The agents of the imperialist American forces may still be operating in Vietnam." He paused and let the interpreter speak. David felt Tuyen's keen attention. David struggled to draw a breath. When the interpreter finished, Tuyen said, "I am doing my duty for the victorious revolution and for the unified Democratic Republic of Vietnam."

The interpreter's voice soared and the little official with a weak handshake beamed. David nodded and went out and after he'd finished registering at a table and he was about to leave, he glanced toward the room where'd he'd been interrogated and the door was shut.

. . .

When David entered the lobby of the Regard, four North Vietnamese soldiers were there. David stopped, but the one who noticed him simply smiled and returned his attention to the ceiling. The four were talking rapidly and in tones of wonder about the cut-glass chandelier. They circled beneath it, pointing, angling their heads. One of them took out a Kodak flash camera and snapped a picture, the pop of the bulb silencing the soldiers for a moment, and then they began chattering again, posing for more snapshots.

David went upstairs and entered his room and locked his door and he sat on a chair by the balcony windows. His first thought was of the old man, his CIA contact, who would be coming in a few hours. There was a danger in that. Tuyen —the new authorities—knew where David was. But it would be more dangerous to try to find the old man and warn him not to come. Things were out of David's hands.

He felt suddenly weak, he felt his strength flowing out of his shoulders, his arms, his chest, down into his legs—he felt stronger there, for a moment—and then it was all gone, his strength had drained from him and into the floor, evaporating in the shadows. There was no single thought that caused this. The faces that had swirled above him yesterday now peeked in through the balcony windows, through the cracks in the door, but he held them off, he remained alone where he sat. He knew that all the confusion and clutter and frustration of these few days in Saigon were meaningless except as the heap where he might find some explanation of his attachment to two people. The boy, Khai. And now, once again, Tuyen.

"My two obsessions," David said aloud, and speaking the word stirred his confusion. Obsessions. That's what they were. And yet, what he valued in himself and in others was violated by the whole notion of an unreasoning drive.

After twice seeing the child, twice seeing Tuyen, and still remaining cut off from them both, David knew he had to resolve all this. He was in a room alone, with his own mind. He'd been alone often enough in his life—he'd sought that isolation—and his own voice would be sufficient now. He had two Vietnamese to understand.

"Khai and Tuyen." He spoke the names and this linkage made him rise from the chair.

"Look at what you've done," he said aloud to himself. "You've put the two together. Before, you'd thought of them separately."

David walked around the room, one circuit, and he answered himself: "What good does that do?"

The answer came quickly. "What do they suggest about each other? Why was the boy a disappointment to you?"

"I can feel nothing for him. Nothing." Saying this was painful. He stopped in the center of the floor. His face felt very warm.

"Why can you feel nothing?"

"He may not be my son."

"How can you tell this?"

"His face."

"Because it's not yours?"

"Because it's not mine. It's alien. I look at his face and I do not see my son and I feel nothing."

"And what of Tuyen? His face is alien too."

David puffed at this. The prosecutor in himself had won his point. "All right. That's true." He thought: perhaps there's no connection between the two after all. David moved forward, opened the French windows, stepped onto the balcony. The street was growing dark. He leaned on the wrought-iron railing. Below, the bars were shuttered. The signs, in English, were unlit. FLOWERS. GOOD TIME. FRISCO.

David spoke softly into the still, twilight air. "You came here to find a son who had your own face. Like David Junior."

He pressed his eyes shut and now tears came. "David Junior," he said. "How can I get back to him?"

He lowered his face and at once he challenged himself:

"And why are you so moved by David Junior? Why does he move you?"

"He's mine."

"More."

"He's me."

David straightened up. He turned and went back into the room. "I love my child only because I see myself in him. I cannot love Khai because there's nothing of me to see there."

He lay down on the bed. He closed his eyes. And then he felt his own father draw near. Images tried to shape themselves, and David squeezed himself shut. Not from anger now, he realized. He expected the images to be bad and he didn't want to hate anymore. Indeed, he felt an odd little prickle of sympathy for his father. The man had never been close to David. For whatever unspoken reason—his face was only vaguely present in David's own, his mind was unremittingly adult in its patterns, he had a fastidiousness about him that would not accept from the beginning a child's incontinence—for whatever reason, the father felt estranged from this child, from David, and the man had no way to pretend that his feeling was anything but what it was. There was nothing to suggest an answer. The man had vanished before David was old enough to think to ask. And yet, David now felt this unexpected sympathy. That was why his father had suddenly come to him in this room in this distant country and David laughed aloud. "I'm your son after all," he said. "We both feel nothing for a child."

David sat up on the bed and the room was very dark. He might have been sleeping, he might have not. But his mind waited to speak, to take up the inquiry just where it had stopped. He swung around, put his feet on the floor, but he did not stand. The street was very quiet. He wondered if it was time for his contact to come. Would his very arrival at David's door be the proof that the new government sought? David was working for the CIA and that would be that. He'd be put away. Could Tuyen do that? Was that what he was warning David about at the very end of their interrogation? He would do his revolutionary duty. But David didn't consider his own peril any further. Tuyen stopped him. David spoke in the dark room. "You still haven't made sense of Tuyen."

"The words on the cell . . ." David began to reply, but his mind grew restless at this.

"You haven't been able to figure out that cell. The trial couldn't and you couldn't. Go back to the child once more. You felt close to an answer when you considered the two together. Khai means nothing to you because you can see nothing of yourself in him. So how did Tuyen compel you to find him? Why does he have a hold on you even now?"

"I liked him. From his words on the cell wall. I liked his mind."

"Liking his mind is far from an obsession."

"Dammit. I don't know. I don't know what the hell drives me."

The room rang with his voice. He realized, with a start, that he'd shouted out loud. Then he realized that he'd been speaking out loud for a long time. "You've been talking to yourself," he said. "Like a madman."

He paused, recognized the irony. "You spoke even that," he said.

"I'm really losing it," he said and he dragged the back of his hand across his forehead. He was soaked with sweat. The air was still. He crossed to the bed and switched on the paddle fan. It began to click softly. The air swirled against him. "You're talking to yourself," he said.

"That's because your own mind is the only one you've ever felt you could talk with."

"Except when you were thinking about Tuyen. Imagining him. And later, by the stream on Con Son Island."

"And you knew him from the wall."

"Yes."

"And what was there?"

"His mind."

"More."

"My mind."

This idea rushed on him and then a great slowness rose inside him. The air moving in the room irritated him. He switched the fan off and he waited as the stillness gathered. Then he opened once more to the idea. David had seen himself on that cell wall; he'd seen the pattern of his own mind, in its aloofness, its irony. Tuyen was not a face, he was a mind, and David had seen himself there as clearly as he'd seen himself when his son was lifted by the nurse.

David sat down on the bed. He was very tired. What he'd learned seemed suddenly useless to him. His thoughts dissolved. He sweated them out, he felt his thoughts beading on his forehead and he lifted his hand and wiped them away. Whatever it was he'd figured out suggested no course of action. Except perhaps one: save himself. He remembered the old man. He turned his wrist so that he could see his watch. The room was too dim. He crossed to the balcony, stepped out. In the faint glow from the night sky he saw that it was past eleven. David had indeed slept. And the old man hadn't come. He'd been arrested; that was very possible. Was David compromised? He could not say. Certainly the CIA could offer him no escape from Vietnam. His desire focused on that now. To escape.

He could have a strong feeling only for those who strikingly reflected himself. But even asserting this, he thought of Khai. Not with any special feeling. The boy remained an alien. But David was reminded of his intention to find Suong for the boy. Then he thought of Tuyen promising to find out what happened to her. And he felt a flush of fear: Tuyen would locate Suong and ask her about David Crowley. Suong had never heard of David Crowley. Only David Fleming. The US Army man she'd known in Saigon. And David would be lost.

He moved slowly back into the room. He closed the French windows and he went to his bed. He lay down to wait for the knock on his door.

. . .

When David woke, there was sunlight in the room. For a moment he was blank, but then he leaped up. It was morning. The knock had not come in the night. This exhilarated him. He'd thought he was doomed, but he still had his freedom; no one had come for him. This release—though he knew it was temporary, though his mind stood off and preserved the deeper fear intact—this release drove him to the French windows, out into the morning air. He had more time: that was how the exhilaration spoke to him. More time for what? He gripped the iron banister.

People were in the street. Casual people. A young woman stood in the door of the bar. She wore pantaloons and blouse, no miniskirt, but her face was heavily made up and she watched the passersby alertly. Soup sellers ladled from pots on the sidewalk. A beggar poked in a rivulet of garbage. Again David thought: I have time. He understood at last what drove him to find Tuyen, to seek a Vietnamese son. But knowing his own motive did not change his feelings. Khai did not move him, nothing had changed, though David thought to return to the apartment. Even as the relief at not being in jail began to ebb now, he felt more strongly that he should go back once more to Trung and the boy. The disappearance of the old man, the phony name being carried to Suong who could do nothing but expose David's cover, Tuyen's intense little speech about the revolution: all this started to drag at him, pulled him back off the balcony, into the room; a room, he realized, that was his registered address, that was the one place the government knew to look for him. And all of this, too, suggested a return to Madame Trung's.

He went out into Tu Do. The whore in the doorway blew a kiss at him. He walked up the street and the beggar straightened by the curb—he was an old man, thin and crusted with skin sores—and his hand groped out at David as he passed by. David moved on more quickly and one of

Tu Do's crab children scuttled out of a doorway, one of the deformed but sassy-faced children who scooted on twisted legs, and he said in English, "Hello, Joe. You give me money. Okay?" The thought David had was that Saigon was getting back to normal. Just that. He walked off the sidewalk around the boy, and began to move on. There was a commotion up ahead. A little cluster of people, shouting. David stopped. He turned and looked back down the street. "Have I learned nothing?" he whispered. The old man was picking through the garbage. The boy was back in the doorway. He looked at David and said, "Hello, Joe." But he did not advance again. David waited. He thought: if he comes out of the doorway, I'll go to him, give him some money. The boy just watched. He did not speak, did not move. The voices up the street surged. David waited a moment more, but he felt awkward. These beggars—he passed hundreds of them, a thousand of them, without a look when he was in Saigon before. He still had no feeling for them, so he waited for another approach of the boy. The child did not move and David turned, waiting for the boy's call, but it did not come and he went up the street.

He stopped at a half-circle of people. Inside the arc were two North Vietnamese soldiers. A young man stood between them. He was hardly more than a teenager—with pointy-toed fake Italian shoes and a pair of sunglasses stuck in his shirt pocket. His hands were bound before him. Probably one of the petty-criminal Saigon cowboys. The soldier nearest him had a megaphone and he said, "People of the tribunal, you have heard the witnesses. This man clearly stole the bicycle."

David looked around at what the soldier called the tribunal. They were people off the street—some soup sellers, a few young women in ao dais, a scattering of older people; passersby, David assumed.

The soldier said, "Everyone in favor of the death penalty raise your hand."

A few of the people looked at each other but most of

them just looked at the young man, who was standing very still. A few hands went up, then more, a clear majority. The soldier looked around and he nodded at the other soldier, who stepped forward, raised a pistol. The soldier with the megaphone said, "In the name of the people," and there was a puff, a sharp sound, and the young man crumpled, a plume of blood rising from his head. The crowd was quiet. David stepped back, turned, moved down Tu Do toward the hotel, stopped. The child was gone from the doorway and David didn't know what to do anyway about the crab children. He wished there were a sea where they could all scuttle in benign silence. Behind him he heard a smattering of applause and of laughter and the soldier's voice, amplified, speaking about justice. David walked away and turned into a side street. He followed the street's angle to Le Loi and found a taxi and he went to the passageway off Pho Duc Chinh.

David's mere presence at the door was enough to bring Madame Trung. She stepped aside to let him come in and he sensed a grimness about her, a hardening in her placid face. Inside, the boy was not visible. David's first thought was that the grimness had to do with the child. He felt a stutter of fear and he said, "Where is he?"

"Sleeping," Madame Trung said and yet there was a faintness to her voice that was drastically uncharacteristic of her; something was wrong.

David looked around the room and he saw, sitting before the shrine, a plain stone urn sealed at the top in black. On the side was taped a card with printing on it. David held back from any speculation. He turned to Madame Trung. "Who is it?" he said and as he spoke, he knew.

"Suong."

David looked at the urn and it had not disappeared, had not moved, had not reshaped itself; its sameness mocked David, that he should be told of this radical transformation and yet the transformation should be held in this plain inertness, it should be rendered as simply a handleless stone urn sitting on the floor. David fought the truth. "Are you sure?" he said.

"They sent some of her things. Clothes, a necklace. I recognized them."

David tried to remember Suong's face, tried in retrospect to see some hint of her future doom in her face; but he knew that nothing was there that could have been read at the time; he sensed in his own face that same invisible potential of the future. "How did you get this?" he said.

"A soldier brought it."

"When?"

"This morning. An hour ago."

David thought: Tuyen said he'd find an answer for me. And then: poor Suong. He wondered how bad the death had been, what she might have gone through. But it all seemed very distant. He could not even imagine her pain. She'd not been part of his life for a long time, had never really been part of it. Poor Suong, he thought, and he grew angry at himself for being unable to feel grief at this moment. Then his will to survive began to stir. "How did they know where you were?" he said.

"Thieu's people always had known. This place was not a secret. I suppose there was still a record of my address."

David felt a rush of fear. The new government could find him in this place, too. But then he realized that Suong was dead when Tuyen's people arrived. Suong was ashes and he was still David Crowley. "Did the soldier ask you anything about me?"

"Nothing."

David nodded. Did that mean Tuyen had indeed recognized him? Or had the man just accepted his identity from the documents without any suspicion?

"You must take Khai now," Madame Trung said.

David turned to the old woman and he drew an odd relief from the desperateness of his own situation. This was a decision he didn't have to make. "Take him where?" David said.

"Out of the country."

"You don't understand. I have no way out of the country. I'm trapped here."

Madame Trung did not reply but moved away, disappeared into the other room. David was alone for a moment. He looked at the open doorway. It would be easy to run. A few steps and he'd be in the passageway; he'd be moving, he'd leave Khai sleeping in another room, out of sight. David could leave now for the third and final time. But for the moment the temptation was weak. His body remained as inert as the urn.

Madame Trung was before him again. She held a thickly bulging brown envelope. "This is for you," she said.

David took the envelope and found it full of money, mostly American currency. Some French. "What is this?"

"Also inside is a location, an address in District Five, on the canal. Tonight at ten o'clock a boat will leave. A sampan with just a few carefully hidden passengers. It will go out into the China Sea and sail to Thailand. They say the river is still open. The North's ships have not moved as quickly as its troops."

"You want me to take the child."

"I was going to take Khai myself. I arranged all this. The money is the final payment. But I decided not to go. I'm too old. I couldn't protect him on the sea."

David looked at the money and he felt empty.

Madame Trung said, "I was wrong to say what I did a few moments ago. You don't have to take Khai. I'm not asking you to take the boy."

David looked up at her. She was calm. Her eyes were puffy—from crying, he knew, crying for Suong, though he himself had not seen her tears. "What do you mean?"

"I want you to have the money. You can go. Save yourself. If you don't want Khai then he would be worse off if I forced you to take him. If you cannot be his father, he is better off with me. He will have a life here. I'm too old to run and your American money will do me no good in a Com-

munist Vietnam. You take it and save yourself. If you want
the boy, it will be entirely your choice. I can't take him out
of the country anyway. He will be no worse off for your
escaping alone."

"In all of that, you didn't once call him my son." David
heard himself say these words—and they were true—but he
felt instantly weary of the inquiry. He could never know the
answer from Trung in a way that would persuade him. He
knew he had to resolve it for himself. Madame Trung was
watching him in silence. He felt the question shaping in
him: is it true that he is my son? But he didn't speak it. Even
to himself now.

David looked toward the bedroom door. He felt as if he
were moving at the bottom of the sea, but he moved. He
would look at the child once more. He would look at the
child and try to find the feelings that he wanted to have. He
wanted those feelings now. He knew that. After understanding in the night that it was his own reflection, nothing more,
that had quickened his life, he wanted to be able to love this
child, this alien child, he wanted to be able to weep for
Suong and embrace this child.

David reached the doorway and he did not pause but
stepped in at once. The boy was sitting up on his pallet. His
face turned at David's entry and it was still the face of a
stranger, unchanged by David's insights or logic or desire.
As plain and unyielding as the urn of Suong's ashes, the face
of this child watched and waited.

David had wanted to study this face as it slept. This
sudden burden of speech was very difficult, but he did not
consider backing out of the room; he stayed and his mind
thrashed about for words. Finally he said, "You were supposed to be asleep."

"No." Khai said this, instantly, sharply.

David hung between two understandings. At first the
word seemed not a reply to what had been said but a petu-
lant rejection of David's very presence in the room. Then,
after the sound had softened a little in David's head, it

seemed that the child had responded to the implicit command in what David had said; he was resisting the order to
go back to sleep. "Are you afraid of me?" David asked.

"No." This time Khai spoke with a surprising noncha-
lance.

After a pause, waiting for more words either from the
child or from himself, David could only say, "Good."

The boy's face watched and would not turn away, would
not come closer. David thought of the beggar boy in the
doorway on Tu Do. But Khai was not asking for anything.
He sat on his pallet in a thin white T-shirt and blue shorts,
his feet bare, his toes as uniformly stubby as an infant's, and
he asked nothing. David thought of Suong's face once more,
looking at him across a sunlit room, a brass mobile tinkling
at the balcony doors, and she would be dead in little more
than four years. He looked at her child who sat before him.
He looked closely at Khai now—not for signs of himself but
for some hint of the boy's future; he looked for suffering
there, early death, as if they might have been passed on from
his mother, the signs discernible with the two faces to com-
pare. And then he could look at himself for the same signs.
But this was foolish. Of course the signs were there. In this
child's face, in David's own face, and in the face of that
young man who'd stolen the bicycle and of Tuyen, as well,
and of Madame Trung and of all the strangers who'd flowed
past David in Vietnam and in the face of Jennifer and of
David Junior. The signs were there: the tiniest movement,
the pull of breath, the warmth of the skin; all these clearly
spoke of an acute vulnerability.

David took a step toward Khai. "Your grandmother told
you I'm a friend, didn't she?"

"Who are you?"

This stopped David. He did not have the will to speak—
what could he say? it was too complex—but he took another
step. The boy's hands went down beside him, palms on the
floor, as if he were ready to leap up and run away. "I'm an
American," David said. He eased forward a little more and

then crouched slowly down and he realized that he was treating Khai like a cornered wild animal. "You said you weren't afraid of me."

"Grandma!" Khai called her with a loud voice but with a certain flatness, a voice hiding its own fear.

David and the boy watched each other as they waited for Trung to respond. The moments passed and the boy looked toward the door and David glanced over his shoulder. No one was there. He looked back to Khai and saw another cry for grandma beginning, but at David's glance a little lift of defiance came to the boy and he tightened his mouth, did not call out. "She trusts me," David said. "Why don't you?"

Khai looked away with forced casualness. He scooted farther off, closer to the wall.

David tried to draw a deep breath and found that he was shaky inside. He didn't know what he was supposed to do next. He had come into the room seeking a feeling that wasn't here. He expected to find it not in the boy, but in himself. And that was foolish, he said in his mind. You learned last night of your selfishness. How could you expect it to be different?

"Because I want it to be different." He said this aloud and Khai peeked at him.

David had spoken in English and he answered the question in Khai's eyes in Vietnamese. "I said, 'I want us to be friends.' I spoke in English."

Khai didn't reply but he did not look away.

"Do you know any English?" David said.

The boy shrugged.

"Does that mean yes or no?"

"Coca-Cola," the boy said.

"Is that all?"

Khai shrugged again.

"Did your mother . . ." David began the question instinctively. He paused, but only for a moment. He felt a quickening in himself. "Did she ever talk to you about your father?"

The boy frowned—a faint frown, showing only in his brow, his stillness. He said nothing.

"Did she say anything?"

"No."

"Are you sure? About your father?"

"My father?" This was spoken with a high, piping child's innocence and David felt anxious.

"Do you know what a father is?"

"Of course."

"Did your mother say anything about your father?" David felt his arms tensing, his legs wanting to move; he might discover the truth yet.

"No."

"Nothing at all?"

"I have no father, I think."

"Are you sure she said nothing?"

David sensed his own intensity only after it registered on Khai's face. The boy moved back against the wall. Tears came to his eyes, his face twisted.

"No," David said. "Please don't. I'm sorry."

Khai began to cry. "Grandma," he said.

David looked frantically around the room. He saw the top. He reached for it. "Here," he said. "Will you show me how this works?"

But Khai was on his feet. He went around David in a wide arc, the tears flowing, still crying for his grandmother.

"Please, " David said, raising the top.

Then Khai dashed out of the bedroom and David heard him crying in the other room, heard Trung's voice soothing him.

David looked at the top in his hand. It was covered with Chinese characters, the tiny little pictures, the forms of life changed into words, not quite recognizable by their original connection to the world, shaped by meanings and connotations that David could not comprehend. He laid the top down and found that he, too, was weeping. He was alone and he was weeping and then Madame Trung was at the door and Khai was in her arms and David rose up but he did not wipe away the tears.

Madame Trung looked at him with a faint puzzlement creasing her forehead. Khai's crying was snubbing to a stop and he peeked from Trung's shoulder and his head lifted in surprise.

David realized that his tears were visible to these two, these Vietnamese. The two were distant from him, as distant as memories of another country, and he knew that this distance was what his own tears were about. "He would never go with me," David said.

"He would do what you tell him," Madame Trung said.

David crossed to them. "Do you want to go to America?" he asked the boy.

Khai responded by hiding his face and clinging more tightly to his grandmother.

Madame Trung said, "Child, you know I've told you someday you'd have to live with someone else. America is a wonderful place. You'll go there."

David's hands rose up to protest this—he had not made a commitment in just asking the question—he couldn't—he had nothing to hold onto with the boy—he had no feeling, no warmth, only fear, only a sense of isolation. Then he thought: I can only do this as an act of the will. He knew what was right. The child's mother was dead, his grandmother was old, he was a mixed-race orphan from a formerly wealthy family in a country of new and crushing rigorousness. David knew what was right. Regardless of the truth about his fatherhood. He could not act from his feelings—he despised his feelings now; he'd learned what his deepest feelings were and he despised them—but he could act from his will.

"All right, " he said. "Yes. I'll take him."

Khai seemed not to hear or not to understand or not to believe. He did not look at David; he clung with arms and legs to his grandmother. Madame Trung nodded at David. "Leave us now. You might not be safe waiting here for the night and I want to have time with the boy."

"What will you say?"

"What does he know?"

"No more than I know. I told him I am from America and I want to be his friend. I'll take him."

"Then I'll talk only of myself and how it will be all right for him in America."

"I can't go back to the hotel. They'll be waiting."

"I have a friend at the end of the passageway. You can stay there until it is time. Number thirty at the very end."

Madame Trung stepped aside and David moved past her, crossed the living room, aware of the urn but not looking at it. He stopped at the door and turned, intending to speak. Trung and the boy had disappeared, but David spoke the words anyway, in his mind: I'll be back.

The woman at the end of the passageway gathered her mother and three children and brother-in-law around her and they all smiled and bowed David into the privacy of a small room. He sat for a long while on a mat and then he lay back with a hard little pillow under his head and a sharp-edged column of sunlight from a high window moved down the wall and across the floor and he heard the voices fade in the other room. He expected to struggle with the fear of what was to come. But he felt very still. He thought instead of Suong, her face and mind and hands ashes now. And her son: for him, she was less even than ashes. The boy had not seen her in over a year. Not since he was barely three, or even younger. When he grew up he might have no memory at all of his mother. David—who had loved her so briefly and so incompletely—would carry more of Suong in himself than her own child. And what could he tell Khai of her? Not even that she'd loved the boy, for he'd existed only as a

mystery back then, a tiny bloom of cells that the two jaded
and distant adults were ignorant of. Was there anything at
all? Any word of Suong's that David could portray to Khai as
a foreshadowing of her love for him? No. David and Suong
had never even spoken of love for each other. He raised his
hands to his face now, pressed at his eyes, tried to force
these thoughts out of his head. He was suddenly very weary.
He had to rest. But he felt a brief ripple of grief over Suong's
death. At last. For all that he'd withheld from her, for all that
she too had withheld, he grieved. Over the false adequacy
of their silence, of the surface of their skin, he grieved. And
over her death.

After a time, the column of sunlight disappeared.
Though the small, high window was bright, the room grew
dim. The grief that had come to David withdrew now and
the feeling that threatened to replace it was fear. But David
held off the fear. He had chosen to take the boy and he had
to wait for the night and this was what his mind had always
been good for, this ability to detach, and he lay as if by a
mountain stream, as if filled with the smell of pine sap and
fresh water. His suspended mind quaked faintly only when
he sensed the space that began outside this door and ran to
the canal and the sampan. And then the Saigon River, flowing into the China Sea. And the sea itself—to Thailand.
David had his money, had his plane ticket, he'd kept them
with him. He squeezed at his pocket. The paper crackled.
Good. He focused on that. He at least had a direction now.
Through the streets, along the canal to the river, down the
river to the sea. He backed off from the nasty little whisper
of danger; he could hear no voices now, only the rush of
water, flowing somewhere.

And then at last it was dark in the room and it was time.
David rose up and went into the passageway; he moved
between lamp-lit windows, faces bowing before rice bowls,
before incense, before sleeping children, and at Trung's he
went in without knocking. The old woman was kneeling

before Suong's ashes; from the shrine a thin track of incense smoke rose, a savor rising like Suong's soul, curling, thinning, vanishing.

David waited, not moving, and Madame Trung closed her eyes briefly and then she stood up. She looked at David and nodded.

"He's sleeping," she said softly.

"Is he ready?"

"Yes." She moved off and David followed her into the room where a candle burned and in the pale light he saw Khai sleeping on the mat. He was lying on his stomach, his face turned this way, his arms straight at his sides.

Madame Trung kneeled before him, bowed her head for a moment, and then she leaned forward and kissed the boy's upturned cheek. She drew herself up slowly and went into the darkness of the room and returned with a shoulder bag.

"Here," she said. "These are a few clothes for him and for you. Also some personal items and a little food."

David took the bag from her.

"You are blessed with a dark night," she said. "Go parallel to the river, staying in the alleys. It's not far. You can be there in fifteen minutes or so, even carrying the child. You know the place?"

"Yes. The paper you gave me said the spur off the canal just past Cong Hoa."

"That's right. The man who will take you is named Quang."

"Quang."

"Go now."

David looked down at the sleeping child. The candle flame flickered against Khai's face. His rest was deep and still and David felt a flickering in himself, a fleeting linkage between Khai and David Junior, a link in the sleep of children; both the boys slept the heavy cat-sleep of children and David bent to Khai and picked him up; the boy rose as if his body itself strove to leave the earth and seek the air, he rose as if with the aspiration of a fish leaping from the water.

David held the child against him, Khai's head falling lightly onto his shoulder, his arms rising in sleep to hold on, and David suddenly felt afraid. There was so far to go before they would finally be safe.

He turned, he moved out of the room and Madame Trung was there, standing beside the shrine, tears glistening in her eyes. David stopped.

"Please take care of him," she said.

"I will," he said, in barely more than a whisper. He wanted to speak with more firmness, but he couldn't. He wanted her to understand that his lack of firmness was only a result of the clutching he now felt inside him, the tightness that could only be eased by running. But he couldn't explain that. He stood waiting because he wanted to say more to her, he wanted to mitigate the sadness of this strong woman. "Madame Trung," he whispered. "Thank you."

"Go now," she said, her hand coming out, touching not Khai but David, touching his shoulder. "Quickly."

David was into the passageway, his burden light, surprisingly light, the child was light against him, clinging ignorantly in sleep. David was concerned about what would happen when Khai woke, but he put it out of his mind; he focused on moving.

At the end of the passageway, he slowed drastically, stopped. The night was very dark; the sky was thick and low; it pressed on his eyes like the darkness in a windowless room. He leaned out to look down the street and it, too, was darker than usual. It depended at night—as did many of Saigon's streets—on the spill of light from the houses and shops. But the curfew and maybe a sense of the new regime's growing severity kept the windows and doorways dark. The darkness of the city would hide David and Khai, but it would hide the North's patrols as well. He strained to see shapes, movement—first up the street toward the central market, where even the traffic circle was invisible in the dimness, and then down the street in the direction of the canal. He saw nothing and he pressed Khai closer to him and stepped out, turned toward the canal, and he moved quickly.

An apartment building loomed on his right and next to it was an alleyway. David turned there and he was heading west now, toward District Five. He rushed; though he had time, he rushed. The child was exposed outside, and David felt something slip under him, his ankle turned, he stumbled and caught himself, gasping. The pain in his ankle sent tendrils up his leg, but he walked on a few steps, testing it, and the pain faded. He stopped and adjusted the bag over his shoulder, lifted Khai a little higher. The boy had stirred briefly when David stumbled. There was only silence now that they'd stopped. David looked around. Nothing was clear, but he sensed on both sides a stacking of back balconies. He'd gone into the night streets of this city before. There'd always been a murmur, a ripple of intense life, but now there was only a deep silence. These people were afraid, he realized. All of them knew once more to be afraid.

David walked on, his footsteps ringing in his ears; too loudly; the people behind these doors were right. He approached his first corner. He slowed and angled closer to the building. Before he could look, he heard a motor muttering, approaching, a vehicle moving slowly this way. He drew back, spun around. Hurry, his mind cried; there was an intensification of the dark beneath a jutting of the building. He moved to it, the engine sound grew, and he bent into the deepest shadows, found a wall, and pressed against it. Khai stirred. Please, David thought. Sleep. The engine was loud now—David expected a beam of light to reach down the alley, expected the vehicle to turn in here. But it passed. The sound grew smaller and it was gone. Khai was still.

David emerged from the shadows and looked both ways in the street and he crossed, entered the next alley. He moved as fast as he could without risking a fall in the litter or cracks of the narrow passage. On one side there was a high wall, on the other, more balconies. In a ground-floor window was a tiny red spot, passing. David determined to keep his eyes set only forward, but he had a vision of all the people behind all these closed doors: they kneeled before the light of glowing incense, their lives were held in a compressed red glow of flameless fire, prayers of smoke. And Khai began to murmur.

David rushed. Another corner, even as Khai's dreams moved the boy to low, unintelligible words. David looked up and down, quickly, and he began to cross. Only then did he hear another engine. He looked and the narrow eyes of a jeep swung into the street. The beams fell short but approached. David lunged into the next alley. Nothing here on either side but walls, smooth walls, Khai's arms lifted. David shushed the boy, stroked his head, even as he ran, even as he listened for the engine, even as he looked for a chink in the wall, an entryway. Khai's arms settled again and David was still in the very center of the alley as the sound passed in the street behind him. He stopped and turned and there was nothing but darkness. He felt his heart beating wildly; he heard it in his ears; it was so loud he expected it to wake Khai. He thought of the new government. It surely hadn't been in power long enough to be able to care what happened in the alleys. Not yet. The risk was in crossing the streets. That was the only risk. And just as his heart began to slow, as he began to move along the alley again, Khai's head rose off David's shoulder.

He felt the child's body go tense. David stopped and he whispered, "There's nothing to be afraid of. Your grandmother said I would take you."

"Grandma!" the child cried. His voice echoed between the walls, rose up into the sky, filled David's head; filled all of Saigon, he feared.

He wanted to drop the child right there in the center of the alley and run. Khai shouted again and David cried out, nearly as loud, "Damn!" He spun around, looked up and down the alley, expecting soldiers to come running, but there was no one. He would put the child down now. Run.

Khai was crying. David's face burned. "Grandma," the boy said again, lower, but his voice full of tears, the Vietnamese word sounding alien, the pitch of the voice making David's teeth hurt. Run away. Run. But David made his own hand come up, made himself gently press the boy closer, made his hand stroke at the back of the child's head. The boy cried and David put his mouth close to the child's ear and said, "Your grandma told you I'd take you to America. That's where we're going now. Don't you want to go?"

The boy's crying grew a little quieter but did not stop. Instead, he began to push away from David, trying to get down from his arms.

"Please," David said. "Khai, listen."

The boy struggled. David knew if he put him down, Khai would run and maybe David himself would run, would let the child go, and he would himself become again the man he had always been, the man he saw clearly last night.

He held Khai close with both arms and he said, "Khai, there's something very important. Didn't you ever want a father?" The child's struggling stopped. "Didn't you ever wonder why you have no father?" Khai's crying stopped.

David stroked at the child's head. He felt the boy's body very still against him and he felt in his own body a trembling beginning. "Khai," he said, and the words to come were small and hard and lodged deep in his throat and he tried to shape the path for them; he felt Khai's stillness beginning to turn to a trembling like his own and David feared the boy's reaction, feared the boy, but he said, "Khai. I am your father."

For a moment there was nothing. David was conscious of the void about him. Speaking the words brought no feeling to him, nothing at all. And the child seemed to have vanished; there was a pressure against David, a vague sense of weight in his arms, but there seemed to be no sentience, nothing living. Then Khai moved. His arms stretched, his legs hooked themselves around David's waist, the boy pressed himself against David, clung to him, and David was lifted, his body felt light, he grew strong and he kissed Khai's head, his fine, dark hair, and he began to run with him.

He concentrated on the pavement beneath his feet, the alley's dark track ahead; the walls and then buildings and then unidentifiable spaces and shapes all passed in this long stretch. David kept his attention ahead. He ran and was glad for the extended block. There were shapes before him and then beside him and then gone and they could have been people, dwellers in the alley, but no one spoke. David ran and he saw a light at a crossing, a street lamp.

He knew it was a major street. Another patrol could easily be there. He slowed and stopped and his chest heaved from the running and he was sweating. "Are you all right?" he whispered to Khai.

Khai responded by tightening his hold. David waited for his own breathing to slow and then he moved forward. The lamp cast an oval of light that came up very near to the mouth of the alley. He approached and there was a wall. But it was on the side nearest the street lamp and David moved to the other side, along a hedge, and he wanted to crouch low. He thought to put Khai down. He knew the boy wouldn't run now. But Khai was his and he couldn't let go of him. David moved slowly forward to the end of the hedge, almost onto the sidewalk and he leaned and looked both ways, quickly, down a wide, long boulevard, and he saw nothing.

He crossed the street at the edge of the lamplight, moving quickly, and he felt good, felt that the emptiness of this street was a good sign and then he was on the opposite side and facing a wall. He jerked his head back, looked at the alley he had just left, tracked it across the street, but there was a wall. The alley did not continue. He ran. Down toward the canal. He'd have to stay on this main street and then turn onto another, Chuong Duong, the street he'd traveled to leave Saigon to go to Nha Be. He looked over his shoulder, then looked up ahead. There was only darkness, but he expected light, he expected a patrol. The sidewalk was smooth, he was running fast here and his chest burned; the child, the bag, were growing heavy, he was pushing himself like a novice jogger, pushing too hard, his legs were growing stiff, his side hurt.

He was at Chuong Duong. He heard the slip of water. To the left there were lights. Far down the street, toward the center of town. In the other direction, his direction, there was only darkness, and he ran, glancing over his shoulder, watching the lights, a cluster of lights, and then two of them—still distant—moved this way. He pushed hard, pushed against his pain. There had to be a turning, had to be. Shops began, their corrugated doors padlocked. He glanced back and the lights were coming. Perhaps three hundred yards. David slowed. The shops began to break up. There were narrow walkways. He went into one, down it, his foot hit a hard object. It scraped. He stopped. He knew he could trip on something in the dark, knock something over, make a loud noise. That would be the end. He waited. The engine approached. Always these engines, these grumbling little jeep engines, pinging from bad Russian gasoline. He looked back the way he came, down the passageway, and a streak of light was there, then a shape, passing, then the engine receded.

David felt very weak. He held the boy closer, tried to renew his own strength from the child. "Khai," he whispered, "you're a smart boy. You know to be quiet."

"Yes," Khai whispered.

David moved along the path, back to the street. The jeep that had passed was just two red spots, growing smaller. In the other direction, the cluster of lights had disappeared. He stepped out, turned west, ran again, a major intersection approached. David felt a chill of apprehension. How many streets could he look down only to find the North Vietnamese at a distance? He knew he was nearing District Five, but he couldn't expect to elude the patrols over and over again. He reached the intersection and had to go out into the middle of Chuong Duong to avoid the lamplight. He crept into the center of the intersection and he saw nothing in all directions. He looked west on Chuong Duong. That would be the most direct route to the canal. But it was a main thoroughfare. Up this cross street there might be a west-ward-leading alley. If not, he would be just as exposed in a futile search for one.

He chose Chuong Duong. He ran west, ran hard once more, a final push, and as he ran, the street was his, there was no sound but his own breathing, no jeep engines, no lights moving. As if his earlier rush of fear had pushed aside the risk itself, he ran freely now, and with a growing confidence. He crossed Cong Hoa, the boundary, he knew, of District Five, and the spur of the canal was coming soon. The street rose and David could see the dark jumble of shanties beside the water.

The instructions from the envelope Trung had given him were very specific. David stopped at the edge of the bridge and came back to the nearest shanty and turned in at a pathway behind it. He groped in the dark and now he could sense the life that had seemed to vanish in Saigon. There were people sitting in the doorways, most of them in the dark but he saw them, he heard their murmured surprise at this intent, passing figure. A candle burned in a tin shack, lighting a ring of faces, a child cried, the hovels jutted at odd angles, squeezing at the path, at David, he pressed deeper in, feeling safer with each step, farther from the street, nearer the boat. And these angles in the dark, these living people, these huddled families buffered him from those who would stop him. Khai clung tightly and David moved and his mind slowed, it felt a sudden ease here; the comfort stretched out inside him and his body, too, slowed a bit. He was looking for a clearing in the shacks, a cistern, his next landmark. There was a figure on a doorstep, a woman, and as he passed, she spoke the friendly Vietnamese expression of surprise—roughly "Hey heaven"—and David greeted her in formal Vietnamese, "Hello, ma'am," and he heard her laughter receding behind him.

The open space came, even before David could think to worry about it, and he turned toward the canal. "How are you, young Khai?" he said.

"All right," Khai said.

"Can you say that in English?"

"Coca-Cola."

"Great," he whispered, and Khai clutched harder with his legs.

David slowed. He guessed he was close to the edge of the canal now. This was dangerous. He could end up in the water. He stopped and peered into the darkness. There was a very faint ambient light—from the sky—and a candle glow from a nearby shack. David had a sense of the canal before him, very near, a chasm. He extended a foot gently, feeling his way, and he found a wooden staircase going down. Just where it was supposed to be from the instructions.

He started down the steps and below he saw a shape in the chasm—the boat, he guessed—set out a bit, and he thought there must be a landing. He went down the stairs carefully; then he felt the warped boards of a little landing and he stepped onto it and stopped.

"Mr. Quang," he said softly.

Suddenly his eyes burned with a flash of light, yellow light, he could not see for this bright light and he drew back but there were hands on his arms, Khai was peeled off him, David lunged for the boy but he was jerked back, a pain across his throat, he heard Khai cry out, wordless, David gripped at the arm around his neck but then a pain bloomed in his head and there was silence.

David woke in a dark place. He was lying on a cot. He could sense the tight walls. A pain pulsed in his head and he moaned aloud, not for this pain but for Khai, for Jennifer and

David Junior, for Suong and for Madame Trung; his mind filled with people and with a fierce anger at himself. There was too much and when he felt a slow spiral begin in his head, gaining speed, he let go to it and the darkness took him.

When he woke again there was a faint light in the room. He looked at surprisingly smooth walls, plaster walls, not rough prison stone. He tried to sit up; his head throbbed but he pushed through the pain, he let the spinning go and it slowed, stopped; he was sitting with his feet on the floor and he raised his head. Though the walls were plaster, it was a cell. A small cubicle with a bucket in a corner, a stench of long-spent piss, an iron door. The light came from a small window high in the back wall, beyond reach.

David knew that his thoughts would soon begin. He feared the regrets that lay waiting for him in this cell; he could not bear them. He looked at the door and stood up and waited for the swirl of the room to stop. Then he crossed to the door and he began to pound on it. He pounded with his fist and his foot and he soon realized it was futile. The sadness of the others—the ones he knew he loved—filled the cell behind him, waiting, demanding that he turn. He stopped pounding and he sagged against the door, not wanting to face them.

Then there was a loud metallic click. He straightened up. An observation slit opened before him and two eyes looked into his and the slit clanked shut. David waited and there were more metallic sounds and the door opened. A North Vietnamese soldier holding an AK47 motioned for him to come out.

David stepped out of his cell and his limbs were heavy with fear. But this was still better than the regrets. He walked ahead of the soldier down a corridor full of other metal doors and then through an archway into a larger space. There were two desks, a rack of rifles, two other soldiers, sitting. A picture of Ho Chi Minh hung on the wall.

David was prodded in the center of his back by the muz-

zle of the rifle and he passed through the space. He reached
a door and a hand from behind stopped him. The soldier
circled David and knocked. There was a muffled voice from
within. The soldier opened the door just wide enough to
step inside. "He's awake," the soldier said to whoever was
in the room. The other voice again, louder now, familiar:
"Bring him."

The soldier pushed the door all the way open and motioned for David to enter. David stepped into a small room
with a wooden table, two chairs. A man sat with his back to
the door, papers on the table before him. He turned. It was
Tuyen.

David felt a pulsing in his head, his own blood pulsing,
and as soon as he felt it, he felt it slow. He waited. Tuyen
stood up and dismissed the soldier with an upward nip of
his head. The door clicked shut. The two men were alone.

Still there was no sign of recognition between them. The
beating in David's head cycled slower and slower and in
Tuyen's face there was nothing, no sign, no flicker of feeling. Then it occurred to David that Tuyen had not asked for
an interpreter. Tuyen knew. He had to know. And yet, even
though they were alone together, he showed no recognition,
no feeling.

Then at last Tuyen said, "Please sit down." He spoke in
Vietnamese, his voice dry.

David would admit the lie of his previous interrogation
if he responded to the Vietnamese words. He glanced past
Tuyen and saw his passport on top of the table. Tuyen had
to know. And the lies were worthless now anyway. He was
prepared to respond, to move, but before he could, Tuyen
motioned him to the chair on the far side of the table. David
crossed to it and he realized that it was foolish to expect
anything from this man. If David had seen his own mind—
seen himself—in Tuyen's words on the cell wall, then of
course there would be no feeling now, only thought, only
distance, at best some irony between them. As he sat, David

smiled faintly: he had sought and freed the very sort of man who could remain aloof at this moment.

Tuyen looked down at the papers on the table. He reached out and put his forefinger on the passport and pushed it a tiny bit in David's direction. "Is this you?" he asked, still in Vietnamese, still assuming comprehension. It sounded to David like a rhetorical question. He said nothing.

Tuyen sat in the opposite chair. "Mr. Quang was arrested yesterday," he said. "Some hours before you and the child arrived at his boat."

"Where is the boy?" David realized only after the words were out that he'd spoken in perfect Vietnamese. He didn't care. It was hard enough to hold back from grabbing Tuyen and shaking him.

"He's safe," Tuyen said, showing no surprise at David's command of the language.

"Where is he?"

"He's with us. I assure you he is unharmed."

"Is he frightened?"

Tuyen did not answer at once. David sensed the man's concentration intensifying. Then Tuyen said, "Don't worry about the boy. He is Vietnamese."

David felt a pulse of resentment at this. But he did not know how to express it and he said nothing.

Tuyen studied David for a few moments more and then leaned back in his chair, placed both hands, palms down, on the table. "We have a few things to discuss."

"Yes."

"You are not David Crowley."

"No."

"You are not a member of this group." Tuyen flicked his fingers at the identification card lying beside the passport.

"No."

"You're an American."

"Yes."

"There's only one organization I can think of that would provide an American with these." He motioned at the documents once more.

David did not reply.

Tuyen nodded faintly. He did not ask the next question, the obvious one. He did not name the CIA. Not for now, at least. He leaned forward and he pitched his voice low. "What are you doing here?"

David struggled to control his breathing. The slowness had changed; he felt a rushing in himself; he, too, put his hands on the tabletop. "Do you know who I am?" he said, breathless by the last few words.

Tuyen hesitated and then said, "I don't think you should be asking the questions." But he said it without any harshness. He sounded almost wistful.

"We're alone this time. Didn't I earn even the right to talk with you for a while? Just talk?"

"How do you think you earned a right?"

"Then you don't know who I am?"

Tuyen's eyes did not move; he watched, waited, did not speak.

David said, very low, "You know who I am. Don't you?"

Tuyen's face did not change. There was no moment of recognition. There was only the word: "Yes." The word came and was gone so quickly that David instantly doubted he'd heard it.

"Who am I?" David said, feeling immediately that he'd pushed this too far, sensing Tuyen's irritation at being probed as if he were the prisoner.

"You are an American CIA agent," Tuyen said.

David withdrew his hands from the table. They were cold. Very cold.

And now Tuyen's face changed. His head dipped briefly, as if to break the tension, and then rose as he said, "If there is something I'm missing, I'm still waiting for an answer to my first question. What are you doing here?"

"I'm the man who took you off Con Son Island."

"I know you are," Tuyen said.

David felt a sudden silence in himself. He blinked it away. "Didn't you understand that's what I was asking?"

"What is your true name?"

"David Fleming."

"Mr. Fleming, what did you expect me to say?"

"Just that you remembered."

"What is the point of that? I am not a superstitious man. There is no place for superstition in a Communist state. But my father would have believed that you are some sort of magical spirit. You appear in my life at the most unlikely times in the most unlikely ways. My father would say that you are clearly not a human being but a spirit creature ready to reshape itself at any moment into a tree or a rock or a tiger. Do you say to such a creature, 'Oh, how are you? I remember you from the jungle stream on Con Son Island'?"

"Of course you don't. So I would expect the reticence you showed to be your father's reaction, not yours. You are a high Communist official with no superstition."

"I am also my father's son."

David's hands rose to the tabletop once more. "Yes?"

"I mean by that, you make me very uneasy. There are unsettling mysteries even without superstition."

"I'm no mystery."

"Something else makes me uneasy. Agents of the American CIA."

"I'm not an agent."

"I find myself asking the question again. Answer this time, please, Mr. Fleming. What are you doing here?"

"I came for the boy."

"The boy?"

"Did you really expect to catch a CIA agent carrying a Vietnamese child onto a refugee boat?"

"Please don't play any more games with me," Tuyen said sharply.

"I'm sorry. The answer to your question actually begins with you. The US Army court-martialed me for letting you go. I was on trial for that, a trial that ended only . . . I've lost track of days here . . . it's not been much more than a week ago." He paused. Tuyen waited, his face a little pinched now; but whether from interest, skepticism, or even perhaps a low-grade superstitious fear inherited from his father, David could not say.

"Go on," Tuyen said.

"I was convicted, but they gave me a suspended sentence. The trial is part of my answer to you because it made me consider my life in Vietnam. There'd been a woman in Saigon. I'd loved her, for a time."

"Nguyen Thi Tuyet Suong."

"Yes."

"We found her . . ." Tuyen hesitated.

"Her ashes. I know."

Tuyen nodded. "There was a child with the old woman. I assume that was Suong's son?"

"Yes."

"And the same boy we took from you."

"Yes . . . When I was on trial I figured out what I'd been blind to before. Suong had broken off with me and I finally realized that she'd been pregnant."

"And the boy?"

"He is my son." The words came easily to David. And they carried a sense of completeness to them. David stopped speaking. He could think of nothing more to say.

Tuyen rose from his chair. David took it at first as a thoughtful gesture but Tuyen did not go anywhere. He stood over David and his face turned hard. "There is no room for superstition in a Communist state. Neither is there room for sentimentality."

David felt himself shrink back.

"Mr. Fleming, I must now understand these CIA documents. A false name, a false passport, even a pretense of being in a group sympathetic with our cause. These are not the artifacts of a search for a lost love and a bastard child."

David leaped up from his chair. Tuyen took a step backward. "Be careful," Tuyen said. "If I call for the guard, everything will be out of my hands."

"I'm sorry," David said. "This is difficult for me."

"Do you expect your interrogator to care about that?"

"This is the truth, Mr. Tuyen. I have an old friend in the CIA."

"What is his name?"

"Kenneth Trask."

"Go on."

"He came to me when I was on trial. I told him I had to get back to Vietnam. I had to find my son. My government would never have allowed me to travel here, even if I'd been acquitted. So my friend agreed to give me documents to get me into Vietnam. I asked him to prepare for the possibility that the South would fall while I was here. That's why I have the ID card in addition to the passport."

"And he put you into a hotel that is known as a contact point for CIA agents."

"I was in Trask's hands. It was the only way I could get here. He acted as my friend. He sent someone to me. But I did nothing for him."

David stopped speaking and Tuyen did not reply. They looked at each other for a moment and David felt Tuyen trying to put all of this together. It was hard for the man. David had to try to see it through Tuyen's eyes. This was all very confusing. Bizarre even. David said, softly, "Are you waiting for me to turn into a tree or a tiger?"

"Perhaps a truthful man."

"I am a truthful man already . . . I couldn't be a CIA agent. My government hates me. I went to Con Son Island four years ago and snatched an important VC official and set him free. Your father would have to be right about the spirit world for me to have changed from that into a CIA agent."

Tuyen lifted his head slightly.

David said, "And what was in my possession as I tried to escape the country? The spoils of an American intelligence agent? No. A four-year-old boy."

Tuyen shook his head slowly. "Why did you do it?"

"He's my son."

"I meant why did you go to Con Son Island and set that official . . . why did you set me free?"

"I never told you." David smiled faintly at this. "I'm sorry . . . it would have made me seem even crazier at the time . . . We didn't say much at all to each other. Not after I convinced you to go with me."

"Why did you do it?"

David was tempted to explain what he'd learned only recently about himself. How he'd seen the pattern of his own mind reflected in Tuyen's mind. How he'd seen himself there. But he didn't want to go too fast. First the surface events. He said, "One day I visited a holding cell at the interrogation center in Bien Hoa. It was the cell where you had been kept as a prisoner. You'd left that very morning, though when I stepped into the cell I knew nothing of you. I was moved by idle curiosity. And when I was there, I examined the walls, looking to see if anyone had written or scratched a piece of graffiti. Again, the simplest curiosity. I found nothing. But then I noticed the rice stand. I thought that perhaps something was behind it. I went to the stand, pulled it back, and there were the words you had written. 'Hygiene is healthful.' Your words . . . caught me . . . they spoke . . . that is . . ." David had grown suddenly inarticulate about all of this. What had been buoyant with truth in his mind began to thump heavily from his mouth. And there was Tuyen's face. It was rumpled now with confusion.

"What was on the wall?" Tuyen said.

"The phrase you'd scratched there. 'Hygiene is healthful.' The . . . ah . . . irony . . ."

"Mr. Fleming, it is true that I was once a prisoner at the interrogation center in Bien Hoa. The cell you were in could very well have been mine."

"The guard said so." David's voice was faint.

"Then I'm sure it was. But as for any words on the wall . . . I wrote nothing there. Those words were not mine."

David's hand flapped out behind him, felt for the chair, found it; he lowered himself into it. For a moment he had no strength at all; his head sagged forward and then he felt a surge in him and he began to laugh. Without a thought in his head, he laughed. Tuyen was sitting opposite him again and David laughed on for a time until there was nothing left but a dry twitching in his chest and he pressed at his temples and he said, "I'm sorry."

"You went to Con Son Island because you thought I'd written . . . ?"

"Hygiene is healthful. Yes."

Tuyen raised his eyebrows briefly and looked away.

David thought this might have been the first time Tuyen had looked away from him since the door had closed. It was over. That's what David assumed. It was all over. He'd looked away. And he hadn't even written the words. Tuyen was suddenly unpredictable, was suddenly alien to David, no different from any stranger in this country. But so was Khai. Khai had once been an alien as well. But now: just thinking of the child made David stir, made him focus on Tuyen's averted eyes, his silence; these eyes, this silence, were great dangers now, these threatened to separate David from Khai forever—and that made him quake with purposeless strength. Khai. He'd thought first of Khai in his fear, but the threat was the same for David Junior and Jennifer as well. Both his sons were in jeopardy now, and his wife, and he said, "What are you going to do with me?"

Tuyen turned his face back to David and he said, "I don't know."

"Do you really think my purpose in coming to Vietnam was to be a spy?"

"We have already acted with less proof than this."

David's words were yanked away. He could only stop his breathing for a moment in response. Only try not to exist in this room.

Tuyen said, "My government has acted already, even since the liberation, in the matter of some of your agents."

The man's voice was stripped of any color, any feeling. It stopped for a moment and David waited.

Tuyen said, "These other cases were up-country. But I have a clear precedent before me."

"What precedent?"

Tuyen looked away again. "To kill them."

"I just came for my son," David said, not caring about the trembling in his voice. He saw only Khai before him and so he had no desire to alter his feelings. "I love my son."

Tuyen turned again to David, but now David looked away. Tuyen said, "Already we're finding that being a government is not so easy. Things are not so clear when you're in buildings with toilets."

David heard something familiar in the mind behind this remark. He looked at Tuyen, whose lips were pursed in thought. David said, "Do you understand who I am?"

"I only understand that it is not so easy to act. Americans are not the simple creatures I had always thought."

"Surely I changed your mind about that four years ago."

"That was something altogether different."

"You must think I am mad."

"I'm not so sure."

"I sounded mad to myself a few minutes ago. Explaining why I set you free. Those words on the wall . . ."

Tuyen waved his hand, stopped David from saying more. "Ever since you mentioned them I've been thinking about those words you saw."

"Yes?"

"That cell was a very difficult place." Tuyen closed his eyes briefly, as if he were in pain. "I was very frightened there . . . I just wonder who it was that could write something like that. What sort of man?"

"I thought it was you."

Tuyen smiled. "I wish it could have been so."

"Couldn't it?"

"No. Not at all. I am not that brave a man. I am too close

to the pain . . . The man who wrote those words was very brave."

David felt drawn again to Tuyen. "When I saw the words on the wall, I thought I knew you," David said. "Now I think that again."

Tuyen rose from his chair. Just like before, just as when he grew severe and challenged the documents. He rose and did not move away, but neither did he speak.

David said softly, "I know who you are."

"Mr. Fleming," Tuyen said, his voice quiet as well, "I find you utterly incomprehensible. But I see nothing in you that is a threat to my country."

David clutched at tiny breaths, holding them, waiting.

Tuyen said, "Do you think you can become David Crowley again? Just until tomorrow morning?"

"Yes."

"We are preparing a plane to remove some assorted foreign nationals to Bangkok. I will put you and your son on that plane."

"Thank you," David whispered.

"You'll need documents to tell your own government that the boy is yours. I will provide those."

"Two sets."

"Yes?"

"One in my Canadian name, for immigration in Toronto. One in my real name for when I return home."

Tuyen smiled. "You have a mind for details, Mr. Fleming. You would have made a good intelligence agent."

David and Tuyen laughed together, briefly, too briefly; David wanted the laugh to go on, but it stopped.

Then Tuyen's face grew serious. "I'm sorry," he said, "but there is much for me to do now. I doubt that we'll meet again."

David rose. "I thought that myself four years ago."

They laughed once more and Tuyen said, "Perhaps my father's superstition is right about you." Then he squared

his shoulders, moved the papers before him, picked up the
passport and an envelope, and handed them to David.
"These are your things. One of my men will give you what
you need for tomorrow and take you to your son." His voice
sounded strained now.

David nodded and he wanted to speak but no words
came, nothing, and he moved to the door. He turned and
found Tuyen beside him.

They looked at each other and David could not say who
initiated it—the gesture flowed mutually—but they embraced. David and Tuyen clasped each other briefly and
then David was mumbling a good-bye and he was in the
outer room and the door clicked shut and Tuyen was gone.

In a phone booth in Bangkok the next morning Khai stood
inside the cubicle with David, clutching his hand and gawk-
ing at the people passing. Finally the phone rang in Baltimore and David heard Jennifer's voice—faint and full of
static—accepting charges, and she cried, "David. Are you
all right?"

"Yes."

"Where are you?"

"Bangkok."

"Did you make it into Vietnam?"

"Yes. And I'm out now. I'm coming home, Jen."

"Thank God."

"Are you and the baby all right?"

"We're fine. If I sound funny, it's because I was dozing.
It's late here."

"Jen, there's a child."

"Yes?" The word was almost inaudible.

"The mother is dead."

For a moment there was only the crackle of phone lines.
Then Jennifer said, "I'm sorry."

"I'm bringing the child home."

There was no pause this time. Jennifer said, "Were you right?"

"About what?"

"Is it a boy?"

"It's a boy."

"David?"

"Yes?"

"Will he like me?"

"I'm certain of it."

"When will you be here?"

"Less than twenty-four hours. Our flight leaves soon."

"David?" Jennifer paused, as if searching for words. But then she said, "I hate telephones."

He spoke gently. "You have nothing to be afraid of, Jen."

"Come as fast as you can."

"We will."

He placed the phone on its hook. The boy was hanging out the door of the booth, watching the people go past. "Khai."

Instantly the boy was in the booth, his arms raised. David picked him up, held him close. David wanted to speak the feeling he had at this embrace, but it was too strong; the exact words would come later. For now he said, "Khai. Are you ready to go to America?"

"Yes."

A NOTE ON THE TYPE

This book was set in a digitized version of Caledonia, designed for Linotype by W. A. Dwiggins (1880–1956). It belongs to the family of printing types called "modern face" by printers—a term used to mark the change in style of type letters that occurred about 1800. Caledonia borders on the general design of Scotch Roman, but is more freely drawn than that letter.

Composed by Dix Type, Inc., Syracuse, New York.
Printed and bound by The Haddon Craftsmen, Inc.,
Scranton, Pennsylvania.

Designed by Virginia Tan.